PRAISE FOR

DEAD BODY LANGUAGE

"Penny Warner's charming debut mystery, DEAD BODY LANGUAGE, is a double hit with a bright, fresh heroine, deaf sleuth Connor Westphal, and a cheery, piquant background, the California gold country."—Carolyn Hart, author of *Death in Lovers Lane*

"Penny Warner has created a fascinating community of eccentrics, a delightfully complex plot and a heroine who is charming, clever and funny. DEAD BODY LANGUAGE is a treasure."—Jill Churchill, author of *Grime and Punishment*

"Penny Warner's witty, courageous protagonist, Connor Westphal, tugs at hearts and engages minds, making for a rewarding read. Way to go, Penny!"—Diane Day, author of *Fire and Fog*

DEAD BODY LANGUAGE

A CONNOR WESTPHAL MYSTERY

PENNY WARNER

BANTAM BOOKS

New York Toronto London Sydney Auckland

DEAD BODY LANGUAGE
A Bantam Crime Line Book/June 1997

CRIME LINE and the portrayal of a boxed "cl" are trademarks of
Bantam Books, a division of Bantam Doubleday Dell Publishing Group,
Inc.

Line drawings by Frank Hildebrand.

ISBN-0-553-57586-4

Published simultaneously in the United States and Canada

Bantam Books are published by Bantam Books, a division of Bantam
Doubleday Dell Publishing Group, Inc. Its trademark, consisting of the
words "Bantam Books" and the portrayal of a rooster, is Registered in
U.S. Patent and Trademark Office and in other countries. Marca Reg-
istrada. Bantam Books, 1540 Broadway, New York, New York 10036.

PRINTED IN THE UNITED STATES OF AMERICA

RAD   10 9 8 7 6 5 4 3 2 1

To Matthew and Rebecca.
And to Tom, my partner in crime.

ACKNOWLEDGMENTS

I very much want to thank the following experts in their fields for assistance on detail and veracity:

Dr. Linda Barde, Director of Special Education Services and Sign Language Instructor, Chabot College, Hayward, California

Joyanne Burdett, Librarian, California School for the Deaf, Fremont, California

Colma Cemeteries, Colma, California

Linda Davis, Features Editor, Valley Times, Pleasanton, California

DCARA - Deaf Counseling and Referral Agency, San Leandro, California

Melanie Ellington, Counseling and Correctional Services, Jamestown, California

David Goll, City Editor, Valley Times, Pleasanton, California

Robert Goll, Managing Editor, Daily Ledger, Antioch, California

Kay Grant, Near Escapes, San Francisco, California

Mario Marcoli, Gold Prospector, Jamestown, California

Donna Melander, Certified Interpreter for the Deaf, Fremont, California

Sgt. Keith W. Melton, retired, California Highway Patrol

Beverly Jackson, Sign Language Instructor, Mt. Diablo Adult School, Concord, California

Mother Lode Coffee Shop, Jamestown, California

Dr. Boyd Stevens, Chief Medical Examiner, San Francisco Coroner's office, San Francisco, California

Jacquelyn Taylor, President, San Francisco College of Mortuary Science, San Francisco, California

Many thanks to the Northern California Chapter of Mystery Writers of America, to Sisters in Crime, and to my mystery critique group: Jonnie Jacobs, Margaret Lucke, Lynn McDonald, and Sally Richards. Additional thanks to Charlie Ahern, Janet Dawson, Lucy Galen, J.D. Knight, Stacey Norris, Edward and Constance Pike, Geoffrey Pike, and Shelley Singer.

And very special thanks to Amy Kossow, Linda Allen, Casey Blaine, Cassie Goddard, and Kate Miciak.

DEAD BODY

LANGUAGE

"Just set where you are, stranger,
and rest easy—
I ain't going to be gone a second."
—Mark Twain
The Celebrated Jumping Frog of Calaveras County

I licked the tip of my murder weapon, then hesitantly sipped my mug of coffee as if it were strychnine.

"Okay, I sneak up behind the principal right after biology, shoot him in the back with the gold-handled derringer, and . . . shit!" I threw down the pencil and ran my fingers through my bobbed hair.

You'd think living in a colorful California gold rush town called Flat Skunk, once famous for its early homicidal heritage, I'd be inspired to knock off the high school principal in some innovative way. It was, after all, part of my job.

I took another swallow of what the Nugget Café served in place of palatable coffee. I tapped my murder weapon on the table, then drew a line through my latest attempt at premeditated homicide, nearly shredding the nugget-imprinted paper napkin I'd embellished with my scrawling.

"Dammit! I can't use a gun to kill the principal. Everyone in the school would hear it—even if I wouldn't," I said.

This confession garnered some attention from the

regulars at the early morning hangout. Sheriff Elvis Mercer halted mid-conversation with a look that clearly said, "Folks around here don't talk to themselves out loud, Connor honey. And they especially don't talk about murdering other folks."

I smiled at the sheriff, then took another look at the hopeless mystery puzzle I was creating for my weekly newspaper, and bit into a piece of toast. "OK, I'll wire the P.A. system so when the principal goes into the office to make an announcement on the microphone about smoking in the bathroom—"

Zap! I jumped. A hand touched my shoulder and I hadn't seen it coming.

It was Lacy Penzance, the self-styled town matriarch, saying something I couldn't make out; her lips barely moved.

I turned up the volume on the hearing aid behind my left ear—the only ear that receives any sound at all—hoping it would help with reading her tight lips. To Lacy Penzance, it probably looked like I was scratching fleas.

"Thorry," I said, swallowing my bite of toast whole and nearly lacerating my throat in the process. I coughed and slapped my chest a few times. "Sorry. What did you say?" I turned so I could see her face more clearly.

"I . . . you are Connor Westphal?" was all I caught.

I looked her over. I'd never seen her up close, although that wasn't surprising even in a small town like Flat Skunk. We didn't have a lot in common, except maybe a love of the historic Mother Lode mining town.

She was silk suits, Mercedes, Brie, women's auxiliary; I was torn jeans, beat-up '57 Chevy, BLT's, and Protestant work ethic. It all added up to money—opposite sides of the coin. Although we were probably only a few years apart—I'm thirty-seven, she looked fortyish—Lacy Penzance and I were generations apart in dollars and design.

"May I sit down?"

At least that's what I thought she said. She really didn't use her lips for much more than sporting scarlet lipstick. I swept some toast crumbs off the table, folded the mystery-annotated napkin, and gestured to the seat across from mine.

Lacy slid slowly and deliberately into the worn red leatherette seat. She removed her peach-tinted sunglasses, revealing red-rimmed eyes bordered by tiny crow's-feet and smudged makeup. There was enough Obsession wafting off her to cause me to lose my appetite, especially for cold toast. But something in the meticulous facade caused me to feel a pang of sympathy for her.

Nervously, Lacy pulled a wad of carnival tickets from the black hole of her purse and set them on the gray Formica table. She spoke again; I understood very little.

Even those skilled in lipreading see only thirty to fifty percent of the words on the lips, so there's a lot of guess-work involved. I usually carry around a little tape recorder in the event I should need something clarified later by an interpreter. But I didn't have it with me this morning. I like to ease into Mondays. As for my hearing aid, it only helps a little. Without it I tend to hear only very low or very high sounds—bass guitars, car alarms. I often turn it off when I'm trying to write.

Without taking my eyes off her lips, I could see the tickets twisting in her slim fingers, but her comments didn't seem to have anything to do with them.

"You own that little newspaper, the one that circulates throughout the Mother Lode?"

Little newspaper? Apparently she'd sized me up, too, and didn't think I looked the part of publishing magnate. Maybe a lone woman in maroon jeans and an old "Oh, My God, I Forgot To Have Children" T-shirt, who talks to herself, wasn't Lacy Penzance's idea of a media baron. I sat up straighter to make up for the image problem and slipped my feet back into the pink moccasins I had kicked off.

"Yes, my office is—"

She interrupted before I could point across the street. "I know where your office is." She looked intently into my eyes as she ripped off two tickets, and placed them deliber-ately on the table.

I was suddenly aware that we were attracting the

attention of some of the Nugget's other patrons. Although my peripheral vision is no better than a hearing person's, I'm not distracted by blaring boom boxes and whispered gossip, so I tend to tune in closely to visual cues. I sensed that our pairing had caused some interest in the café.

Lacy Penzance leaned in closer. "I stopped by there a few minutes ago. The gentleman in the room next to yours said you were here."

Gentleman? I must have misread her lips that time. I would not call my office neighbor, Boone Joslin, a gentleman, even when he was clean and sober.

Jilda Renfrew, part-time waitress with manicurist aspirations, interrupted with a toothy smile much too bright for a Monday morning, and delivered the hot chocolate I had ordered. When Lacy sat back abruptly, I took a moment to pour the chocolate into my half-filled coffee cup. It had been an adjustment, breaking the Starbucks addiction, but the benefits of trading Forty-Niner football tickets for the forty-niner heritage had outweighed the modification. It was a minor change compared to the others I'd made since my move from San Francisco to Flat Skunk.

"What can I do for you, Ms. Penzance?" I asked, after a warming swallow of do-it-yourself mocha.

Lacy glanced around, licked her lips, then began to speak. I studied her nearly motionless mouth, feeling the onset of a headache from the intense concentration.

"I can't talk to you here. Could you buy one of these raffle tickets for the frog-jumping contest this weekend? Everyone will assume that's what we're talking about. Then I'll meet you—" She looked down at her purse and I missed the rest.

I reached a hand forward. "I'm sorry—what? You'll meet me . . . ?"

"I've got to go," she interrupted, suddenly looking a little frantic. "Twenty minutes. In your office. Please. It's about my sister . . . she's missing . . ."

I thought that's what she said anyway. Before I could clarify, she cut me off again and I missed what she said. She had a frustrating habit of interrupting me. It couldn't have been much—a couple of words—but I was really curious as to what she wanted from me.

After all, this was Lacy Penzance, widow of Reuben Penzance, former mayor who had recently relocated to Pioneer Cemetery. She was an icon in Flat Skunk, a relic of elegance and wealth from the heydays of the gold rush in this now rustic, gold-stripped town. When she wasn't selling tickets for charity, Lacy spent most of her time living alone in the Victorian Penzance mansion over on Penzance Street, not far from the renovated Penzance Hotel.

The storefronts, when not sporting some form of the word "gold" to attract tourists, often featured the name "Penzance": Penzance Video Rental Store stood next to 'Nother Lode Diaper Service, Penzance Development and Real Estate rented space adjacent to the Slim Chance Health Spa. You couldn't take two steps without seeing the ubiquitous name.

In the early 1900's the Penzance family had attempted to rechristen the town after themselves. But the residents wouldn't hear of it. The name Flat Skunk lingered like a bad odor. It could have been worse. Many of the original Mother Lode town names are unprintable. The rest are just as creative as Flat Skunk: Gomorrah, Humbug, You Bet, Whiskey Slide, Poker Flat, and Git-Up-And-Git. I'd meet her if only to find out what could be so important that she needed me. Hopefully Jeremiah Mercer, my part-time assistant, would be there to interpret for me. I didn't want to miss a word.

"Fine. My office," I said. I hoped I said it quietly.

"That will be four dollars, please." This time I had no trouble reading her lips. Her exaggerated mouth movements were no doubt a performance for the onlookers. So, she was going to stiff me for a pair of frog-jumping tickets I didn't even want. If it was a scam, she was quite a con artist.

I forked over the cash and thanked her for the tickets with little enthusiasm. I stuffed them into my jeans pocket as she moved on to the next unsuspecting diners. Curious to see her try to stiff them with her sales technique, I slurped my not-quite-mocha and unfolded the napkin with the mystery puzzle.

"Got a deadline, Connor?" Sheriff Mercer asked, as he stopped by my table on his way to the cash register. At least, that's what I thought he said. It wasn't easy reading his lips with that toothpick dangling from his mouth. Thank God he had given up the tobacco-chewing habit that was so popular around Skunk.

"Eight thirty-seven in the morning is much too early to be planning the perfect murder, Sheriff. Deadline or no deadline."

"Who you gonna kill off this week? I got the one last week. I knew the dentist did it. You never fooled me." He grinned proudly and tapped the table with a sausage finger.

"Might as well give it up, Connor. We'll take care of any mysterious murders that occur around here. You better stick to writing the obituaries." He hoisted up his khaki pants at the waist and sauntered out the door as if he didn't have a care in the world. That calm exterior was what made Sheriff Mercer so effective in his job. And damn if he didn't solve every one of my mystery puzzles.

I stared out the window at the bubble-gum blossoms of the flowering plums that framed the old Pioneer Cemetery across the way. Those pink puffs gave the crusty old mining town an incongruously delicate fluffy trim, like the cake crumbling with age in *Great Expectations*. Around here it didn't matter if I couldn't hear the hoot of the owls or the rustle of the rivers—I could feel the heartbeat of the forty-niners in the antique town I now called home. I didn't miss San Francisco a bit; I loved everything about the Mother Lode.

In the early mining days, murder had been a preferred form of recreation in this Mother Lode town of Flat Skunk. According to my Cornish great-grandmother, Sierra Westphal, 836 gold-diggers were axed, hacked, hanged, shot, or stabbed to death during the five years that followed the 1848 discovery of gold in California. Sierra, or Grancy as my father used to call his grandmother, wrote in her tattered diary: "If you ask me, the mortuary is the real gold mine in this Califoyrna town." She's partly responsible for my being here.

Back then, more brothels and saloons flanked the muddy "gold-paved" streets than all the churches, banks, mortuaries, and jails put together. Today the gold country is part of California's attic, a tame collection of tourist traps, trendy boutiques, bed-and-breakfast inns, and bogus gold-mining expeditions. About the only threat to safety is stepping into the line of fire of a tobacco-chewing spit-shooter.

And this coffee.

"More?" asked Jilda, crinkling up a Cornish nose that was common among long-time residents from Rough & Ready to Angel's Camp.

She relaxed her squint and poked at her frizzy, permed hair with sparkling fingernails. I'd made a promise to myself early on not to take her up on her offer of a free introductory manicure. Otherwise I'd probably be sporting bejeweled inch-long acrylic nails, dipped in Neon Magenta.

"Didja hear me, Con?" she said, raising the coffee pot to illustrate her question.

"Got an antidote?" I replied as she poured. Before I settled here, I used to think any mouth-breather could work at a diner like the Nugget if they could chew gum while using a pencil and didn't have cholera. But Jilda's ability to pour coffee from a height of three feet without spilling a drop had changed one of my many stereotypical attitudes.

I tried to shake my thoughts back to the matter at hand—my weekly deadline—as I stared at the false front of the hotel across the street. The bucolic picture faded from view as one of the town's good ol' boys headed toward the café from across the street. The man's lumbering gait and self-conscious mannerisms distracted me from the frothy view of the trees and my halfhearted attempt at completing the next mystery puzzle.

Mickey Arnold, wearing the ubiquitous 501's and a khaki sheriff's department shirt, grinned, waved, and needlessly tucked in the shirt as he approached the café window. It wasn't vanity that caused him to straighten up, more like insecurity, I thought.

I waved back at the thirty-something deputy sheriff, even though his body language was telling me more than I wanted to read. Despite being deaf, I don't possess super X-ray vision as some "hearies" seem to think. Where I am not able to notice a change in tone of voice or notice a subtle vocal nuance, I can read a face and interpret body language well enough to see what many hearing people overlook. A twitch of an eyebrow or a shift in body weight often speaks louder than words.

Did Mickey realize his current swagger and strut were shouting all kinds of messages? It didn't matter—all that was about to change dramatically. The still attractive, impeccably dressed Lacy Penzance, her attention focused on the tickets she was stuffing into her bag, was moving toward the door—and heading right toward Mickey.

I waved a warning hand at him, but he apparently mistook it for flirtation. He gave the window reflection another glance, smoothed his buzz-cut hair, and checked his belt for kinks and twists.

"Watch out!" I mouthed through the glass. But Deputy Arnold was too busy primping to read my lips. I'm self-conscious when I raise my voice in public. When I lose control, I'm told I sound squeaky and distorted. I held back for a few moments, then yelled just as he made a turn. Too late.

Too bad, because he didn't look at all attractive in the Nugget Café doorway, sprawled on top of a startled, gasping Lacy Penzance.

The impact was solid and forceful, obvious from the aftermath. I almost felt it myself. Lacy's roll of tickets and the contents of her purse had scattered in all directions—under tables, counters, and feet—while the deputy's hat and sunglasses bit the dust at top speed. He'd smacked into Lacy Penzance so hard, it's a wonder he hadn't knocked her unconscious.

Perhaps if he had, I wouldn't have gotten poison oak, my underwear would still be in my top drawer, and a few more Flat Skunk citizens would still be alive.

As several diner patrons jumped to the rescue, I stared at the usually immaculate Lacy Penzance as she lay gasping at the bottom of the wreckage.

The self-styled first lady of Flat Skunk had been flattened like road kill, her belongings spiraled out around her. I felt sorry for her.

Deputy Arnold clambered to his feet, his face a kaleidoscope of colors. After awkwardly assisting the disheveled woman to an upright position, he knelt down and fumbled with her spilled purse and tangled frogjumping tickets. I watched him gather up an assortment of coins, keys, papers, letters, makeup, pills, tissues, and other can't-live-without items and stuff them into her purse. By the time he'd brushed Lacy off and offered his apology, he'd long forgotten about me.

But as flustered and self-conscious as the deputy was by the encounter, Lacy Penzance appeared unruffled. Three generations of cold hard cash did wonders for a person's carriage, equilibrium, and self-confidence. Although her skirt was slightly off center and her blouse modeled a new smudge, she moved away from the spectacle as gracefully as if she had just danced *Swan Lake*.

When the performance was over I told myself to get back to work before I caused any more damage. I hoped Mickey would be too embarrassed to join me. I don't much enjoy small talk, since lipreading is always a challenge for me. And I was definitely not interested in Mickey romantically. Besides, I had work to do.

"Deadline, deadline, deadline." I chanted my mantra as I stabbed a pat of butter with the latest weapon I'd been turning over in my hand.

"What if I used a knife?" I said, checking my teeth in the shiny reflection. "I could go into the office while the students are at an assembly, close the door and—damn! That won't work, Connor. This is supposed to be a locked-room mystery. You can't use a knife without being in the room. And if you leave, you can't lock the door. Unless—"

I glanced up from the knife and caught Deputy Arnold's concerned look, as well as a series of side-glances from the few remaining café patrons. You'd think they'd all be used to my verbal idiosyncrasy. After all, I was becoming accustomed to theirs.

Wolf Quick, sometime gold-mining guide and free-lance jewelry designer, gaped at me like a slack-jawed mackerel with a forkful of Hangtown Fry. The ponytailed man cursed as the unique mixture of eggs, bacon, and oysters tumbled back onto the plate. I had been by Wolf's jewelry store only once, to have him melt down a gold bracelet. I wanted the gift returned to its original nugget state, as a keepsake of five years wasted with the wrong man.

French McClusky, owner of the Memory Kingdom Memorial Park, and Celeste Camborne, the mortuary's grief counselor, shared a look of moderate concern before resuming their probable discussion of designer headstones and color-coordinated casket liners. Between the balding, middle-aged man and the big-haired, thirty-something woman lay a coil of Lacy's tickets.

French, looking more like a cheap lounge singer than

a mortician in his discount suit and drugstore toupee, owned a chain of mortuaries in the Mother Lode, an area heavy with prospective business thanks to the influx of aging retirees. Celeste, dressed in clothes too young and frilly for her age, served the customers during their time of sorrow by offering a shoulder to cry on, an ear to listen, and a nice sharp fingernail to point out the best buys in bereavement accommodations.

Luckily I hadn't yet had any use for their services in Flat Skunk.

Even the old prospector, "Sluice" Jackson, paused in his relentless muttering long enough to peek at me from under his caterpillar eyebrows.

"It's one of those locked-room puzzles, you know . . . a solve-it-yourself whodunnit, for my newspaper. I'm on deadline and I'm sort of . . . stuck," I said to no one in particular, as I made a two-fingered jab to my throat—the sign for "stuck." Sometimes a sign expresses a concept better than two dozen words. But I could tell by the way Jilda snapped her gaping mouth shut and the rest of the diner patrons glanced at each other, that I hadn't convinced anyone of my sanity.

I ran my fingers through my hair again, a habit I'd developed since I'd cut it on impulse the day I left San Francisco. I felt to see if my side part was straight, then stretched a knot out of my back. Anything to avoid work, as William James once advised. This damn puzzle was not coming together easily and I had other news stories demanding attention.

Like those who long to sing at the Met, play pro ball, or strike it rich in the gold mines, I'd dreamed of owning my own weekly newspaper. After six years of writing, editing, and fluff-reporting for the *San Francisco Chronicle,* I had abandoned everything to become publisher of a Mother Lode tourist guide, reviving the name my great-grandfather had christened it back in 1864: *Eureka!* It fit me; I, too, had found something.

Sort of.

I surprised the hell out of my hearing parents and ex-lover when I renounced urban life for a claim in rural Flat

Skunk nearly six months ago. But when my grandparents died several years earlier, they left the Westphals their antique printing press and a run-down fifties diner in Flat Skunk. When I asked my parents if I could take over both, they never thought I'd actually pick up and leave. But I never looked back. I feel at home here, at least more than in the city.

Except I do miss my mocha.

I gave my audience a reassuring smile, then turned to the window and stared out at the distant sprinkle of evergreens freckling the Sierra. That was the trouble with a small town. Everybody heard you when you talked to yourself—especially when you were plotting a murder.

Everyone but me, that is.

Being deaf isn't really a problem. A nuisance now and then when there's a new song on the radio everyone's buzzing about, or when a siren comes up behind me on the freeway, but that's about it.

I contracted meningitis when I was four, which left me with almost no hearing in either ear. By that age I had a fairly good foundation for language and speech. People who hear me speak for the first time often ask if I'm coming down with a cold, or if I'm from the Midwest.

Aside from not being able to sing on key, my biggest frustration is trying to read a pair of mumbling lips or exaggerated mouthings. And the ignorance. The misconceptions are worse than the silence. That's how I ended up working for a newspaper. When I write, there is no silence.

I took another bite of toast. I was glad not to be in San Francisco, writing stories about workout wear, paying too much for a one-bedroom condo overlooking an alley, and waiting for my boyfriend to make a commitment to monogamy.

In addition to the small inheritance, Sierra Westphal's diary was also responsible for my being here. Flat Skunk seemed just the right place for a displaced person like me, a town built out of gold dust and spit by a bunch of hardluck gamblers who came to make their fortunes in the rich ore buried beneath the red clay. Only a few had made their claims in gold. The rest had just gotten dirty, gone hungry, and died broke.

Except my great-grandfather William "Corny" Westphal, Sierra's husband, and old Septimus Penzance, two of the luckier gamblers in town. Corny had made his living off the miners, selling eggs at two bucks apiece and bacon at five dollars a slab. Old man Penzance had struck it rich buying up land when the first depression hit. Corny had launched the newspaper, which my grandfather, Jack, had continued until the town nearly died when the gold mines dried up.

As for Septimus, his bloodline ended just before my arrival in town, when they pulled the bloated body of Reuben Penzance from the Miwok Reservoir, his feet tangled in fishing line, a hook caught in his nose. The full story had never been explained to me. But town folks said old Sluice Jackson hadn't been the same since.

I was scratching out the fifth in a series of mystery puzzle dead ends when a shadow danced on my annotated napkin. The heavy scent of hair spray made the latest bite of toast taste like bad French cologne.

Jilda stared down at me with her mouth agape—it seemed to be the style around here. Her ill-fitting uniform was too short to please the feminists and her blouse was buttoned too high to entertain the new generation of miners. I was tempted to give her a few tips on subtlety, but with two pots of hot black liquid balanced on a pair of breeding hips, she was unfairly armed. Besides, she was sweet, always cheerful, and knew everything that was going on in town. She was a great source for my paper.

"More coffee, Con?" she asked, raising one of the pots.

"Better run," I said, and downed my not-quite-mocha.

If I had known how busy the next few days were going to get, I would have stayed. I never did finish that mystery puzzle.

"Damn!" I said, looking at my watch as I pushed through the door of the Nugget. Where had the time gone? Taking in the pungent air that gives Flat Skunk its name, I jogged across the street, hoping to make up for lost time. I headed up the back stairs of the old Penzance Hotel two at a step.

The *Eureka!* newspaper office, such as it is, occupies a large room on the upper floor of the hotel. Built in 1861, the rambling, hodgepodge structure has been renovated numerous times over the years, serving periodically as a church, an assay office, a jail, a morgue, and at its peak, a brothel for lonely miners.

When gold mining dwindled and respectable women started moving west in greater numbers, the brothel was revamped as the decorous Penzance Hotel. About five years ago the Penzance Development Company decided to close the hotel, but preserved the historic landmark by dividing it up into rentable offices and touristy boutiques, in keeping with its gold fever heritage.

I entered the tiny hallway that linked a number of small offices on the second floor. Boone Joslin, part-time private investigator/attorney/notary public and whatever else he could do to make a buck, occupies the first office; mine is next door. The remaining cubicles are currently vacant except for a room down at the end of the hall where Jeremiah Mercer, the sheriff's twenty-five-year-old son, runs a combination comic book/skateboard/used CD/computer games store. I help support Miah's business by paying him for interpreting services and light office work.

I had just slipped the key into the lock when I felt the vibrations of a heavy thud through the floorboards. I looked around for the source of the disturbance, thinking Miah had dropped a skateboard or Boone was rearranging the furniture in his office again. I couldn't tell where the jolt had come from so I backed up to the detective's door and tried the knob. It was unlocked.

I opened the door expecting to see Boone at his desk reading another Kinky Friedman mystery. But his chair was stacked with a pile of papers. Instead of the fiftyish, gap-toothed, balding Boone Joslin, a younger man stood in the middle of the room. Midforties maybe, with a mouth full of perfect white teeth and a head full of dark brown wavy hair, almost long enough to wear in a ponytail. In contrast to all that dark hair, his beard had a startling amount of blond.

It looked like the guy had been tearing the place apart. Filing cabinet drawers were pulled open, file folders, papers, and boxes of stored junk were dumped unceremoniously around the floor.

It was even messier than usual.

"What are you doing?" I asked the man in the middle of the chaos holding a filing cabinet drawer in his sculptured arms.

"I pulled it too far ... it slipped out ... I was ... Hey, are you Connor, uh, Westphal?"

The bearded man set the drawer down, swiped at his hair with thick, callused fingers and reached out to shake hands. I ignored the gesture.

"Who the hell are you?" I said like I owned the place. "What are you doing in Joslin's office? Where's Boone? I think I'd better call—"

"Wait! Hold on a second." He raised his hands as if he were being held up in a robbery. As I reached for Boone's phone he placed one of those rough hands over mine; I pulled back. Of course there was no way I could use Boone's phone in a meaningful manner, but this guy didn't know that. I get a lot of distance out of bravado.

Besides, if I had to, I could dial the sheriff's number and just talk and talk and talk and eventually someone would pick up the phone on the other end and hear me. But I didn't get the chance.

"Listen, I'm not a burglar or anything. I know this looks kind of funny—" He turned his head and swept the room with his arm, then faced me again. I missed a few words.

". . . this mess. I'm Boone's brother. My name is Dan Smith."

As long as he didn't turn his head away, I could follow every word. Maybe those perfect white teeth made it easy. Or maybe it was the way his mouth was outlined by that disconcerting blond beard. Or maybe his lips—

"You don't believe me," he said, breaking my wandering train of thought. I must have looked unconvinced. Deaf people tend to show their thoughts and feelings through vivid facial expression and body language. I was apparently an open book.

"Here—" He pulled an ornately tooled wallet from the back pocket of his jeans, removed the driver's license, and handed it to me.

Daniel Webster Smith. Address: Truth or Consequences, New Mexico. Born forty-two years ago. Six foot two inches tall. Six inches taller than me. Two hundred and twenty pounds—almost twice what I weigh after a week on Slim-Fast. Brown hair, blue eyes. Donor. License recently renewed.

But the picture wasn't recent. His hair was shorter, there were no indications of newly sprouting gray along the temples, and he was clean shaven. I returned the license and watched him stuff it into his wallet.

He extended his hand again and this time I shook it,

quickly, noncommittally. His hand was dry and softer than it looked. I let it go, then glanced around the room at the disarray.

"Your name's different from Boone's. And you don't look like him, either. Where is he, anyway? And what are you doing here?" I shook my head at the mess.

Dan Smith pulled out Boone's swivel chair, removed the stack of papers, and gestured for me to sit down. When I passed, he sat down himself.

"Well, the truth is, we had different fathers. Boone's my half-brother."

I blinked and waited for him to go on. He could tell I wasn't satisfied.

"Our mother remarried after he was born and I came along ten years later. Kind of a surprise."

At first I thought he said his mother's name was "Mary," but that didn't fit the context so I tried "remarried" and it worked. I took a closer look around the office, trying to figure out what had happened, then looked at him for an explanation.

"It was like this when I got here."

The place hadn't been vandalized, exactly. There weren't any overturned tables, menacing words written in lipstick on the windows, or other indications of a break-in. But drawers had been pulled open and papers were strewn about haphazardly as if someone in a hurry had been searching for something important.

Dan Smith looked pensive, as if waiting for me to speak. It was a look I was familiar with. He'd probably said something while my head was turned and was expecting an answer. I said "What?" just in case.

"Got any idea who might have done this?"

"Frankly, I thought it was you. Boone's a slob, but he's not this bad. So where is your brother, anyway?" I was still not convinced they were blood relatives.

"I don't know. I thought he'd be here. He knew I was coming to visit for a couple of weeks. I was . . . thinking of staying a while, if things worked out. But he didn't show up at the train station in Whiskey Slide so I rented a car and drove over. He mentioned you a couple of times, said you had the office next door. Told me I could get his key from you if he wasn't in. Turns out I didn't need it. The door was unlocked." He paused then said, "You *are* Connor Westphal, aren't you?"

I nodded reluctantly. I wasn't sure it was any of his business. "He's probably out on a case. He sometimes takes off for days at a time. And he's kind of bad about remembering things. I guess that's why he gave me a key, which I've had to loan him on a number of occasions. But you know all this if you're related. Funny he'd forget to mention his own brother, though."

Dan brushed his hair back slowly. His eyes darted suddenly to a dark corner of the office. I turned to see a very fluffy gray cat creep out from under Boone's desk, circle around a pile of papers, and finally make itself at home in an open filing cabinet drawer.

"What's that?" I asked. I'm sure I looked a little horrified.

"That's Cujo."

"Cujo?"

Dan leaned over and gave the cat a scratching under the chin.

"Boone doesn't have a cat. Boone hates cats. What's it doing here?"

"She's mine. I brought her with me."

"You brought your cat?" I grimaced. Wait until Boone came back. The fur would really hit the fan. I made a mental note to be there. I wasn't big on cats either. They always creep around the house and then jump out at you when you least expect it. With a dog, you know where you stand. At least with mine, I do.

"Did that lady find you all right?" Dan said.

"What lady? Oh. You mean Lacy Penzance?" I'd almost forgotten her. I checked my watch. I still had a few minutes until our meeting. "Yeah, thanks. How'd you know where I was?"

I looked him over as I spoke, trying to figure out how much of what he had told me was the truth. Except for the eyes, he didn't much look like Boone. Dan was more muscular, with large arms and broad shoulders. Boone was kind of flabby and stooped. And Dan's smooth, tan face set off his deep-set eyes better than Boone's ruddy, splotchy complexion. Little of his appearance confirmed him as Boone's brother.

"I watched you go into that café after you checked in this morning. Guess you didn't know I was here." He looked out the window, then looked back at me. "It's a nice view from these windows. You can see just about everything, from the main street to the Sierras." He smiled a strange smile, kind of a smirk.

I suddenly blushed and felt the heat turn my neck into raspberry kisses. God, I hoped I hadn't tugged at my underwear or tripped on my way to the Nugget while this voyeur was watching me.

"Did you call the sheriff about this mess?" I asked, changing the subject.

He scratched his beard, much like he'd stroked the cat. "Not yet. I was sort of checking it out myself first, to see if there was really a reason to report it. Besides, Boone doesn't like cops much. You probably know that. I don't think he'd want them sniffing around his office."

He was right. Boone hated cops. But that was no reason not to call the sheriff if someone had broken into his office. Unless . . .

"Are you some kind of investigator too, like your brother?" I asked, fishing a little. The pond still looked murky.

"Not really. I'm . . . a teacher. Was. At the University of New Mexico. I also taught a few classes at the C.F.— the correctional facility," he said, glancing back toward the window. Though he wasn't looking at me, I think I followed him fairly well. "I'm from New York originally. Needed a change, so I moved to New Mexico, but I got kind of burned out in the desert and thought I'd check out the job market here. Make a career move. Boone seems to like it here."

"Flat Skunk is probably very different from True or False, or wherever you're from."

He showed me those teeth again, white and evenly spaced, with a tiny chip off one of the front ones. When you stare at people's faces all the time you really notice the details of their mouths.

"Truth or Consequences. Actually Flat Skunk doesn't seem so different. Country music stations around the dial. Home-cooked meals at the café. Cowboy hats and pickup trucks. Of course, it's nothing like New York. You know, you don't sound like you're from around here, either, with that accent of yours." Dan Smith raised a dark eyebrow. "Where'd you get it?"

In the corner of my eye, I caught flashes of light coming from the hallway. I grabbed my backpack and headed for the door.

"Meningitis," I said, and sprinted for my office.

Lunging for my office door, I saw the bright light of the TTY, a teletypewriter device for the deaf, flashing urgently through the translucent glass pane.

I dug through my backpack and located my keys at the bottom of the abyss. Jamming them into the lock, I pushed open the door, and dove for the phone. But by the time I set the phone receiver on the TTY, the flashing white light had been replaced by the small red wink of the answering machine. "Damn phone," I said out loud.

I plopped my overloaded bag onto the paper-stacked desk and sank into my padded swivel chair for a quick stress-releasing spin, which only made me dizzy. I had a deadline to deal with—I would have to leave the Boone Joslin/Dan Smith puzzle alone for a few moments and get back to my own mystery puzzle. Hoping for some fresh inspiration in the office environment, I dug out the embellished napkin and spread it out on top of a frog-leg recipe I was preparing for Saturday's edition.

"Ho-hum," I said as I scanned the office for clues that would help me find a solution to my locked-room puzzle. But I got no assistance from my color poster of the cherried up '57 Chevy I hoped my "needs-work" car would one day be, nor the reproduction of Wayne Thiebaud's "Lipstick"—the one that makes a routine cosmetic look like a menacing bullet.

In my office, the walls not papered with "Far Side" cartoons, MAD Magazine art, and comic book covers are lined with books on subjects like women who've cycled cross-country, hitchhikers who've traveled the universe, and desktop publishing manuals for the computer-addicted. Nothing led me to a brilliant revelation. Even my *Little Lulu* and *Heckle And Jeckle* collection let me down.

The blinking red light of the answering machine kept distracting me from my murderous thoughts. Wondering who had called always drove me crazy. Damn. When were those brilliant telephone scientists going to create a printout answering machine for the deaf that I could afford? I would be in the dark until Miah decided to get his cute little butt to work. According to my watch, he was long overdue.

At that moment, Lacy Penzance stuck her head in the door. In the confusion of seeing Boone's office amok, meeting Dan Smith, working on the mystery puzzle, and missing the telephone call, I'd forgotten our appointment. I got up and tried to cover.

"Ms. Penzance, I was just—" I puffed up my cheeks and shook out my hair, then searched my desk for an ending. I was having problems with closure today.

Lacy Penzance didn't seem to notice. I checked my watch again. Where was Miah? I really needed an interpreter for this tight-lipped woman.

She sat down in the padded folding chair across from my desk and removed her sunglasses. I reached for my tape recorder. She looked at it, then squarely at me.

"No recording, please. What I have to say is personal."

I tried to explain my need for a backup listener but she shook her head. I let it go.

"I want to place an ad in your newspaper—an anonymous ad. I'm . . . trying to locate my sister. We were . . . separated at a young age, and I've just learned she may be living in the Mother Lode area somewhere. I understand your newspaper is distributed all along the gold chain, so there's a chance she might see my message—or perhaps someone who knows her might see it. I've written everything here."

I may have missed a few words but that was the gist of it. She pulled an envelope from her purse, opened it, and passed me a folded sheet of lavender paper. Her finely lined hands, trimmed with gaudy gold rings, trembled slightly. I unfolded the paper and read the neat, curlicue printing. She had probably practiced those circles and swirls a lot in junior high school.

"Anyone knowing the whereabouts of Risa Longo, write in care of the *Eureka!*"

The ad promised a $5,000 reward. I looked up at her.

"How much will that be?" she asked. She sat with her back very straight, gripping her purse with whitened fingers.

"Five thousand dollars?"

She blinked and pulled back. "I'm sorry. How much?"

"Five thousand dollars for information about your adopted sister? You're going to get all kinds of weirdos if you put that in the ad. Especially around here, where it doesn't take much for someone to catch gold fever."

She considered this, then said, "Just make it 'reward' then." She pulled her designer wallet from her designer purse and opened it, revealing lots of designer green.

"Now, how much?"

I was still having trouble comprehending her request, but it had nothing to do with my lipreading skills. Maybe she was eccentric—wasn't that the stereotype of the lonely, rich widow?

"It's a dollar a word—ten dollars minimum. We're probably looking at about fifteen bucks. If you want a bigger display ad—"

"Here's twenty." She separated a crisp bill from its comrades.

"I'll bill you. Shall I send the responses to your home or—"

"No," she interrupted again, placing the money on the

desk and tucking her wallet back into her purse. "I don't want anyone to know I placed the ad—not even the mailman. You know how people are around here. Everyone knows everyone else's business. I'll be by to see if there's been any response. Will it be in tomorrow's paper?"

"Saturday. It's a weekly." A real fan. "I'll write you a receipt."

As she rose to leave, I stood up in response. She replaced the peach-tinted glasses she had removed earlier and curled a lock of hair behind one ear, exposing a small thin scar just above the ear. I looked at her eyebrows—the same tiny lines just under the ridge. Maybe she wasn't forty-something after all.

Lacy pulled the glasses off, wiped the fog that had formed on the lenses with a tissue from the box on my desk, and I noticed her watery eyes. She replaced the glasses and stuffed the tissue into her purse. "I hope the ad will help—" She stopped.

I waited, then said, "What about hiring a detective? I mean, that's what most people do when they want to find someone. Boone Joslin—"

"I hired Mr. Joslin about a week ago, paid him a large advance, and haven't heard a word since. I've been trying to contact him but apparently he's on one of his notorious 'vacations.' I haven't much . . ."

I figured she said "time," but it could have been "charm" or "lamb" or any number of words with an *m* in it. Of course, "charm" and "lamb" didn't make any sense, but then neither did "time" when you thought about it.

Before I could ask any more questions, Deputy Arnold burst into the room, dangling a set of keys from his fingers.

"Oops. Excuse me. Sorry to burst in, but I hoped I'd find you here, Ms. Penzance. Found these after you left. Must have fallen out of your purse when I bumped into you, back at the café. Tried to catch up with you but I got sidetracked by the sheriff. Then you were gone. Thought you might need them." He grinned a hero's grin.

Lacy Penzance took the keys from the deputy with a

smile but didn't thank him. She glanced at me one last time, and left.

I didn't see her again until the funeral.

"REWARD!"

I keyed in the last word of Lacy Penzance's ad on my desktop publishing software using a fancy Galleria font, then added a graphic of a kid waving her arms to attract attention. It hadn't been easy getting rid of Mickey. He had wanted to chat. I suspected he'd held off returning the keys just to have an excuse to stop by.

But I was too busy trying to make a headliner out of a common bar brawl. Some guy had refused to leave the Spittin' Cotton Saloon when "politely" asked. A hundred years ago he probably would have been tied up with a good solid rope, hoisted up the nearest tree, and hanged for his misbehavior. There was a lot of that going around back then, especially in nearby Placerville, once known as Hangtown. Dummies still hang in effigy from the tops of restaurants and saloons there, in an effort to attract the tourists. This time the guy got off easy. Deputy Arnold took him down to the drunk tank for the night.

Flat Skunk currently seems to be going through its adolescence, caught between two cultures, the past and the present. Somewhat like myself, being deaf in a hearing world. Skunk is having a difficult time figuring out whether to cling to its rustic tough-guy image of an old-fashioned gold-rush town or to embrace the 1990's interpretation of a cutesy neo-yuppie village. In spite of all the cappuccino stands and porcelain nail "shoppes" popping up like pimples on a preteen, the old mining town wasn't about to change without a tantrum or two.

The next interruption in my morning occurred around eleven o'clock—a flashing light on the telephone. I lifted the receiver, placed it on the TTY handset, and typed "GA," meaning "Go Ahead," on the keyboard. As glowing red letters began to appear on the monitor, I read the message inching its way across the console.

"CONNOR ITS MIAH. CALLED EARLYER BUT MISSED U. SORRY IM NOT THERE YET BUT COMIX

CITY IN WS HAS THE SGT ROCK IVE BEEN LOOKING
FOR. KNEW U WOULDNT MIND. ILL WORK LATE
TO MAKE UP. BE THERE SOON. OK? GA."

The "U" meant "you" and the "WS" meant "Whiskey
Slide" but I was half tempted to correct his spelling before
I replied. I promised myself to get Miah a portable spell-
checker and a typing tutor with the next paycheck. But I
was glad he had the portable TTY with him, which plugs
into designated public telephones. At least we could keep
in touch.

I typed back, "OK MIAH BUT ONLY IF U GET ME
A *FOX AND CROW* OR *LITTLE LOTTA* WAIT
MAKE THAT *BETTY AND VERONICA*—1950–1955
THX. AND HURRY NEED YOU DESPERATELY GA."

"NO PROBLEMO. HOW ABOUT ANOTHER
LITTLE LULU TOO? SEE YOU SOON BEST BOSS IN
THE WORLD. GA. SK."

Signing off with an "SK" for "Stop Keying," I went
back to my work. I received several other phone calls but
only one on the TTY. The rest were recorded by the
answering machine for interpreting later by Miah. The
TTY message was a strange one that came in just before I
took a lunch break. The caller had typed "lacy penzance,"
then hung up. But my deadline didn't allow much time for
contemplating that little mystery.

Around one o'clock my stomach started asking questions, so I "saved" my newspaper copy in the computer
and called it a morning. After securing my office, I stopped
next door to check on Dan Smith. I wondered if he had
discovered anything more about the upheaval in Boone's
office or had had any news from Boone himself. No one
answered my knock. I tried the door. Locked.

I grabbed a quick Cornish pastie at Dilligaf's deli-bar-
bait shop-and-video store across from the cemetery. The
tourists always ask who "Dilligaf" is. I like to tell them he
was a famous outlaw from the forty-niner days—they love
that—but it's really an acronym for "Does It Look Like I
Give A Fuck." A little redneck humor from the owner.

I hopped on my mountain bike, rode no-handed three
miles down to the Miwok Reservoir, and settled under a

bristlecone pine to eat my lunch. Watching the water slap the shore, I ate a cold, soggy meat pie that smelled like my ex-lover's Nautilus bag, and read my competition—the daily-except-weekends *Mother Lode Monitor*. The self-promoting rag was strictly a glorified ad for where to dine, sleep, and spend money in the gold country. The *Eureka!*, although smaller, was much classier.

I was alone by the small, secluded reservoir—just the way I like it—except for Sluice Jackson, the ragged old miner, wearing his floppy beaded hat. The beads are actually dangling earrings that Sluice makes and sells to the tourists as he shuffles up and down the main street. At the moment he was hunched over a leather bag mumbling to himself. He looked around anxiously as he pulled out what appeared to be a small metal dowel glinting in the sunlight. Another one of his old mining tools, no doubt.

I had to admit, the old guy made me a little nervous. Mainly because I couldn't understand a word he said when he talked to me. But then, I don't think most folks really understood him. Sometimes, when working late at night down at the newspaper office, I've seen him on his way to the cemetery where he does odd jobs, talking to thin air as if he were Cosmo Topper entertaining spirits.

Sluice caught me watching him. He tightened the straps on his backpack, rubbed his wayward eyebrows, then started in my direction. I quickly packed up my lunch remnants and, tossing a few crusts to the squirrels, made a leap toward my bike. I felt sorry for Sluice, but I wasn't in the mood for a mumble-fest. It was hard enough reading the lips of those who spoke meaningful sentences.

Too late. He toddled faster than I leaped.

"I din't take it. I din't do it. It wern't me. It wern't." He was shaking his head and clutching his leather sack and talking to me as if I had accused him of stealing.

I smiled weakly and tried to look as though I knew what he was talking about.

"It wern't me," he said one last time, then he turned and walked away. I watched him go down the hill toward town, shaking his head, still in some kind of denial. I wondered, briefly, what he didn't take. He probably didn't know himself.

It was just after one forty-five when I arrived back at the Penzance Hotel. As I reached the top step I spotted Miah in the hallway, arms loaded with comic books.

"Hey, Miah," I called. I shook my index finger in the air, made a twist at my nose with the manual alphabet letter "F"—which looks like the common gesture for "OK"—then opened and closed my thumb and index finger at my mouth, signing: "Where's my *Fox And Crow*?"

He smiled apologetically and shook his head, tossing the too-long blond forelock over his eyes. He said something aloud but I couldn't make it out at that distance. I gave the universal sign for "What?" by screwing up my face.

"Wait—" he managed to sign, wiggling his fingers with difficulty under the armload of comics. He disappeared into his tiny shop, then returned moments later carrying a few comics in one hand and signing with the other.

"No *Fox And Crow*—sorry. Got a couple of *Little Lulu*s. And check this out—a 1956 *Betty And Veronica*. You want it?"

I'm taking some liberties with American Sign Language here. Basically a few superfluous words are omitted and the syntax is reordered—it somewhat resembles Chinese. But that was the gist of it. What he actually signed was more like, "None, Fox, Crow, none. Sorry. Got few Lulu—Look! 1–9–5–6 B-E-T-T-Y, V-E-R-O-N-I-C-A. Whoa! You want, you?"

Miah does a great job of matching facial expression to content, which helps with comprehension—head shakes, eyebrows raised, that sort of thing. He gets his point across most of the time and that's what counts. To tell you the truth, I have a little crush on him. He has these long, smooth, lanky fingers that were born to sign, among other things. So what if he's only twenty-five.

I don't really need to use signs with Miah. Most of the time I can understand his speech, when he isn't trying to shake his long forelock out of his face. But we primarily sign to each other to give him more practice. Part of the job requirement at my newspaper was the knowledge of sign language, but there weren't a lot of folks in the area who knew ASL. Miah was willing to learn, had taken a course down at the local community college, and in the past six months had become proficient enough to interpret for me in most situations. He was a natural.

"Both *Lulu*s have Witch Hazel," he signed, crooking his finger across his nose in an unsuccessful attempt to make the sign for "witch."

I laughed. "Thanks a lot. You just called me 'ugly.' " I showed him the correct way to move his crooked index finger to make "witch"—arched outward from his nose, not dragged horizontally across the middle of his face. He shook his head and spoke without signing. "Damn! I always get those two mixed up!" Then he made the sign for "pea brain."

I unlocked my office door and asked Miah to take down phone messages and start typing ads while I checked my desk for the damn mystery puzzle I had scrawled on the restaurant napkin. I'd had a great idea at the reservoir about how to kill the high school principal without having to unlock the door and was ready to finish it up. But the search proved useless—the napkin seemed to have mysteriously disappeared, until it occurred to me where I might have left it.

I knocked on Boone Joslin's office door and turned the knob. This time the door opened. I pushed it slowly—remembering the surprise I'd received the last time I had burst into Boone's office.

But it was the smell, not the sight, that stopped me cold this time.

"Whoa!" I shouted, then inhaled again as if it were my final breath. "Is that sourdough bread? I haven't had real San Francisco sourdough since I left the city! Where'd you get that?"

Dan Smith was hovering over the hot buttered bread and a file folder on Boone's desk, tapping his pencil in a rhythmic beat. There was a trace of butter on his mustache that he licked off as he looked up.

I knew the radio was playing because I could feel the vibrations of a bass guitar or drum through the floorboards.

"Murrf," I think he said. I don't know what it meant. He was a little hard to read with his mouth full of sourdough bread. He gulped down the large bite with a swallow of cola, wiped his mustache and lips with the back of his hand, and extended the remainder of the loaf to me. "Want a bite?"

I tried to shake my head, but I don't think I looked very sincere. "Where'd you get it? Not in Flat Skunk."

"Stopped overnight in San Francisco on my way here. It's day-old, but I heated it up in Boone's microwave.

Tastes like fresh." He set the torn loaf down next to the open file and steam wafted up, along with the pungent aroma. Warm bread. I tried not to drool.

Boone's office was practically a home-away-from-home, complete with all the necessities—a microwave oven, convertible sofa bed, exercise bike ("like new, never used"), portable TV and VCR, and Nintendo Entertainment System. Everything a good private investigator needs.

I moved in slowly, my attention temporarily distracted from the bread by a legal-size envelope on the desk. It was tinted the shade of raspberry sherbet and almost obscured by the file Dan had been reading. Peeking out from the envelope were enough twenty-dollar bills to wallpaper my office.

"I . . . I think I lost my napkin in here." With great effort, I tore my eyes from the money and glanced around the room, which looked considerably tidier than earlier in the day.

"You need a handkerchief?" he asked tentatively, pulling a white hanky from a deep Levi's pocket.

"No, I wrote something on a paper napkin from the café. I thought I had it with me when I stopped by this morning and now I can't seem to find it." In my once-over search for the napkin my eyes fell upon the cash again. I looked up at Dan Smith.

He did a quick body search, then shrugged. "Sorry. Seems like quite a few things have disappeared around here lately."

"No word from your brother?" I asked, edging toward the desk for a closer look at the bills.

He frowned and rubbed his jaw. "Nothing." He looked at the envelope, then at me. "It's five thousand dollars."

I picked up the envelope. Five thousand dollars. That rang a bell.

"Where'd it come from?" A familiar perfume rose from the envelope.

"Believe it or not, I found it in the microwave when I went to zap my bread. Boone's always hiding his stuff in strange places, ever since he was a kid and Mom found his *Playboy* collection in the all-too-predictable bottom drawer. I assume this is what our mysterious office visitor was looking for. Guess he missed it."

I frowned. Something wasn't adding up. Too many odd things had occurred since Dan Smith had arrived in Skunk.

"Did you call the sheriff?"

He scratched his beard again. "No. I didn't think it would be a good idea. Like I said, Boone doesn't like people going through his stuff, especially the cops. But I am getting a little concerned about my brother. That's a lot of money to have lying around. Why didn't he take it with him?"

I studied Dan Smith as he stroked his mustache back and forth with a thick, tanned finger. The stroking was disconcerting. "You think the money has anything to do with that file you've been looking at?" I indicated the folder on the desk.

He picked it up and closed the cover.

"I found it on the floor near the filing cabinet. Nothing inside, only 'Whiskey Slide' written on the cover and a name on the inside. The rest of the files seem intact. I'm afraid it doesn't tell me much."

"What name?"

He looked puzzled.

"What name was written inside?" I repeated, more insistently.

"Lisa . . . uh . . ." He pulled open the cover. "Risa Longo."

Risa Longo! The woman Lacy Penzance was searching for. The long-lost sister. Had Boone found her in Whiskey Slide?

"I think you should have called the sheriff," I said, watching him for a reaction. His face remained blank and he had stopped rubbing his mustache. "I realize Boone has a habit of going off for days when he's working on a case. But this—this is different. His office has been broken into. One of his files has been tampered with. And all that cash . . ."

Dan's eyes shifted suddenly toward the door, and a chill ran up my back. I turned around abruptly.

Miah was standing in the doorway looking very upset.

"What?" I signed, turning my palm up and shaking my open hand forcefully.

"Phone. Someone—" He signed without mouthing the words, presumably so Dan wouldn't understand him. But the curious expression on his face told half the story. "Woman. Refuse leave name. Said, tell you run ad—not! Sounded like she crying, upset, much. Finish, hung up."

I turned back to Dan to see if he had caught any of this. Some of the signs were obvious—telephone, crying, hung up—but he looked more puzzled than Miah. That was fine. Miah and I had an understanding. When talking business in front of others, we don't use speech.

"What's up?" Dan asked.

"Uh, got a phone call. From . . . my mother. Her car . . . broke down, you know how it is."

Dan didn't move.

"Gotta go," I said bluntly. I pulled off a small hunk of bread, then followed Miah back to my office.

It was probably Lacy Penzance—she was the only advertiser who could have been upset about the ad she placed, unless the woman with the lost poodle had heard bad news. The rest of the ads were the usual collection of garage sales, help wanted, and run-of-the-mill lost-and-found. I keyed in a computer command and watched Lacy's ad appear on the screen.

"Damn! I didn't get her phone number when she was in this morning," I said to myself out loud, then turned to Miah. "Try the phone book. If you can't find her number, maybe it'll be in that frog-jumping committee file. Or the Friends of the Pioneer Cemetery file. If you find it, give her a call and I'll tell you what to say."

Bless Miah—he had some surprising talents. He got the number by calling Mickey Arnold at the sheriff's office. Mickey was like an older brother to Miah, what with the sheriff being Miah's father and all. It didn't hurt that the deputy had a little crush on me either. He was a great source of information at times.

Miah dialed Lacy's number but there was no answer. What, I wondered, was her problem now? Had she found Risa Longo herself? Was that why she was canceling the ad?

Reluctantly I told Miah to pull the ad, then I gave up on Lacy Penzance for the time being.

By seven that evening half of the inside pages were neatly ready to go to press—mostly ads. In the next two days I had to finish the front and back pages—mostly news— plug in a few fillers, and complete that damn mystery puzzle, which had become a mystery in itself. Although everything was done by desktop publishing on my PC, it would take me all of Thursday to add the finishing headers and footers, graphics, and fonts. Then I had to get it over to the printer in time to publish by Friday night for distribution Saturday morning.

It might be tedious work to some, but I loved every minute spent at the computer creating my newspaper. Being a deaf student in a hearing high school, I was prepared primarily for the secretarial route. My teachers thought that was about all I could do in life with my disability. But I mastered the computer, read every manual ever written for my word processing and desktop printing programs, and watched my growing expertise open doors at a number of interesting jobs. That, along with a degree in journalism, helped me get the position at the *Chronicle*. I'm convinced the computer will change the Deaf community's way of life in the very near future.

I grabbed my backpack and rode my bike the half-mile home, eager for dinner.

My home, if you can call it that, is a reconverted fifties restaurant once known as the Claim Jump Diner. It was owned by my grandparents, Jack and Constance Westphal, until they died a few years back. The place had sat empty for longer than that before I took it over. I've been as faithful as I could be to the original *art moderne* style, restoring and recovering the small booths and stools in red-and-white Naugahyde, refinishing the countertop with swirled black-and-white Formica, and replacing the peeling linoleum with black-and-white tiles.

Old *Life* magazines helped a lot with decorating ideas. So did my grandmother, who had saved a lot of the original decor in storage. Only the kitchen has been modernized, with all the latest accoutrements—dishwasher, microwave, espresso maker. You want to take authenticity only so far in the kitchen.

I even kept the fifties look in the back room where I live and sleep, accessed through swinging doors in the kitchen. The entire place consists only of the diner and the small back area that provides my living quarters, complete with a tiny bathroom. I have a print couch that looks like a Disney version of the space age—something the Jetsons would covet. A blond wood couch frame with jutting arms and stubby blond legs supports four cushions covered in circular design fabric. A couple of wing chairs flank the couch, alongside two blond end tables. The almost matching coffee table sports a heavy marble ashtray, now used for holding chocolate candy that I take for medicinal purposes. I found a couple of black cone-shaped pole lamps at a garage sale, and an old RCA Victor TV console that I gutted and replaced with a new Zenith screen inside that features captioned viewing. Though I haven't been able to realize it yet, my dream is to open the diner as a haven for the mocha-less of Flat Skunk. Ultimately, I'd divide my time between my two loves, the *Eureka*! and caffeine.

Opening the door, I got an exuberant greeting from my other love, my signal dog Casper, a cream-colored Siberian husky who "hears" for me, and responds to sign language when she's in the mood. After a hands-and-knees workout with the dog, I helped myself to a stomachful of leftovers which I shared with her, and a hot lilac-scented bubble bath which I didn't. I changed into a long oversized T-shirt, and plopped on the couch with an ice-cold Sierra Nevada ale. Thinking momentarily of Dan Smith, I made an uncompleted TTY phone call to my ex-boyfriend, then downed the beer to take the edge off the loneliness. The last thing I remembered was lying on my couch watching Jimmy Stewart peer out his rear window at a murderer.

When I awoke the next morning to the flashing lights

of daybreak television news, with kinks in my neck, arm, and side, I was staring at our own Sheriff Elvis Mercer waving an arm in a long shot of Flat Skunk's Pioneer Cemetery.

I sat up, checked the time—7:35—and tried to read the captions as they danced across the bottom of the screen, but I only managed to catch the wrap.

"I'm Robert Goll and this is Channel Five News."

I stood as the story ended abruptly with a freeze-frame. A very lifeless body lay on a stretcher next to a waiting ambulance. A corner inset on the screen featured a snapshot of the victim's familiar face.

It was Lacy Penzance.

Lacy?

I dug frantically into the couch pillows for the remote.
I found it under my left foot and switched the channels,
hoping to catch another report. Channels 3 and 7 featured
flapping mouths, serious eyebrow work, and plenty of
photographs of Lacy Penzance, but neither station was
captioned at that hour.

What had happened to her? I had just seen her the
previous day, and now she was—dead? God! She'd been
asking for my help . . . it was unthinkable!

It took only a few more seconds to realize I could
cover the story for my paper—if I got myself to the
sheriff's office fast enough. The hell with my column on
frog fricassees. This was a real story, the solid kind of
story I had been wanting to write since I got here. But did
it have to be this? The death of Lacy Penzance, who
already seemed to have her share of sorrow lately with the
death of her husband such a short time ago. I would have
settled for a nice sex scandal or drug bust. This wasn't just
a story. This was someone's life. Someone's death.

I headed down the hall for a quick change, ran

brushes over my hair and teeth, and washed my face, adding the becoming mandatory moisturizer and makeup. Relatively clean and markedly fresh, I rummaged through my clean laundry pile for just the right outfit to wear to a sheriff's office. Pulling on a pair of brown jeans, I searched until I found a long-sleeved beige cotton sweater that I felt conveyed the casual confidence of an investigative reporter. I slipped on my black Converse All Stars and black blazer, grabbed some muffins and a carton of juice from the fridge, poured Casper the dog food equivalent of a bacon-and-eggs breakfast, and hopped on my bike.

The most populated part of Flat Skunk is Pioneer Cemetery, where the interred bodies outnumber the living residents. Its five acres are a nationally registered historic site and attract almost as many tourists as the depleted gold mines and booming cowboy bars.

I rode through town and cruised slowly past the cemetery where the televised action had taken place, honoring the yellow "Police Line—Do Not Cross" barrier. The crowds and reporters had dissipated, and only a few town residents remained on the periphery, pointing, whispering, and shaking their heads. I turned around and rode back to the sheriff's office at the other end of town.

The Flat Skunk sheriff's office, more like an outpost, is housed in an old brick building that was once an assay office. Sheriff Mercer uses the barred section on one side as a temporary holding cell for the few crooks and criminals we get on occasion—mostly drunks. The other side is a large room taken up by three desks: the sheriff's, Deputy Arnold's, and the dispatcher's. No one was in the office when I opened the door and let myself in, but the smell of lingering cigarette smoke told me someone was nearby.

I pulled the bran muffins and orange juice from my backpack, set them on the sheriff's desk, and called his name. Then I scanned the top of his desk for information that was probably none of my business. I spied two burglary reports, two assaults, one DUI, and a handful of business cards from the local television stations.

Nothing about Lacy Penzance.

I lifted a few more papers and spotted the Polaroids

tucked into a large manila envelope. Suddenly the scent of cigarette smoke grew stronger, so I snatched my hands away from the pile, and turned to greet Sheriff Elvis Mercer, forcing a casual grin.

"Hi, Sheriff." I sat on the corner of his desk trying not to look guilty. He came out of the bathroom buckling his holster and tucking in his shirt, the cigarette dangling precariously from his lips, and greeted me with a wave of his hand when it finally became free.

The sheriff's hands were smooth, hairless, and nicely manicured; not what you'd expect from a person who was supposed to whip a lot of butt, slice a lot of karate chops, or fire a bunch of high-powered weapons in the course of duty. These were office hands that typed reports, answered phones, and patted victims of stolen bicycles.

"C.W.! Didn't know you were here!" he said, removing the cigarette from his lips and dousing it in an old cup of coffee on the deputy's desk. He smoothed his wandering eyebrows, wiped something from the corner of his mouth, then went to his desk and began to search among the pile of papers.

In the short time I'd been in Flat Skunk, Sheriff Mercer and I had become friends for a number of reasons. One, I needed information for the weekly police blotter and he graciously supplied it, as long as I spelled his name correctly.

Two, I'd hired his troubled son to help out around my office, and Sheriff Mercer appreciated the respite from his single-parenting duties. Three, on occasion I brought dinner to the station and we shared a pastie or corned beef sandwich while we talked about our favorite cop shows, mystery writers, or hockey teams—"How about them Sharks!"

And four, we both had severe computer fixations. We shared our latest software and sent jokes back and forth via E-mail messages. I sent him stupid criminal stories and he sent me stupid newspaper headlines. It was a sort of competition. He was ahead, three to one.

"I called your name. Guess you didn't hear me." I poured orange juice into his chipped "Fifty Isn't Old If

You're A Tree" coffee mug. The caffeine residue inside the cup turned the orange juice the shade of burnt sienna.

"I was in the W.C." He lifted some papers from his desk, then catching a glimpse of himself in the window reflection, he patted his chin and neck. "Do you think I'm getting, you know, kinda fat?"

"Naw. You look good. Especially on TV—I saw you."

"Guess you heard the news, huh, along with everyone else in Calaveras County?"

I shrugged. I'd learned not to be too eager when trying to pull information out of a mouth that's supposed to stay shut. I took the "who-cares" approach. I'm sure he saw right through it, but he didn't let on. It's a game we play.

"It's certainly a shock," I agreed. "I can't believe Lacy Penzance is dead. I just saw her yesterday. So what happened?"

"Mickey videotaped the broadcast. I looked kinda puffy around the eyes." He tapped the puffiness.

"No. You came across great. Really natural and poised. Very professional." Truthfully, I hadn't noticed how he'd come across. I'd only caught the ending. But he'd been complaining about feeling old lately, and I figured it couldn't hurt to tell him what he needed to hear.

The sheriff, in his midfifties, was basically trim except for the impending middle-aged spread and the beginning of a slumped and burdened set of shoulders. There was a sprinkling of gray around the ears and in the tangled eyebrows. His smooth, even mouth was easy to read when it wasn't smoking, chewing gum, or eating the muffin he had just popped in.

"Gotta cut down on these muffins. My cholesterol's up again." He sat down at his desk, grabbed a handful of papers in one hand, and finished the rest of the muffin without even looking at it.

The sheriff is not your typical stereotype of a macho law enforcement officer. He's patient, caring, hardworking, fair, and even a little neurotic about his job, as well as his appearance, and his personal life. He buys self-help books to help him deal with his divorce. He sees a therapist to help him work on his relationship with his son. And he attends singles events at the community college, hoping to meet the right woman.

His only real flaw is a bad habit of abbreviating words. When he shortens a word or uses only the initials, I really have to struggle.

"You look ten pounds lighter on TV, really."

He tried not to smile. It was time to push the fat aside and chew on something solid. I sat down in the chair opposite him and leaned back, my hands folded across my chest.

"Sheriff, what happened to Lacy Penzance?"

"Don't know exactly. Kind of odd circumstances. Won't know anything until we hear from the M.E. Don't tell me you're thinking about writing something for your newspaper. This isn't your usual stuff."

I fluffed my hair, attempting to appear nonchalant. "Maybe not. But I'm getting tired of reporting the occasional untimely amphibian death. I thought I might look into it, see if I can give it a personal slant. She was well thought of in this town, wasn't she?"

Sheriff Mercer shrugged, took another sip of orange juice, a bite of a second muffin, and talked with the wad of food shoved to one side of his mouth. He was nearly incoherent, but I turned up my hearing aid and caught the main thrust. The trouble with being deaf is you have to keep your eyes on the speaker. It's tough to do that and appear only mildly interested in the conversation. That constant eye contact comes across as intense to many hearing people.

"Well, it looks like—and I do mean 'looks like'—Lacy Penzance may have committed suicide. Right there on her husband's grave."

"What?" I said, losing my poker face. "I can't—that's not—" All I could do was open and close my mouth.

Sheriff Mercer washed down the muffin with a giant gulp of juice and jotted down a few notes.

"At this point in the P.I.—preliminary investigation—we're tentatively calling it a suicide, and I do mean tentatively. She was found on her husband's grave, dressed to kill you might say, with a knife stuck in her middle. There was no sign of a struggle. It could have been self-inflicted."

I leaned in toward the sheriff, my hands gripping the edge of the desk. "But, Sheriff! A woman doesn't stab herself when she wants to commit suicide! She takes pills. She turns on the exhaust. Maybe she jumps off a bridge. But she doesn't use a gun or a knife. You know that."

He patted his chin again. "I know, I know. But it appears she was U.I.—under the influence. She reeked of it. The M.E. will tell us more."

"Still, how can you think it might be suicide when—"

He looked at me directly for the first time since he'd sat down. "She left a note."

I fell back in my chair, flabbergasted. "A suicide note?"

He nodded solemnly. "Apparently she was despondent over the death of her S.O."

"S.O.?" This one stumped me.

"Significant Other. Isn't that the P.C. term? Reuben, her hubby. Maybe she had a few too many mai tais, took a stroll to the cemetery, and decided to join him. Maybe she sat down, said her good-byes, set out her note, and poked a knife into her gut. Hard to say for sure, but that note's puzzling. We'll know more when the D. and C. comes back from the M.E."

"D and C?"

"Dice and culture. The autopsy."

I had a little hot flash at the mention of the autopsy. Lacy Penzance was going to be cut open and—I shook away the visual that loomed in my mind. God, poor woman. First on display for the television viewers, then the final invasion of privacy.

"What about that note?" I asked. "What did it say?"

"Can't comment on it until next of kin have been notified. If she has any."

While the sheriff's attention was called to the blinking red light of the telephone, I took a deep breath and tried to think where to go with all this disturbing information. Lacy Penzance had been in my office yesterday, asking for help in locating her long-lost sister, Risa Longo. Today she was dead, an apparent suicide. Presumably she'd stabbed herself to death in the cemetery.

From what I knew of her, that wasn't her style. First of all, what woman would use a knife to commit suicide when pills were so much gentler, kinder? Why would she do it in such a public place, a reserved woman like her? And why did she change her mind about running that newspaper ad about her sister, if she was so anxious to find her? The whole thing made no sense. Granted the sheriff was experienced in things like this, and he wasn't stupid, but—

The sheriff hung up the phone and turned back to me.

"Sheriff, Lacy Penzance came to see me yesterday. She wanted to put an ad in my paper . . ." I stopped. She hadn't wanted me to say anything. Was I betraying a confidence, now that she was dead?

"What for? Wanna sell her car or something?"

"No. More of a want ad than a for-sale. She was . . . searching for something. Sheriff, would it be all right if I went over to the cemetery and looked around a little?"

The sheriff puffed up a little, trying to look official. "Sorry, C.W. I've got a line there right now and you can't cross without an escort."

I figured he meant some sort of police line. "Haven't you already investigated the scene?"

"A prelim., yes, but we may need more. I'd take you but I'm overwhelmed with paper work this morning. Until we hear from the M.E., it's off limits. Maybe later." He looked searchingly around his desk. I pointed to the envelope of snapshots. The sheriff eyed me suspiciously, then opened the envelope and spread the photos on the desk.

They were difficult to look at. But they were also a little unreal. Lacy looked almost posed, lying in front of the gravestone. There was little blood in the picture—just a small spot where one of her hands lay near the knife in her abdomen. The other arm lay limp at her side. Her legs were spread open, a rather unladylike stance for a woman who cared so much about appearances.

The sheriff gathered up the pictures and returned them to the envelope. I stood up and headed for the door, unable to shake the feeling that Lacy's body language was odd, even in death. When I glanced back to say good-bye, I caught the tail end of a comment.

"What?" I said.

He patted his stomach. "Thanks for the muffins. What were they—tree branch?"

"Bran. They're good for you. No fat, no sugar, no salt."

"No flavor," he said, and went back to his work.

I closed the door and spotted Mickey Arnold walking toward the sheriff's office. The deputy's mouth was shaped as if he was sucking up a straw. I figured he must be whistling, even though I didn't know what whistling was exactly. Someone explained it to me once as air blowing out and making a high-pitched sound. Didn't help. Looked stupid.

"Hey, Mickey. I was just heading for the cemetery. Have you been over there yet?"

Mickey smiled and signed "good morning" as stiffly as an arthritic in a high wind, but I appreciated the attempt. I signed it back, then retrieved my mountain bike from the side of the sheriff's office.

"Thought maybe you could tell me what you figure happened over there. I was thinking about writing something for the paper. Maybe I could give it a slant, you know, like how a sheriff's deputy investigates an unusual death in a small town."

Mickey had been responsible for a recent drug bust that I'd featured in the *Eureka!* He'd caught the Penryn brothers growing pot in their bathroom.

"Uh, sure," he said, standing a little taller. Then he glanced at the door to the station and his shoulders sagged a bit. "Just let me check in first . . ."

"Okay, but be warned. The sheriff's not in the best of moods. There's an awful lot of paper work on his desk he's looking to pass out."

Mickey thought about it a moment, sucked in his lips, then fell in behind me as I began walking my bike down the street. I turned around, gave him my sweetest smile, and let him catch up.

"All right, I guess I've got a few minutes. But you can't touch anything. And you better watch your step. The medical examiner said there might be some more evidence we haven't found yet, so we can't go walking all over . . ."

His jaw kept on moving as we headed toward Pioneer Cemetery. I haven't a clue what he was babbling on about. I was too deep in thought to pay attention.

The cemetery still bore a few stragglers, although the media vans were nowhere in sight. No doubt they were on the hour-long drive back to Sacramento, anxious to edit their video footage for the evening news. How would Flat Skunk appear to the public after some creative "packaging" by the editing techs?

That's all we needed. The kind of publicity that would bring in the borderline nuts and maniac militia. If nothing else, perhaps an honest and thorough report on Lacy Penzance's death in the *Eureka!* could equalize the sensationalism of the tabloids and talk shows.

Flat Skunk is an interesting town. I appreciated it every time I walked from one end to the other. As the deputy and I headed for the cemetery at the edge of town, I couldn't help scanning the rustic storefront facades that had been built decades earlier by what looked like a Hollywood set designer. Reuben Penzance had wanted his town to retain the look and feel of the old mining camp it once was. He'd hired a prop constructor to "authenticate" the buildings by creating false fronts, horse hitching posts, wooden sidewalks, and brick streets. Behind each western-style facade stood ordinary structures, hidden by bravado from public view.

I glanced over at Mickey and caught him midsentence as we neared the cemetery.

". . . and you know why I like your mystery puzzles, Connor?"

"Because you're a cop?" I offered.

Mickey used meaningless hand gestures to illustrate his explanation. "Huh-uh. I like them because at first, no one has a motive for the crime. At least, that's the way it looks. Then you start uncovering their secrets and you find out *everyone* has a reason to kill the victim. Secrets. That's why I like 'em. Nothing is as it appears. That's why I love police work, too." He ended his speech with his palms turned up, a childlike open-mouthed grin on his face.

"Thanks, Mickey. Glad you're enjoying them. I think my next one will be a takeoff on Dick Lupoff's comic book killer. Someone comes in and steals a valuable *Little Lulu*."

"I remember *Little Lulu*! I used to love those comics!" He stopped in his tracks as he spoke, as if stunned by this mutual interest.

"My favorites were the ones with Witch Hazel," I said.

"Yeah! She was great. Always scaring Little Lulu. God, Connor, we have a lot in common."

I smiled and walked on. Always scaring Little Lulu. Ha. Nothing could scare Little Lulu. Not even Tubby. I looked back and started to offer a retort, but Mickey had turned away. He seemed to be calling to the meager crowd at the cemetery, waving his arms and shaking his head.

It was mostly kids on skateboards, Roller Blades, and bikes, a couple of older women talking, nodding, and point-ing, and some of the good ol' boys, chewin' and spittin'. I spotted old Sluice Jackson on a small knoll, tending some bushes outside the police line. His rheumy eyes locked on us as we approached the barrier.

Deputy Arnold told the kids to get lost, with quite a lot of official bluster and self-importance. They ignored him and kept on staring at the police line up the hill. I felt a little sorry for Mickey—he didn't command the same respect as the sheriff. But he was a dedicated police officer who took his job seriously, and I respected that. I just thought he should lighten up a little.

A kid, maybe ten or eleven, ran out from the corner of the roped-off section of the cemetery. Spotting the deputy, the boy dropped to the ground in an effort to hide himself.

"Get on out of there, Brian Hurley, or I'll throw you in the slammer," the deputy said, his face tight, his arms waving. Brian Hurley got up and walked toward his friends, who gave him a hero's welcome. They all took off down the street to celebrate his victory of crossing the police line without getting arrested.

"Stupid kids," Mickey said, tucking in his shirt in an effort to recapture his composure. "That area there is full of possible evidence, not to mention poison oak. They'll be itching and scratching by tomorrow." The deputy scratched his arm vigorously in empathy, and led the way up the hill.

The front of the park was dramatically different from the older part of the grounds beyond the ridge, where the early settlers were permanently settled. Pioneer Cemetery had begun its career as a traditional burial place for the forty-niners and their families, with large stone markers, fancy engravings, and poetic dedications. The mounds were uneven, the gravestones chipped, broken, weathered, and discolored, and the plots were as varied as the clapboard houses in Flat Skunk. It was here that silent history could be heard, if you listened the right way. I paused to read a headstone before following Mickey up the hill.

Here lyes a loving, caring wife,
A soft and tender mother;
A friend who's free from pain and stryfe,
There never was another.

The old Pioneer Church that had originally welcomed the citizens of Flat Skunk had long since been torn down. According to Mickey, after French McClusky bought the property to add to his Memory Kingdom chain, the massive and unused front acreage had been converted into a modern memorial park with expansive lawns and immaculately tended grounds, complete with benches, a children's playground, and picnic tables. The newer area featured flat marble-veneered markers instead of the upright headstones found in the older section. This was a park for the living as well as the dead. If you gazed at it from a distance, you almost couldn't tell it was a cemetery at all.

We walked up the hill to a section in the older part of the burial ground where the police line had been erected. Mickey ducked under the barrier and held it up for me. I followed him into the silent city.

"Over there is the Penzance plot," Mickey said. "Watch where you walk. We've pretty much covered it, but you never know."

We tiptoed carefully along the border of the Cornish dead. Nearly one-half of the population of Flat Skunk was descended from Cornwall, England. The rest were a mixture of European and Asian ancestry. Their early settlers all had one thing in common: the lust for gold.

Septimus Penzance's monument was in the center, a dark and weathered obelisk that stood seven feet tall, with softened engravings on each of the four sides. The rest of the family lay around him, enclosed in a foot-high stone fence.

"Baby Penzance, born September 26, 1864, died September 28, 1864," was nestled in a marble crib. "Blenda Penzance, our loving daughter," had died just short of her third birthday in 1898. The family plots were filled with children who hadn't survived the harsh conditions or contagious diseases of the era.

Reuben Penzance's tombstone at the edge of the plot was the traditional upright granite marker. It was fresh and unmarked by time, weather, or vandals, but the dark stain of what I imagined was blood at its base made me shudder. Next to it stood Lacy's stone, marked only with her name and birthday, the final date yet to be inscribed. She had probably purchased it when she had bought her husband's stone—they were identical in design, lettering, and wear.

"Ever read *Pet Sematary*, that book by Stephen King?" the deputy asked as he glanced around, breaking the pensive spell. "This old section kinda reminds me of that book. Creepy, you know."

Mickey waved to Sluice Jackson, who was digging haphazardly around a tree, then squatted down next to the tombstone. I squatted, too, so I could read Mickey's lips. Being so close to the grave, I was aware of a peculiar smell, not unlike the white paste I used to sample in kindergarten. Or was it the stuff we used to use in science class—formaldehyde? My imagination was getting to me. Had I pithed too many frogs to shake the association of this smell with death?

"She was found here . . . ?" I prodded, allowing him to assume I knew more than I did. It's a good technique for getting information.

Mickey ran his eyes over the blood stain. "Yeah, about seven this morning, by the Clemetson kid who cuts through the Pioneer on his way to school every day." With a bend of his head he indicated the opposite side of the hill. "Scared the bejesus out of him, I'll tell ya. Came running into the office like a rabid skunk screaming, 'There's a dead body in the cemetery. There's a dead body in the cemetery.' Over and over." Mickey waved his hands like a frightened kid. "So I says, 'Yeah, and I'll bet you got Prince Albert in a can,' and . . ."

Mickey laughed, then noticed my blank expression and shrugged. "Anyway, the sheriff wasn't in yet, so Craig, the kid, he drags me over here and sure enough, there's Lacy Penzance lying here against this grave, her hand covering a circle of blood, the knife—" Deputy Arnold rubbed his forehead, as if trying to rub away the image. "So I radioed the sheriff."

"Sheriff Mercer said it may be a suicide."

Mickey raised both eyebrows. "I suppose so . . ." He glanced over at Sluice and cocked his jaw.

"What do *you* think?" I prodded, with an emphasis on the "you."

Mickey took his eyes off Sluice and looked at me. He spoke slowly, deliberately. "I don't know. There was a knife in her chest. That's not a common way to commit suicide, man or woman. But it's possible. One of her hands had kinda dropped down to her side, as if she had let go of the knife after using it. You know, it reminds me a lot of one of your mystery puzzles."

I thought about the Polaroid pictures I'd seen at the sheriff's office. "So you have your doubts, too."

He rubbed his forehead again, which was beginning to turn a little red from all the attention. "I figure, if she wanted to commit suicide, why here? Why with a knife? But if somebody killed her, why do it on the grave? How'd they get her here? There aren't any tracks like she was dragged. And who would want to kill Lacy Penzance? Like I said, it reminds me of one of your puzzles."

He paused, scratched his arm again, and surveyed the area. I urged him on. "Can you show me what she looked like when you found her? You know, her body language?"

Mickey sat down on a nearby grave to demonstrate. It took him several seconds to get into position. "She was sort of like this." He lay across the grave, his legs open, one hand on the ground, the other at his side, his head tilted to the side.

I tried to visualize Lacy Penzance in that awkward, unladylike position. "What was she wearing?" I asked, remembering only a skirt and blouse.

"A skirt, black. Kinda tight. It was open, there." He pointed to the area between his knees. "Had a sweater-like thing on top—pink, with black decorations on it, like little circles. Lots of jewelry—all gold. An earring was missing from one ear. Hasn't turned up yet. No coat, even though it was fairly cool last night. She ran the knife right through her sweater. Didn't even lift it up."

"What kind of knife was it?"

Mickey thought for a moment, his eyes shifting to Reuben Penzance's grave, as if to conjure up the image. "It was a fancy one, not one of those you order from the TV ads. The maid showed me her kitchen stuff this morning. A similar knife was missing from a collection she kept on a rack on the counter. I figure it was hers."

He stood up, shook out his pant legs, and brushed off

the back of his jeans. "I think I'll take another quick look around. Never know. I got a feeling we might've missed something."

"Okay to touch this?" I asked, referring to Reuben's gravestone. It was covered with a patina of white powder and red dust.

Mickey nodded. "It's been printed."

I ran my hand over the inscription. The stone was cold, hard, and disturbingly new. According to the date cut on the marker, Reuben Penzance had died last October. He was fifty-two years old.

While Mickey searched the site, I tried to recall what I knew of Reuben's death. I'd heard he'd been on a hunting trip with old Sluice. The story was that Penzance had fallen over in the boat and drowned. The sheriff said they had investigated and ruled it accidental. Jilda said Sluice Jackson, the lone survivor, hasn't been the same since.

I caught the deputy waving his arms to get my attention. "Hey, Connor, I gotta get back. Didn't find anything. I don't think the earring's here," he mouthed exaggeratedly. I hated when he did that. It made him look like an ape.

"So what happens next?" I asked as we headed back toward the street.

"Wait for the medical examiner's report. Then we should know more. But I wouldn't be surprised if they call it something other than suicide." He stopped abruptly and looked at me. "That's off the record, Connor. There's no story yet. Just supposition. I don't want to read about any of this in the *Eureka!* until we know what's what."

"Don't worry," I said, although I hated that phrase. It was something my ex-lover had said to me every time he wanted to skirt an issue. But noncommittal came in handy for the moment.

"Well, gotta go. Maybe we could have coffee later? Or I could rent that movie, *Children of a Lesser God*, and bring it by your place tonight. With a pizza?"

Children of a Lesser God? It was a good movie, but it wasn't the only movie a deaf person wanted to watch. I

suppose if I'd been Asian, he'd want to rent me a Jackie
Chan or Bruce Lee film.

"Yeah, maybe. Call me." I smiled lamely and waved
him off. He signed "See you later"—with an awkward
twist of an "L" in midair—and headed down the street
toward the sheriff's office.

I glanced back at the cemetery, paused a few minutes
until Mickey was out of sight, and decided to take another
look at the area surrounding the police line. The barrier
enclosed only a small section, leaving the rest for friends
and families to wander about and visit their departed
loved ones. I walked down the path, through the newer
area, moving deeper into the past. The farther back I
walked, the older and more decaying the cemetery
became.

I revisited my great-grandmother, Sierra Westphal,
honored by a modest marker amidst her own pioneering
family. She was lying next to her husband, William, and
not far from her sons, Cullin, Cosmo, and Jackson Westphal. She had lived to be eighty-six years old, dying in
August of 1915. Curiously, she had lived only a month
longer than her husband. The inscriptions on the twin
graves were difficult to read, aged by the elements, but I
could still make out the archaic poem that had been
inscribed on Sierra's stone:

Here lyes MOTHER,
Moved Above;
Gone and Left Us
With Her Love.

I passed by several other stones, wondering who had
died from smallpox, cholera, typhoid, tuberculosis, and
other long-lost diseases; who had died from broken hearts;
whose lives had been cut short by greed, fraud, jealousy,
or revenge; who had died of unknown causes.

Vandals had come and gone over the years, doing
damage to the Flat Skunk heritage, until finally French
McClusky had taken over the funeral business. He orga-
nized the Friends of the Cemetery, a charitable group that

offered time and money to preserve the historic site. Lacy Penzance had no doubt been on that committee, too.

The Friends had reconstructed many of the broken monuments, patched chips and cracks, and carefully rescued the land from weeds and erosion. Even so, many of these markers that had been created to last forever were on their way to becoming dust themselves.

> Darcy Muff Sutton.
> Died of thin clothes
> And no shoes.
> April 17, 1889, aged 16 years.

I walked the cobblestone path through history, curious about what life had been like in the gold country over a hundred and fifty years ago.

> Sacred to the memory of
> Major Jeffrey D. Knight
> Who was killed by the accidental discharge
> Of a pistol by his deputy.
> 14th April 1878.

> Neglected by his mother,
> Ill treated by his wife,
> Ignored by all his children,
> He gave up on life.
> Good-bye Leonidas W. Smiley

> Beneath this stone a woman lies;
> Her heart a broken shell,
> The man she loved, he died too soon,
> Now she is dead, as well.

No name was inscribed. Had Lacy Penzance died of a broken heart too? I turned away from the solemn markers, full of troubling questions about the Pioneer Cemetery's next resident.

I got on my bike and rode the short distance to the hotel. Although the May nights were still cool, the morning was already beginning to warm up the town, and the sun cast a diagonal spotlight on the main street. As usual, the early morning air was scented by the town's namesake.

The reality of Lacy Penzance's death was beginning to sink in, and I had an uneasy feeling. I wanted to know more about the distant but charitable woman, and not just for my newspaper story. I couldn't shake the sense that I owed her somehow.

I climbed the hotel steps, two at a time, and entered the hallway. Boone Joslin's door stood ajar as I walked by. I pushed it open slowly.

Dan was facing the window overlooking the street, his weathered cowboy boots propped on the desk. He was tapping a pencil and waving his feet to a beat. I looked over at the radio and saw the "on" light lit up.

"Hi," I said, quietly. Must have been too quietly. He made no move. "Hello?!" I said again.

Dan turned around, pulled his feet down from the

desk, and stopped the beat of his pencil. "Connor! Hey. How you doing?"

I shrugged halfheartedly. I wondered if he'd heard the news. "What are you listening to?" I said.

I didn't know different types of music by sound, but I knew them by reputation. I found that the kind of music people listened to told me a lot about them. Most folks around here favor country-western tunes, and worship the likes of Clint Black, Garth Brooks, and Dwight Yoakam. My old boyfriend used to say I was better off deaf when it came to country music. He only listened to jazz. That's when I learned about music snobs.

"Music," he said.

I made an "I-know-that" face.

"It's called Zydeco. From Louisiana. Kind of like—"

"Soul, country, polka, and French all rolled into one."

He gave me a "how-did-you-know-that?" look. "You know much about music?"

I shrugged again. Better to maintain a little mystique. "Heard from your brother yet?"

Dan tapped his pencil, double-time, and shook his head.

"Did you hear about Lacy Penzance?" I asked.

"That the woman who killed herself in the cemetery?" He slowed the pencil rhythm.

"Yeah. How did you find out?"

"The waitress at the coffee shop told me. What's her name? Jilly or something? Said the woman stabbed herself on her husband's grave."

"I suppose she told you why, too?"

"Said she was unhappy about the death of her husband or something. Left a note."

What, I wondered, was the point of having a newspaper in this town? Everybody knew everything before it even hit print. Maybe I could learn Lacy's dress size or where her birthmarks were located if I spent more time at the Nugget Café.

I pulled up the folding chair and sat down across the desk from him. "Don't you think it's kind of weird that she supposedly killed herself when—" I paused. Maybe I shouldn't say too much. After all, Lacy had taken me into her confidence. Just because she was dead didn't mean I could go blabbing her secrets.

"When what?" Dan asked. The pencil paused. "You think there's something more to it?" he added.

I squirmed in the chair a little, trying to get comfortable. "No, I just think it's strange, that's all, to commit suicide on your husband's grave in the local cemetery in the middle of the night. Especially when—" I stopped myself again. "Well, it's just not something I would do. But then, I'm not much like her."

Dan smiled. It was a disconcerting smile. I frowned and stood up.

"I better get to work."

I turned and headed for the door. A wadded-up paper hit the wall in front of me. People were always throwing wadded-up papers at me. I turned around; Dan was grinning widely at what he thought was a clever way of attracting my attention. I picked up the tossed ball.

"Connor, I'm planning to go to Whiskey Slide to see if I can find Boone," Dan said, dropping the smile. "I think he may have gone up there on a case. I may be away awhile. Thought you might want to know."

I said nothing, but silently decided it was time to find out a little more about Dan Smith. I pressed the ball of paper tightly in my hand, raised my arm, then threw it back at him. Got him, right in the heart.

With the advent of the TTY, we deaf people finally came out of the Dark Ages in terms of long-distance communication. It's only been in the past few of decades that we've been able to use the telephone via the teletype system, then electronics. Before that we relied on the tedious methods of writing letters or asking neighbors and friends for emergency telephone assistance. Our hope for the future: a TTY/computer in every home and office. I'm not holding my breath.

Fortunately, most government offices now own TTY's, and those that don't are accessible through the California Relay System, which offers telephone interpreting services. The New Mexico Corrections Facility owned a TTY, I discovered, after I switched on the device, placed the receiver in the handset, and dialed the long-distance number. After a short delay, electronic letters began to move across the glowing red display terminal.

"Dept. of Corrections. Sgt. Bruce Taylor. GA."

You can often tell when a hearing person is using the TTY as opposed to a deaf person. The deaf tend to use all capitals, omit punctuation, and use common abbreviations. Hearies type more formally, as if writing a business letter. I adapt to the caller.

"This is Connor Westphal from the *Eureka!* newspaper, Calaveras Co., CA. We're interviewing an applicant for police beat position and need references verified. Was a Daniel Webster Smith in your employ recently? GA."

I typed as quickly as I could and kept it brief, but the TTY was still a relatively slow process taking sometimes four to five times longer. And it cost more than a long-distance call because of the time delays.

"Hold on . . ."

The cursor flashed for a few moments, then came to life with more electronic letters.

"Daniel Webster Smith worked for the Dept. for 8 years, until June of last year. Job title was 'Instructor, Dept. of Corrections.' GA."

Instructor. What did he teach the prisoners? I wondered.

"Could you tell me what courses he taught? GA."

Another delay. "According to the file, law. GA."

Law? "Is he an attorney? GA."

Pause. "Says 'Instructor.' That's it. GA."

"Does the file give a reason for his resignation? GA."

Another delay. "Didn't resign. Says here, 'Employment terminated. Conflict of interest.' GA."

"Does it say anything about next of kin or who to call in emergency? GA."

"Nothing here. GA."

I thanked the sergeant and keyed off.

Dan Smith was terminated from his job at the correctional facility for conflict of interest. What kind of conflict?

Was this guy Boone's brother or not? I tried to imagine the two of them side by side, but the contrast was too extreme. Dan was tall, well built, with arms you wanted to capture in photographs and hang on your walls. Boone was short, mostly paunch, with hairy arms and ruddy red hands. Dan had a well-trimmed blondish beard, hair a little too long to work in law enforcement, and blue eyes that probably glowed in the dark. Boone had chins where a beard should have grown, a scalp like a crystal ball, and red-rimmed green eyes that looked especially appropriate at Christmas time.

Siblings. My thoughts moved to Lacy Penzance and the sister she had been trying to locate with the newspaper ad. Risa Longo. Who was she? Shouldn't she be notified of her sister's death, even if she didn't know she had a sister? And where was she?

I set the receiver in the TTY handset again and placed a call to Sheriff Mercer, who also had a TTY.

After a few moments, "C.W.? GA." appeared on my screen. He must have known my ring. Either that or I'm the only deaf person who calls him.

"Hi, Sheriff. Got a question for you. Know anybody by the name of Risa Longo? GA."

"LOngo. YEah. HOw do yuo know her? GA."

I ignored his question and his typing skill. Like father, like son. "What can you tell me about her? GA."

"I'm not so surre I shoudl." There was a pause. I waited it out. "All I can say is, taht's the name written on the back of a business card found in LAcy Penzance's purse. RIsa LOngo. NOw, wanna tell me who she is?"

I loved the way he typed—omitting letters here, throwing extras in there, hanging onto the shift key a little too long. I waited for the GA, thinking this might be another pause. Half the time the sheriff forgot to add the "Go Ahead" signal. After a few more seconds I gave up and resumed keying.

"Not sure, Sheriff. Just heard her name mentioned recently. What kind of business card was it? Did it say anything else? GA."

"THat was all. IT was a busines card from MEmory KIngdom. WITY? Whos this Longo woman? GA."

WITY. What's It To You. One of his favorite abbreviations. "I really don't know yet. Memory Kingdom—the one in Flat Skunk? GA."

"Whiskey Slide. WHat are you nott elling me, Connor Westphal? Spit it out. OR should I say spell it out? GA."

"Nothing yet. Just trying to write a decent story about Lacy's death for the paper. Was there anything else in her purse? GA."

"JUst a bunch of makeup, a roll of tickets to the frog-jumping contest, acouple more business cards, ssome cash, women's stuff, you know. Thats about it. GA."

"Did the other business cards have anything written on them? GA."

"NOpe. 1 from a dr. Reed NIemi in Whiskey slide. 1 from dr. Enid SChantz here in town. 1 from a dr. KRistin Larsen in Sac. 1 from Beau's B & B. Nothig on the back of them tho. Whats this all abuot? GA."

"I'm not sure. I'll tell you if anything comes of it. Thanks for the info. GA. SK."

"COnn . . ."

I hung up before he could continue. I was more than a little puzzled. Risa Longo's name was written on a business card for a Memory Kingdom outlet in Whiskey Slide. The same town Dan Smith was headed for in search of his brother. The brother that Lacy hired to find her sister. The town that was written on the empty file folder.

Risa Longo and Memory Kingdom?

Maybe Risa Longo was dead too. Maybe Lacy Penzance discovered somehow that her sister had died—saw an obituary notice or something in one of the papers, and located her through the funeral home in Whiskey Slide. Maybe Lacy was overcome with grief at losing her only known relative and—

Oh, get real, Connor. Lacy Penzance is not going to kill herself because of a sister she's never known. Still, I had a feeling the sister had something to do with her death. And the only connection I had was the Memory Kingdom funeral home in Whiskey Slide.

It was noon by the time I stopped puzzling over all the loose ends. So what was all this to me? I was curious, naturally. I am, after all, a newspaper reporter. And if I could find out something that wasn't already common knowledge to the entire town, it would make an interesting story. Hell, let's face it. I loved a mystery.

But most of all I felt I had a little unfinished business. Yesterday I was taking Lacy Penzance's ad. A few hours later I was seeing her on television—dead.

I stretched my back, shook my hair, bent my fingers back to release some tension, and decided all this thinking was making me hungry. Time for a lunch break. I left a note for Miah, then stopped off at the Nugget for a BLT and a Sierra Nevada Pale Ale.

On my way out I picked up the Tuesday edition of the *Mother Lode Monitor* to scope out the competition. I was halfway across the street when I saw Mickey Arnold coming out of Gold Dust Drugs wearing a new pair of motorcycle-cop sunglasses. I supposed he wanted to look the part of a tough cop, but the price tag dangling by one ear tempered the effect.

"Deputy Arnold," I said cautiously, after seeing his face light up. He was a likable kind of guy, but I didn't want to lead him on. He wasn't the type you'd want to French kiss in front of the fireplace. Still, he had his appeal—the enthusiasm for his work, the awkwardness of his flirtation, the genuine love for his hometown.

The Terminator wannabee waved when he saw me, removed his glasses, and twirled them in his fingers while he played nervously with his gun belt. But the twirling was too great a task for his coordination and he fumbled them to the ground.

After a quick rebound, he stiffly finger-spelled, "Hi, Connor," then signed, "What's new?" At this point he began to talk. "Learn anything more for your story?"

"Not much. Just filling the pages with the same old fluff—ground-breakings, fund-raisers, frog profiles, cemetery suicides. The usual."

Mickey laughed, making one of those gagging motions that remind me of watching a cat choking on a furball. He brushed back a few wisps of moussed hair that had become dislodged from his slicked-back style.

"Thanks for the guided tour through the cemetery this morning. Any news on Lacy yet?" I asked, as coyly as I could muster. Shame on me.

"Not much." He checked over his shoulder and stepped in closer, as if someone might hear us. "The report from the medical examiner came back. They don't think that knife actually killed her." He looked pleased with himself.

"Really? You were right! So what do they think it was?" I leaned in too, even though I didn't need to. Deputy Arnold looked around again for spies. No KGB in sight.

"Well, this is strictly off the record so you can't print it in the paper yet, but the M.E. couldn't identify it. Said it was something . . ." He whipped out a tiny notebook, flipped a few pages, and read his scribbling. ". . . long, thin, and sharp."

"But not a knife."

Mickey shook his head and pursed his lips, dramatically.

"What do you think it was?" I pumped away.

He tried to look casual, dropping one shoulder and placing a hand on his gun belt. "Well, here's what I think, but it's only a theory I'm working on. She was found at the cemetery, right? There wasn't a lot of blood, just that dark stain on her blouse and some on the stone, right? A person holds about five pints of blood, you know. And the thing that killed her was something long and sharp—"

"Like an ice pick?"

He shook his head. "I don't think so. Something thicker, more like a . . ." He looked around. ". . . a knitting needle or maybe one of those things they use at the hospital—a catheter. But—" He pressed his lips together then mouthed the word so firmly his lips turned white. "The sheriff is fairly certain it's not a suicide."

"What about the note they found?" I asked, leaning closer still. I hated myself when I used my feminine charms. But a girl's gotta do what a girl's gotta do.

"I found it, actually," he said humbly. "Anyway, it just didn't sound right, you know. All that stuff about—well, I better not say. You know."

No, dammit, I didn't know! Come on, Deputy, out with it!

I waited but he said nothing more on the subject. "I gotta get back to work. Going to the Jubilee for a little frog-tasting this weekend?"

It was hopeless. "Wouldn't miss it," I said with a sigh, and climbed on my bike.

Mickey Arnold pointed to his eye, then to me. "See you," he signed, crudely. I had to smile.

"Oh, great!" I said, scanning the headline of a special edition of the competition when I got back to the office.

DOWAGER DEATH STUNS SKUNK

Another winning slug from those masterful word-smiths at the *Mother Lode Monitor*. They even had a photo. The sheriff looked like a dweeb.

The article was overwritten, ungrammatical, and full of hyperbole, but it had sure scooped the hell out of the *Eureka!* How did they manage to print the story so fast? The by-line read Harmony Blaine.

Lacy Penzance, well-known philanthropist and widow of former Flat Skunk mayor, Reuben Pen-zance, died yesterday of an apparent stab wound in the local Pioneer Cemetery.

Her body was found by ten-year-old Brian Hurley on his way to school at 7:05 A.M. this morning, and immediately reported to Deputy Mickey Arnold at the Flat Skunk Sheriff's office.

Initially labeled a self-inflicted knife wound, further investigation by this reporter has revealed there may have been a second weapon involved that caused Penzance's death, laying question to the theory of suicide.

At this point in Sheriff Elvis Mercer's investigation no suspects have been identified. The sheriff is still pursuing a number of leads.

Damn! Beat out by a throwaway bird-cage liner. I rolled up the paper and tossed it into the trash. It was time for a little old-fashioned newspaper war.

I stopped down the hall at Miah's comic book shop. Miah looked up from his *Batman: The Death of Robin* special edition and signed, "What's up?" by shaking an upturned hand in the air.

"Miah, I'm going to Whiskey Slide for a little while and I probably won't be back until late. I need to finish that story on gourmet frog fare by tonight. Think you could do it for me?"

I signed at a moderate speed and moved my lips to help him understand. He seemed to follow every word. I can tell when beginners don't understand my signs. They just nod their heads rhythmically, then give me a blank stare at the end of my speech.

Miah brushed his index finger up the front of his chin, for "Sure," then shook his head while signing "problem," meaning "No problem."

Since he owed me, I gave him two more assignments—one about the frog play given by Mrs. Stadelhofer's fourth grade class, and one about the history of the Frog Jubilee in Calaveras County. In appeasement, I promised to look for a couple of *Dark Man* and *The Stranger* comics at Whiskey Slide's Comic Central store.

"By the way, someone called while you were out, but they hung up when I said hello. Happened twice," Miah said, his fingers illustrating his statements.

I responded with face language—a frown.

"Oh," he continued. "And that guy staying in Boone's office left a note. It's on your desk."

I returned to my office and picked up Dan's note from the desk.

"Connor, forgot to ask a favor. Would you feed my cat while I'm gone? Food is in the microwave. Thanks. Dan."

I tossed the note into the garbage can and gathered up a few things before heading out.

I never saw it coming.

I was halfway home, pedaling furiously on my all-terrain bike and no doubt looking like the demoniac Margaret Hamilton in *The Wizard Of Oz*, when a bright red Miata pulled out right in front of me.

I grabbed the handlebars—I was riding with no hands, a skill I'd learned early so I could sign to my riding partners while biking—then jerked the bars sideways to avoid a collision, nearly swerving into a roadside ditch. It was the small pothole I didn't see that caused me to kiss the pavement.

I took the handlebars in the chest, knocking the wind out as I landed on the graveled red pavement, a pretzel of body and bike. For several seconds I lay on the ground, gasping for breath like a fish out of water. As soon as I could speak, I said only one word, unfit for print in my family newspaper.

What I thought was pavement turned out to be red clay mixed with bits of rock. I stood up stiffly, brushing the crimson patina from my once-beige sweater and brown jeans, and surveyed the damage.

At first glance it looked like I could ride the two-wheeler home, providing I didn't need to sit on the crooked seat and I didn't mind steering with reversed handlebars. I straddled the front wheel, twisted the bars into forward position an inch at a time, then checked the rims and wheels for further damage. Two popped tires clinched it. I wouldn't be riding my bike home.

Until this point I'd felt no real pain except for a tightness in my chest from getting the wind knocked out, and a little stinging on my legs. But my knees were starting to throb, so I took a moment to check them. Peeking through my newly shredded jeans were a pair of scarlet kneecaps glistening in the sunlight. The twin circles were bright red except for the small dark circles that dotted the circles. I bent over; a closer look revealed the horror I had feared. Tiny pebbles were embedded in my bloody knees.

"Fuck!" was only one of the words I used while reviling the jerk who caused all the damage. That was followed by more creative language I had picked up at deaf camp as a kid.

The car, nothing but dust on the horizon, had pulled out of the nearby parking lot of the Mark Twain Slept Here bed and breakfast inn, one of the most popular overnight lodges in the Mother Lode. I badly needed some clean water and a couple of hefty Band-Aids or I'd never make it home. Feeling a little dizzy and short of breath, I propped the bike against a nearby tree, and hobbled up the short flight of steps to the inn's front door, trying not to imagine how bad I was going to feel when the numbness dissipated.

The ten-room, trigabled Victorian mansion, which now took in honeymooners, traveling salesmen, and city-weary executives, had once been the boyhood home of Reuben Penzance. Built by his great-grandfather, Septimus, it had been passed on to his grandfather and later his father. According to a local guidebook, the home had finally been sold when Reuben was in elementary school, as the Penzance family prospered.

The wrought-iron fence surrounding the grounds sported a bronze plaque that defined the architecture and

gave the original date as 1853. Considering gold was discovered in 1848, it hadn't taken old man Penzance long to
build his first dream house.

Now, standing among the lodgepole pines, the home
had been renamed the Mark Twain Slept Here Inn, after
the Mother Lode's favorite historical character, who did in
fact spend a night as a guest of the Penzance family. The
mansion was now coated with what must have been a
dozen layers of paint—this time a distracting shade of pink
with lavender and blue gingerbread trim. The word "cute"
didn't do it justice. Cinderella could have worn a version
of the monstrosity to the ball.

I considered knocking on one of the two front doors.
They both featured a pair of tole-painted old miners that
had been added since I'd last been to the Mark Twain. I
opted for the knob instead, after encouragement from
both the "Welcome Forty-Niners" sign overhead and
doormat beneath my feet.

The door opened to a cozy foyer, where Beau Pascal,
the current owner, had added a rolltop front desk. I
tapped the summons bell, then placed my palm on the
desk to feel the vibration. I'd once rung a doorbell for fifteen minutes before the occupant opened the door by
chance and told me the bell had been disconnected.

I was studying a wall display of miners' picks, pans,
and assorted tools when a wad of sticky paper, like a giant
spit ball, bounced off my head, followed by another, and
another.

"You've got a serious termite problem here, mister,"
I said, looking toward the assault weapon's point of
origin. Leaning over the upstairs railing was a slim,
slightly balding man in a Bloomingdale's T-shirt. Upside-
down, his thinning hair hung in delicate wisps like spider
webbing.

"Hey, Connor. How you doin'?" I'm not entirely sure
that's what he said, since he was hanging upside-down
over the balcony. Talk about a lipreading challenge.

I met Beau when I'd first arrived in Flat Skunk.
Needing a place to stay until I fixed up my own place,
we'd struck up a bargain. He'd just reopened the inn and

could use some publicity to get started, so he'd given me a cut-rate room in exchange for discount advertising in the *Eureka!*

Beau bounded down the stairs in a kind of two-step manner. The man never seemed to run out of energy. I suspected a coffee addiction.

"Finally ready to give up that Diner From Hell you poured your life savings into, Connor? Want to move back here 'til those condos are built over in Whiskey Slide?"

The catty remarks about my home were part of a running joke between us, the old my-house-is-better-than-your-house routine. He was currently hanging new wallpaper, which gave him the lead for the moment.

"The offer is tempting, but I'm not leaving the diner without a proper fight. And so far I've beat the electrical, the plumbing, and the dry rot." I looked down at my knees. The stinging felt like a multiple needle attack.

Beau followed my glance. "Whoa! Looks like you've lost the latest fight, Connor! What happened? Finally take a header on that bike of yours? I told you to keep your hands on the handlebars. But you have to be a show-off!"

He pulled out a small first-aid kit from beneath the desk, made a close-up inspection, and grimaced.

"Some idiot pulled out of your parking lot right in front of me as I was riding home."

"Well, looks like I'm gonna have to amputate," Beau said, brandishing a mean pair of scissors and a reckless, evil grin. "The pants, that is. Hope you got them on sale."

Thirty minutes and several snips later I was wearing a pair of fifty-dollar cutoffs with dark red fringe. Beau had me sitting on the toilet seat with my legs propped up on an antique chair, while he performed surgery in the bathroom. A small pile of tiny rocks lay on a piece of paper toweling on the counter. The Mercurochrome covering my knees hadn't kicked in yet, nor had the liquid anesthetic Beau had offered from the minibar disguised as an old mining cart. My knees hurt like hell, not to mention my hands, my elbows, and my right shoulder.

"You should have been a nurse," I told Beau over a second glass of freshly squeezed orange juice when the surgery was over. I took it with another shot of whiskey for the pain.

Beau grinned. "Always wanted to be a plastic surgeon. Then I could do a little surgery on myself and change my nose every time a new look comes along. Hope you don't mind but I gave you a little knee-lift while I was digging out those boulders. Michael Jackson, eat your heart out."

As I finished my spiked juice, Beau and I talked about Lacy Penzance's death. Of course he had heard about it—it was the topic of the hour, which reminded me of something the sheriff had said earlier.

"Beau, Sheriff Mercer mentioned that Lacy had a business card from the Mark Twain in her purse. Did you give it to her?"

Beau pressed his lips together, then said, "No. She's never been here, as far as I know. Of course, the door's always open during the daytime and anyone can walk in. Maybe she picked up a card to give to someone visiting the area when I wasn't around."

"Who are your guests right now?"

Beau pulled out his registration book from the rolltop desk. "The McDonalds have been here a couple of nights. They're from San Francisco, getting away from it all. There are two women in the Roaring Camp room from Denver, here on vacation, Lucke and Richards. The Jacobs family are taking up two rooms—the Red Light room for the couple and the Claim Jumper room for their two teenage boys. They're here for the frog festivities this weekend. The Jacobs boys won last year in two divisions: Best name for a frog—Ribbet. And cutest outfit—they made a little Superman suit. Then I've got a single guy in the Miner room. Name's Russell. James Russell. In fact, he left just a few minutes before you—"

"Red Miata, right?" I said, as I watched the recognition dawn on him.

"Yeah! Was he the jerk that ran you down?" Beau asked. "He's a looker. Dresses like one of those guys in the Aramis ads, you know. Unfortunately, I haven't seen much of him. Stays in his room mostly, then goes out late at night. But you know how I like the mysterious type," he said with a mischievous grin.

Although I liked to think a few of the men in this town find me attractive, Beau wasn't one of them. Being gay, he hadn't initially been the most popular guy in the macho atmosphere of Flat Skunk. But once people got to know him, things seemed to change. The folks in town became a bit more tolerant of those who wore their Stetsons cocked to a different side. Beau and I had a lot in common; we both felt a little alienated from the mainstream.

I stood to leave and winced at the dull ache that had set in nearly everywhere. "I don't care how cute he is, stay away from him when you're biking. He's a menace on the road."

I thanked Beau for the medical care and took him up on his offer of a ride home. He carried my mangled bike to my front door as I followed him gingerly from the sidestep pickup, walking like an old lady with arthritis, osteoporosis, and hemorrhoids. Beau wouldn't leave until I promised to come by for Sunday breakfast—blueberry scones, broccoli quiche, and raspberry mocha.

It was an easy promise to make. Beau made breakfast to die for.

I pulled out my keys to the diner and stuck them in the lock. Flat Skunk isn't the kind of town where you have to lock your doors yet, but being a deaf, ex-city girl with a suspicious nature, I locked my home, car, and bike automatically. I pushed open the door, picked up the mail that had slid through the door slot, and waited for Casper to attack me.

But when I closed the diner door behind me, I had a funny feeling, a weird sort of déjà vu. Not like when you feel you've experienced something before, but as if something very familiar had changed.

Casper appeared in a matter of moments, having finally pushed through her doggy-door, but she wasn't her exuberant self. I gave her a soft pat, then passed through the diner to my room in the back and slowly took in the small living area. There was nothing I could put my finger on, but something triggered a semiconscious alert as I set down the lastest packet of mail on the coffee table. Yesterday's mail, still resting where I had placed it last night, was different.

I picked up the first envelope and peeked inside. The coupon booklet was still intact. Thank God. I checked the next envelope and the next, a bill from the computer software catalog company, and a letter from my old boss. Nothing missing. Nothing wrong. Except the pile of envelopes itself.

I have this habit of arranging things. Got it from my father, I guess, another slightly obsessive-compulsive. As I go through the mail, I sort the letters by size and lay them on the table, largest envelope on the bottom, smallest on the top. Makes sense to me.

Last night's mail was out of order; big envelopes mixed in with small. I would never have done that to the mail.

I walked around the room slowly, looking for other signs of tampering. I checked my junk drawer by the telephone, pulling it open slowly and dramatically, like I'd seen in those horror movies where the teenage girl opens a drawer and out jumps her cat or something. No cat, and the drawer was still a jumble.

I headed for the dresser where I hid my valuables. The sheriff had once told me the bottom dresser drawer was one of the most common hiding places for secrets. If someone had a reason to look for something, that was the first place to check. I kept my stuff in the top drawer.

If I ever got in a car crash, my mother would be happy to know that my underwear drawer was clean and neat. Underpants on the left, bras on the right, nylons in the middle, and sexy stuff in the back just in case I ever needed them again. Underneath all this satin and lace was where I kept my valuables—mostly love letters from my ex-boyfriend and a collection of little gold charms in the "I Love You" hand shape that I got from my first deaf boyfriend.

There was no doubt about it. Some kinky weirdo

freak had been fooling around in my underwear drawer. A pair of my sexiest panties was in the bra section.

I dug down for the love letters—still there, but not in order. And they had been read—I could tell by the way they'd been reinserted into the envelopes.

I shuddered. Who the hell had had his hands in my drawers? And why? Was it possible the intruder was still here? The back of my neck prickled suddenly.

Catching movement from the corner of my eye, I spun around and screamed. Poor Casper. Nearly scared her to death.

I patted my leg—the sign for "Come here, girl"—calling her back from the hallway. She returned timidly, wagging her tail between her legs. "It's all right. I think," I said, while I signed "Good dog."

Casper responds to about fifty signs. Although she's not an officially trained hearing dog, I taught her myself, from the first day I got her as a puppy. A fluffy white-and-cream-colored Siberian husky with transparent blue eyes, Casper learned her first sign—"stay"—in two hours. Now she responds to basic signs like "wait," "stop," "come," "lie down," "door," "food," as well as concepts such as "where?" "listen," "quiet," "bring me," and "what's that?"

Right now she was using body language to let me know I had frightened her with my scream. That made two of us. I still wasn't sure we didn't have a reason to be scared. But at that point I figured if there was an intruder in the house, he or she would have made his presence known by now.

Armed with a two-foot wooden pepper mill I made a timid search of closets, corners, and cupboards, but found nothing. With two bandaged knees, several decorative bruises, a splitting headache, and a doubled heart rate, I was in no mood for this latest intrusion into my life.

But someone had been eating my porridge and it was not only scaring me, it was pissing me off.

"Sheriff . . ." I typed, after I'd given my living quarters a second, more intensive search. "Someone broke into my place while I was out this morning. Can you come over and dust for prints or do whatever it is you guys do to catch burglars? GA."

"COnnoor? WHat are you talkig about? GA."

There he went again with his creative keystrokes.

"Sheriff," I typed more slowly, thinking that might help. My fingers trembled over the keyboard. "Someone broke into my diner. My things have been . . ." I paused. The cursor pressured me into a word choice: ". . . disturbed. Can you come take a look? GA."

"SOmeone broke in? How? ANYthing missing? ARe you sure the perps gone? GA."

I took a deep breath and resumed keying. "Yes, someone broke in. I don't know how they got in. I keep the place locked all the time. Nothing is actually missing— so far. At least, I don't think . . ."

Another pause while the cursor blinked like a demanding instructor tapping a foot, waiting for an appropriate answer to an inscrutable question. I had no idea what the creep had come for—or if anything truly was missing. And I wasn't absolutely certain he was gone.

"COonnor? You there?" he broke in.

"Yeah, I'm here. I'm pretty sure whoever it was is gone. I don't think anything was taken, but some of my things are . . . messed up. GA."

There was a long pause on his end. The pulsar winked rapidly at me in time to my pounding heart.

"MEssed up? what do you mean exactly? RAnsacked? DAmaged? DEStroyed? OVerturned? what? GA."

I realized I was beginning to sound a little odd. "No, actually, everything's very neat. Nothing's been broken or destroyed. But—it's not the way I left it. GA."

There was another long pause before the sheriff came back on line. His hesitation was beginning to irritate me.

"ok. YOur things are messed up. DId you leave the dooor open? A window? MAybe your dog got into your stufff. GA."

"Sheriff, I NEVER leave my door unlocked! And I don't think Casper has much interest in my mail or my underwear drawer. Everything's . . . just . . . well, different! GA."

"Different. ok. WHat did the 415 do exactly? GA."

I typed a little more forcefully and hoped he felt my irritation on the other end. "THE 415 WENT THROUGH MY MAIL! MY LETTERS ARE BACKWARDS FROM THE WAY I STACKED THEM. AND HE WENT THROUGH MY . . . MY UNDERWEAR! GA."

There was yet another long pause. Sheriff Mercer was probably having a good chuckle over this one. No doubt sharing it with Mickey and the dispatcher and anyone else who happened to be in the office.

"HOld tight. I'll come take a loook at your underwear drawer when I get done here. I may be a couple of hours tho if its not an emergency. GOt another urgent call and stack of forms for the M.E. I have to process before I can deal withh suspected mail disarray and felony underwear dishevalment. YOu're SURE someone was in your place? I mean, its possible in your hurry to gett to your newspaper this mornig, you might have left the diner open or messed up things yuorself? GA."

He wasn't taking this very seriously. Maybe more exclamation points would help. "NO, SHERIFF!!! I KNOW WHEN SOMETHING'S NOT RIGHT! SOMEONE'S BEEN HERE! CAN'T YOU COME OVER NOW? GA."

"Ill get over as soon as I can. Maybe I can get Mickey to cruis by when he comes in."

"I can't wait long for him. I have to go up to Whiskey Slide this afternoon on business. I don't want to leave the place open." I hated the thought of the deputy or the sheriff rummaging through my Calvins without a chaperone.

"10-4. We'll do the best we can. GA. SK."

I signed off, feeling more exasperated at the sheriff than frightened by the intruder. I headed to the closet for a change of clothes, peeking and scanning before taking too many steps, just in case. I pulled my favorite denim skirt and white cotton top out of the clean laundry pile next to my couch-bed, then I thought about something the sheriff had said. The front door hadn't been damaged, but maybe a window had been pried opened somewhere.

I checked the diner's front windows, then the living area windows in the back. All secured. Barefoot, I stepped into the tub in the tiny adjacent bathroom and checked the small smoked porthole window. Locked.

I stepped back out and felt something gritty beneath my bare toes. I raised one foot and brushed it off. Fine red clay drifted down like snowflakes.

Dirt in my bathtub. I wasn't usually *that* dirty when I took a bath.

I stepped back into the tub and examined the powdery dust, then stood up and looked out the window again. The window was definitely locked, just as it had been this morning when I left. But the thin layer of dust along the sill had been wiped clean.

I wasn't that clean, either. I never dusted this early in the week. Frankly, I never dusted.

I went out the back door, examined Casper's doggy door, then moved around to the bathroom window. There weren't any telltale footprints in the red clay beneath the window, but one of my white poppies and yellow monkey flowers looked a little squished. And the dirt around the area seemed unusually smooth.

I examined the window for signs of tampering. The glass looked untouched, as did the wood sash and sill.

Nothing.

No signs of breaking and entering. The diner was locked up tight. I finished dressing and opened the medicine cabinet to renew my bandage accessories. A nearly empty box of Road Runner Band-Aids hid behind a bottle of piña colada-scented suntan lotion. I pulled out the box, helped myself to half a dozen, then replaced the box next to the lotion. I started to close the cabinet door, then stopped.

They say you can tell a lot about people from their medicine cabinets. Not surprisingly, I keep things all lined up in neat little rows, tall at the back, short at the front. Kind of like my mail.

Something was missing. There was a gap between the hearing-aid earpiece cleanser and the hydrogen peroxide. Whoever had invaded my cabinet had moved back a short bottle to disguise the space. But I couldn't for the life of me remember what was gone. And it sent a chill up the back of my neck.

Once I was certain my diner was a fortress again, I finished getting dressed, stuffed a pair of blue jeans, a red rugby shirt, and a pair of sneakers into a backpack for a comfortable change, and grabbed my reporter's notebook, along with a handful of personalized business cards.

I thought about calling my old boyfriend before I left to let him know about the intruder, make him worry about me a little. But I knew it was just an excuse, and I was feeling vulnerable. With a last look around the diner and a curse for the unknown invader, I headed for my Chevy and Whiskey Slide.

Whiskey Slide is a thirty minute drive if you take Highway 49, even longer if you opt for the back roads and hit every podunk mining town along the route. I took the long way. I liked the ride and I didn't get many opportunities to drive my classic car.

Aside from getting a giggle or two out of the town names, I'd found most of the old camps were nothing but dry creeks or large pits in the landscape. Early settlements like Lousy Ravine, Humbug, Poverty Hill, Bogus Thunder, Poker Flat, and You Bet weren't much more than dusty markers on the side of the road now.

My personal favorite, Git-Up-And-Git, still sported an

old weathered waterwheel, but the land was mostly a series of dug-up mounds that look like oversized burial plots. The entire town gave the impression of being one big cemetery.

Whiskey Slide, however, had managed to survive the influx and desertion of the argonauts. Like Flat Skunk, it had become a tourist mecca full of boutique overkill and gold-panning lures for weekend wanderers, only on a much larger scale.

Larger in acreage and population than Flat Skunk, Whiskey offered additional amenities: a decent discount clothing mart, a computer store, and one good Mexican restaurant. It was worth the trip from time to time.

I pulled into a gas station/bait shop and filled up the car before locating a telephone booth that still housed an intact directory. Searching the *L*'s for Longo, I found nothing between Samuel Longnecker and Zachary Longueville. Rats. On to Plan B.

Whiskey Slide is one of a handful of towns in the Mother Lode that doesn't offer mail delivery. With such a small population, folks just keep a post office box and make the daily trek to town to pick up their mail.

I entered the post office building, found the postcard machine, and dropped two quarters into the slot. Voilà! Instant stationery. The one I chose featured an old prospector holding a nugget the size of a tooth. Appropriate, since he was missing a few canines himself.

I wrote a vacation cliché in the blank space—"Having a wonderful time! Wish you were here!"—then signed it and addressed the front to Risa Longo, filling in a post office box number that matched my age.

"I'm not sure I have her right box number," I told the clerk as I handed him my bogus correspondence. "Could you check it for me, just in case?"

He mumbled something, looking down at a large envelope he was taping closed for a previous customer.

"What?" I said, as I leaned in.

He repeated his question but I still couldn't understand him. I stared at him blankly, shaking my head and tapping my ear.

He glanced up, looked at me for a moment, then nodded. "You're deaf?"

I smiled as he pushed a notepad over to me.

"I can lip-read, if you speak clearly and look at me."

He began to speak again, exaggerating his mouth and talking slowly as if I were a child just learning the language.

"Longo? Let me see," the clean-cut middle-aged man said, scratching his left eyebrow with his pinkie ring. He looked at a well-worn plastic-covered list and shook his head, causing a handful of loose neck skin to ripple. "I think it's fifty-four. Fifty-four. Fifty-four. Yep, here it is. You're way off. There, that'll do it," he said, drawing a line through the thirty-seven and replacing it with the correct number.

After thanking the man for his invaluable assistance, I went outside to find a comfortable spot under a tree, hoping I hadn't already missed Risa Longo's mail pickup. I pulled out a dog-eared Dick Francis mystery and read with one eye on the page and one eye on the post office. A number of people went in and out, but none seemed to fit the bill of Lacy Penzance's sister.

I was all the way to the part where the horse trainer gets killed when a woman in a silk jumpsuit brushed past me and entered the post office. She was approximately Lacy's age, but that was the only similarity to Lacy, as far as I could see from a distance. This woman was plumper and shorter, with close-cropped dark hair and ringless hands. As I had done with all the other post office visitors, I watched her as surreptitiously as I could from my vantage point, then moved in closer so I could see the rows of boxes more clearly.

Fifty-four. Bingo. It was Longo.

I turned around and pulled out my compact for the old pretend-to-check-my-face trick while the woman retrieved her mail. Peering over the top of the case, I watched as she paused at a nearby counter and sorted through the stack, discarding nearly half into a trash bin with a blank expression. When she reached my postcard, she stopped, read it, flipped it over twice, glanced around the room, and frowned. I pretended to struggle in my backpack for some change to use in the stamp machine. Did the name I had signed at the bottom—Lacy Penzance—ring a bell? Or was Lacy a stranger to this woman? I couldn't read Risa Longo's puzzled expression.

With a second glance outside the door, she tucked the card into a copy of *TV Guide,* stuffed the mail she'd saved into her oversized carry bag, and left the post office. I was right behind her.

As I ducked behind my Chevy, I watched her walk to her BMW parked across the street. When she arrived at her car, she pulled the postcard from the small magazine, frowned again, then replaced it and got into her car.

I knew one thing for certain. She was soon going to need major collagen treatments for those deepening frown lines.

Following a suspect looks easy in the movies. You jump in the car, keep your distance, and eventually you both end up at the same destination.

But anticipating the direction a real live person is actually headed when she doesn't use her blinker, she drives too fast, and she's three cars ahead, is about as easy as lipreading.

With lipreading you're on target maybe thirty to fifty percent of the time. The rest is guesswork. I'm able to guess most words that come over the lips, so I suppose that makes me a good lip-reader. Stuck in the middle of tourist traffic behind Elmer Fudd and the Mrs., I was not so good at guessing which way Risa Longo had suddenly turned.

When Fudd slammed on the brakes to point out a statue of Mark Twain to Mrs. Fudd, I rear-ended him while trying to get a lock on my suspect's new direction. A common misconception about the deaf is that we seem to have a sixth sense, some sort of ESP, to make up for the hearing loss. Not me. But I do have insurance.

"Shit," I cursed as I slapped my hand down on the

steering wheel. It must have been audible because Mrs. Fudd turned and gave me a disgusted look. My language must have upset her. Or maybe it was the minor dent I had nicked in their oversized puke green Lincoln.

Suffice it to say, the bump in his fender was barely visible to the naked eye, while the front of my classic two-tone '57 Chevy had turned ugly. While the Fudds and I exchanged insurance information, I caught the Mrs. saying to her husband, "I didn't know deaf people could drive cars."

We pushed my car to the side, after backing up traffic on the two-lane road and drawing a nice gawking crowd. Thanks to a new wheel alignment created by the impact, I had to walk to the nearest garage three blocks away to arrange repairs. The mechanic on duty said no problem, piece of cake, and I thanked him profusely as I sat down ready to wait it out with a few more chapters of my mystery. That's when the guy in the overalls named Ed smiled and shook his head.

"What? You can't fix it?" I asked.

"Oh, we can fix it all right, but it won't be ready until tomorrow. Gotta get a part from Sonora. Don't have any Chevy parts that old in stock. Don't suppose you wanna sell it?"

I said no, thanks, and walked back to my car to get a few things. Now what? I had just pulled out my backpack and shut the door when someone touched my shoulder from behind. I jumped and dropped my bag.

"You gave me a heart attack! Don't you know better than to come sneaking up on a deaf person?" I hate when that happens. And it happens all the time.

Dan leaned against the red-and-white fin of my side-lined Chevy. He was wearing a blue work shirt which matched his eyes, jeans that fit like a glove, and his tanned leather cowboy boots.

"Car trouble?" he asked, grinning. I surveyed the front-end damage and explained the ineptitude of the camera-burdened Fudds.

"So what are you doing here anyway?" he asked. "Following me?"

"No. I have business here. But my car . . ." I looked helplessly at what now appeared to be a hunk of classic junk.

"How about a beer?" He nodded toward the oak-and-stained-glass door of the He's Not Here bar across the street.

I ran my fingers through my hair, wiped possible mascara shadows from under my eyes, and followed him into the popular refreshment getaway. Dan motioned toward a small burl table in a dark corner but I opted for one by the window. I could read him better there, and perhaps spot Risa Longo on the chance that she might decide to cruise the Main again.

"What do you want?" asked Dan, standing halfway between the table and the bar. I ordered a Sierra Nevada and Dan returned with two frosty bottles and glasses. Neither of us poured the beers into the glasses.

"So. What are you doing here?" Dan repeated, his upper lip frothy with beer foam. It caused me to lick my own lip, which in turn caused him to smile. "And where's my cat? Fine cat sitter you turned out to be."

"Your fur ball is fine. I left it with Miah, along with complete instructions on how to care for it and the name of a good personal injury lawyer in case he's scratched to death during your absence." I took a swallow of beer and tried to think of something profound to say. "Thought I might run into you here." Very profound.

"Easy to do," he said, after taking a deep pull from the bottle. He had a disconcerting habit of licking the mouth of the bottle before taking a drink. "Another small town with one main street. You looking for something to put in your newspaper?"

I decided to tell him the truth—at least some of it. I didn't fully trust him yet, especially after the TTY chat with New Mexico's corrections facility. But the little he'd said so far had checked out. And what I had to share wasn't anything he probably wouldn't hear at the Nugget. I explained about Lacy's advertisement for her missing sister, since keeping it to myself no longer made sense.

And I told him about the name written on the back of the mortuary business card.

"So you thought you'd come up here and try to find Lacy's sister? Why?"

"I don't know. Thought it might add to the story I'm working on. There might be a connection between Lacy's search for her sister and her own death. The sheriff doesn't think it's a suicide any more, even though it was made to look like one." I waited for some sort of surprised body language.

"I know," he said simply.

"You know? What do you know?"

"That it may not have been a suicide. Everyone's talking about it."

"Figures. There are no secrets in Flat Skunk." The bartender dropped off a bowl of pretzels and asked if we wanted another round. I passed. Dan nodded. "Actually, I feel I sort of owe her," I said.

"How?"

"I think she wanted my help in some way. She seemed so upset, desperate to find her sister. I wasn't very . . . encouraging."

Dan stuck the end of a pretzel in his mouth and munched it like a chipmunk, in little bites, until it disappeared.

"How about you? Any news about Boone?" I asked.

Dan took another gulp of beer. "Not much. No one saw him except maybe the bartender here. He said a guy who looked like Boone came in for a couple of beers about three or four days ago. He hasn't seen him since and doesn't remember much else. No one I've talked to knows anything."

"You'd better call the sheriff."

"I did. He doesn't know anything either."

"What are you going to do?"

"I filed a report. Other than that, look around a while longer. What about you?"

I checked my watch. It was nearly five P.M. The car wouldn't be ready until morning. I could either take the bus home and back again, rent or borrow a car, or wait it out, pick up my car tomorrow, and try to follow Risa again. And hope my newspaper didn't fold in my absence. I could call Miah to cover—there was lots of busy work. And maybe he'd appreciate the extra pay.

"I've got to make some phone calls. Want to help me out? I left my portable TTY in the car."

"You mean like talk for you, over the phone?"

"Yep."

Dan downed the rest of his beer, then followed me to the pay phone in the corner by the bathroom. I gave him my office number to talk with Miah.

"No answer," he said. "Machine. You want to leave a message?"

I nodded and reached out my hand to take the phone. "Did it beep?" Dan paused a moment, then handed the receiver over.

"Miah, this is Connor. I'm stuck in Whiskey Slide. Would you do a couple of things for me?" I gave him instructions to feed Dan's cat and my dog at home— clueing him in on the well-hidden key—then asked him to finish a couple of articles that were ready to be typed, and prepare the copy for print. He'd done it all before so it shouldn't be a problem—I hoped. Then I hung up, dialed the sheriff, and gave the phone back to Dan. In a few seconds he began to speak.

"Hi, uh, this is, uh—I'm calling for Connor West-phal." He paused, then looked at me.

"Tell him I'm stuck here and won't be back until tomorrow. How's my house?"

Dan repeated my words in his own way, paused, then covered the receiver and spoke to me. "He said he doesn't know how your diner is on the inside, but no one's reported any other break-ins in the area. Said he'll cruise by there again tonight, and check it out tomorrow when you get back."

Another pause, then, "I'm on hold."

A couple of seconds passed before Dan said anything else. Then he frowned and covered the receiver again. "He's asking me, 'who's this talking?' "

"He's probably confused, since I'm not using my

TTY. Ask him to check on my dog when he's out there."
Dan relayed the message to the sheriff, then interpreted the
sheriff's reply back to me.

"He said he's not a dog sitter. Says you feed that dog
better food than he eats. Says your dog doesn't like him.
Says what are you doing in Whiskey Slide? Says hurry
back before something bad happens to your underwear.
Says who the hell is talking for you."

Dan pulled the receiver from his ear. "Connor, I—"

I cut him off. "Tell him thanks. I'll make him a nice
dinner on Sunday. Something low in cholesterol and fat.
Tell him the guy interpreting for me is . . . never mind. Just
say good-bye."

After relaying the message, probably edited slightly,
Dan hung up. "What was that all about?"

"I'll tell you over dinner. Where are you staying? That
guest inn on the way into town—Breakfast in Bed?"

"No, the Black Bart Motel. It's cheaper and it's got
one of those all-you-can-eat buffets right next door. You
staying over?"

I decided it would be the best idea. Dan offered
to make a call to the Black Bart and find me a room.
While he did, I freshened up in the bathroom, then asked
the bartender for a dining recommendation. I didn't feel
like stuffing it in tonight at the buffet, and the thought
of Mexican food just didn't sit right. I hoped he'd recommend some place nearby that was inexpensive and
Italian.

"Room with a view for fifty-five bucks," Dan said as
he started to pay the bar tab. I pulled out my own cash
and left a few bills. "No pets, no room service, no cable
TV, but they do have claw-foot tubs and a candy machine
in the lobby. And they're serving fried chicken at the
buffet."

I winced and he caught it. "Don't suppose a light fettucine primavera sounds good to you, does it?" I asked.
"Garlic bread? A fresh garden salad? Zabaglione for
dessert?" I hoped to make him change his mind by the
mere description.

"Hey, I'm half Italian," he said, accenting the statement

with pinched fingers, much the way the Godfather might gesture. "Lead on."

Mama Leone and Alfredo di Roma have nothing on Hasta Be Pasta's fettucine carbonara. The pasta was perfecto, the wine intoxicating, and the conversation stimulating. Although I learned little more from the tight-lipped Dan Smith, I managed to tell him my whole life story. He seemed to have a way of getting me to talk about myself. He would have made a great reporter.

"So what's it like being deaf?"

"It's really cool," I said facetiously.

He laughed and the delight spread across his face. "You know what I mean."

"I don't cry over it. I'm used to it and don't find it such a big problem. A little frustrating now and then, but more of an inconvenience than a handicap."

"How'd you learn to speak so well?"

"My parents sent me to 'normal' public schools with hearing kids and I had a lot of speech training. Since I was hearing until I was four, I'd heard and used language for a couple of years. That helped."

"What about sign language?"

"I learned it when I got older, hanging around other deaf kids at camp and deaf clubs. My parents wanted me to belong to the hearing world, but I felt pretty much out of it most of the time. By the time I learned sign language, I really wasn't a part of the Deaf culture either. I'm kind of caught between two worlds."

"But you get along so well."

"I guess. Even though my parents didn't really understand what it's like being deaf, they helped me believe I could do just about anything I wanted. I fell for it."

"Teach me a sign."

I nodded, and showed him a simple phrase made by intersecting a couple of V's.

He repeated it a few times before asking, "What does it mean?"

" 'Have a nice day,' " I said with a smile.

He signed it to the waitress as she brought us the bill.

Good thing she wasn't deaf. I don't think she would have liked being told "fuck you."

Thanks to the wine, my head was spinning a little as it hit the pillow in the room named after bandito Joaquin Murietta. I'd been having a little trouble lip-reading Dan Smith's interesting lips as the evening went on. But I had no trouble dreaming about them.

Morning comes early in the gold country, especially when you've downed a half carafe of the house red the night before. I headed to the breakfast buffet for a shock of coffee and some all-you-can-eat toast. I found Dan reading the *Mother Lode Monitor* over a cleaned plate of what may have been an order of Hangtown Fry.

"Any headlines?" I asked, as he folded the newspaper away.

"Sale at Norma Jean's Who Did Your Hair salon, over on Jail Street. Perms half off. And Prospector's Hardware's got wheelbarrows marked down, with the purchase of a load of manure."

"Thanks for sharing," I grumbled, trying to revitalize myself with black fluid. I poured in some milk and dropped a Hershey's Kiss from a nearby candy bowl into the cup for a makeshift mocha. I checked my watch and washed down my toast with something that tasted like motor oil. What I would have given for a Starbucks.

"Well, I've got to get going," I said. "I don't want to miss Risa Longo. The post office opens at nine. And I've got to get my car. You staying awhile?"

"Yeah. I still have a few things to check out. I should be back in Flat Skunk by tonight though, if nothing develops here."

"Me, too. Lacy's funeral is tomorrow and I don't want to miss it. But I'm getting really worried about Boone, too. You've got to find out what's happened to him."

Dan didn't say anything for a moment. I collected my bag and stood up. When I turned back to say good-bye, he was already speaking.

"What?"

"I said, I had a good time last night. It was a nice evening."

I smiled. I guess I had understood what he'd said after all. I just wanted to see him say it again. As I waved good-bye, he gave me the "fuck you" sign. I hoped he still thought it meant "Have a nice day."

I had just pulled up to the post office in my good-as-new-thanks-to-Visa vintage muscle car when I caught a glimpse of the Party On store across the street. Not wanting to wait around another whole day for my victim, I ducked into the store. In a matter of minutes I had bought a bouquet of helium balloons and was headed for the Whiskey Slide newspaper office down the street.

"Excuse me," I said to the woman at the front desk. "Could you tell me where a woman named Risa Longo lives? I have this balloon bouquet to deliver for her birthday and I've lost the address. I expect she's a subscriber."

The woman looked me over. I tried very hard to look like a balloon person.

"I'm sorry, we can't give out our customers' addresses."

I shrugged, wished her a nice day, and moved on to the next store. Surely one of these shops would have an address and a free-information policy. At the seventh shop I got lucky. Risa Longo was a regular at the Naughty Lingerie Boutique.

"She's out on Buzzard Road. Go left out of town and follow the road until you get to Buzzard. She's down at the end."

I thanked the woman profusely, bought myself an irresistible pair of silkies, and handed the balloons to a little kid as soon as I was out of sight of the store. Just as I was backing out of my parking space, I spotted Risa's car.

All that trouble to find her and she practically taps me on the shoulder.

I drove right behind her down the main street determined not to lose her. The traffic was light, and I had no trouble keeping up. I followed her around a winding road until we were a good ten minutes out into the countryside. She turned onto a dirt road with a hand-painted street sign, decorated with small blue-and-white flowers, that read Buzzard Road. I pulled over and watched as she drove the car around a bend and out of sight.

It was time for Plan C.

Plan C was right up my alley. Go up to the front door, ring the bell, and lie. The hard part was coming up with the premise. That took me all of the walk to her front door.

As a newspaper reporter, I've had lots of experience ingratiating myself into places I don't belong. Since I've never really felt I belonged anywhere, it comes easily. If I take on the stance, facial expressions, and gestures of the people I'm with, I can fake myself into financially troubled hospitals, closed political meetings, poorly run schools, suspect public offices, even crooked senior bingo games.

My desktop publishing software adds the finishing touches to my chameleon act. I've become somewhat of an expert in creating bogus letterheads, phony business cards, and official-looking but absolutely artificial documents with my little P.C. With over five hundred fonts and two thousand graphics, I can create fake birth certificates, brochures, even personal correspondence that look authentic.

Still wearing the denim skirt and not-so-white top, I made my way to Risa's front door. I pulled out a business card from my wallet collection and flipped open a page of official-looking documents on my leatherette clipboard.

The house was a lengthy, rambling adobe affair, nestled behind red-barked manzanita trees and framed by an expansive lawn. Parked in the circular driveway and blocking the front door from my sight was the tan BMW I had followed from town. The trunk lid stood open. I peeked inside and spotted several full grocery bags.

As I reached for the bell, the carved oak door swung open, startling both the opener and myself.

"Goodness! You scared me!" The woman slapped a hand on her ample chest. She was wearing a long V-neck top and tight stirrup pants in baby blue. Casual but expensive, youthful but discreet.

"I'm sorry!" I said, as my racing heart slowed. "I was just about to ring the bell. I'm . . . Connor Westphal. From the agency?"

"Oh, we're not interested in selling the house." She started out of the doorway to retrieve more groceries, but I stood in her way and didn't move.

"I'm not a real estate agent. Didn't anyone call to tell you I was coming?" I opened my notebook. "You are Risa Longo, aren't you?" If I just kept talking, she wouldn't have time to think.

The woman frowned, rested her hand on her chest, and backed up slightly. "No one called me about any agency. What agency?"

"Adoptions and Records," I said, still leafing through my notes on Frog Fricassee. Luckily they were illegible to anyone but myself. "I'm representing a client who was adopted at an early age. She's been searching for her—" I checked my notes, "—adopted sister for several months now and your name was referred to us as a possible link to the missing sister's whereabouts."

I pulled out my phony business card and handed it to her. It read: "Calaveras Consultants. Connor Westphal." The generic but nonexistent company had come in handy on a number of occasions. The card included a phony number, fax number, E-mail, and snail mail address. As a

Roadrunner fan, "Acme" would have been my second choice.

I looked up to read the woman's face, but it was blank. Not a wince or a twitch or a ripple on the whole canvas. Was I not convincing as an adoption counselor or did she have a hearing problem, too?

"I realize this is a delicate matter and that you may have obligations to shelter someone's privacy, but I have to ask, for the sake of my client. She's quite anxious to discover more about her heritage. She's . . . hoping to become pregnant and . . . needs a medical history."

"I don't know anything about any adoptions. Who is this person you're representing?" Her eyebrows formed a kind of check mark across her forehead—one sloping down, the other up. Luckily her red-outlined lips were easy to read, even if her face wasn't so clear.

"I'm not at liberty to say. I'm sorry. The truth is—and I hope this doesn't come as a great shock to you—my client indicated that you might be her biological sister."

"What!" The woman slapped her chest again, making a red mark above the low-cut V. "Me? Adopted? You've got to be kidding!" She laughed as she spoke, thoroughly entertained by the bizarre suggestion. "I used to hope I was adopted every time I had a fight with my parents. But I haven't fantasized about being an orphan since adolescence. I'm sorry, your client is mistaken."

I pretended to check my notebook for my next question. It gave me a moment to think.

"Would it be possible that you were adopted at such a young age you weren't aware of it, and your parents never told you?"

"No, it's not." The laughter faded. She was beginning to show a little irritation in her face—pinched lips, increasing frown, tight neck.

"But how can you be so sure?"

"Because I am."

"But—"

"Listen. My father had cancer. I was one of the few people who matched for a bone marrow transplant. We were about as close as two people could be for the compatibility test. He's definitely my father. And if you think my mother isn't really my mother, well, come here. I'll show you."

Risa Longo swept open the door and led me to a sunken living room filled with an eclectic collection of memorabilia from what must have been a well-traveled life. Money can't buy you happiness but it can buy you a lot of trinkets. She pointed to an ornately carved ivory table where a number of photographs were mixed in with some Asian, African, and South American art objects.

"Look here," she said, holding up a picture of herself several years younger. Next she picked up a picture of another woman who could have passed for her twin sister. Neither resembled Lacy Penzance.

"This one's me, taken ten years ago with my first husband. He died last year. That's my mother there, about the same age as I was then. Now tell me I'm adopted."

She was right. I couldn't. They had the same drooping eyes, the same sculptured nose, the same puffy lips, the same romance novel cleavage.

I set the pictures down carefully. Lacy Penzance said she wanted to track down her adopted sister. But Risa Longo was obviously not related. Had she been a link to Lacy's real sister? Or could Lacy have been adopted out of Risa's family?

"Did you have any brothers or sisters, Ms. Longo? Could it be that my client was put up for adoption by your parents before or soon after you were born?"

Risa Longo shook her head. Her chest danced. "My mother had three miscarriages before I was born. She was desperate to have a child. It took them ten years to finally have me. My mother died six months after having me. Who is this client you're representing? Maybe if you'd tell me her name I could help you in some way."

What did I have to lose? There really wasn't an issue of client confidentiality any more.

"Her name was Lacy Penzance. Did you—?"

I didn't need a course in reading face language to comprehend her immediate reaction. Before I could finish my sentence the woman had visibly paled, her mouth pulled back into a grimace, and her eyes narrowed. Her hands began to tremble. She grasped her elbows as if to calm and protect herself at the same time.

"Who are you? What do you want? I don't know anything about this Lacy Penzance, but I'd like to know what's going on. Are you from the police?"

"No, Ms. Longo. I'm not from the police. And I really don't have much to tell you. I'm just trying to locate Lacy Penzance's sister. That's what I was sort of hired to do. Did you know Lacy's dead?"

"Yes," she mouthed gently. She glanced away and shook her head as if to clear her mind.

"They were calling it a questionable suicide at first. But the sheriff suspects . . ." I didn't finish the sentence. Instead I said, "Have the police contacted you?"

She shook her head again, still not looking at me.

"If you have any connection to her at all, they may want to talk to you. She . . . may have been murdered."

"What?" The woman grew considerably more shaken. She sank down into a silk-covered ottoman. I sat in the chair opposite her. "She was just here. . . . I—"

Risa Longo turned her head away and I didn't catch the rest of her statement.

"What did you say?" I moved so I could read her lips.

"She was here, the day before yesterday, in the evening. I didn't know who she was when she came to the door. She wouldn't give her name. Just said she needed to ask me some questions. She was really agitated and making these wild accusations."

"About being your sister?"

"No! Nothing like that! She asked about my husband."

I blinked. "Your husband? What did she want? Was she—"

"She asked to see a picture of him. I didn't know what she was talking about, but she seemed frantic. A little incoherent really. She started pleading with me to show her a photograph of Larry."

"Did you show it to her?"

"I wasn't going to. She was starting to scare me a little. My husband's gone a lot and I'm out here by myself most of the time. When I started to close the door on her, she pushed me aside and ran in. She kind of looked around as if searching for something, then made a beeline for my photographs here. She grabbed the only picture I have of him, taken in Las Vegas at our wedding last year."

"She actually took the picture?" I asked, surprised at Lacy's odd behavior.

Risa Longo nodded. "Yes! Just stuffed it into her bag and ran out the door crying and muttering things I couldn't understand. I called the sheriff right after she left, but I didn't know who she was—she never said her name—so they couldn't do much. Then I saw her face on the TV and recognized her as the woman who had taken off with my wedding picture. And she was dead!"

"Did you call the sheriff?"

"No. What for? I didn't think—"

"Ms. Longo, what does your husband say about all this? Does—did he know Lacy?"

The suddenly tired-looking face drooped even more. "To be honest, I haven't talked to my husband for a few days. I haven't been able to reach him. He's an archeologist, so he's away for long periods of time. Maybe she had something to do with his work. Sometimes they make remarkable finds, you know, valuable. Worth a great deal of money . . ." she drifted off for a moment. "I wish he'd call. I'm a little worried about him. I've been wanting to ask him about her, but now, well, now I'd just like an explanation."

I stood up and walked back over to the photo gallery, trying to make some sense out of Lacy Penzance's activities.

"You don't have any other pictures of your husband?" It seemed odd to me that there was only one photograph.

"No. We've only been married for six months. And he's gone so often. It's hard enough getting him to take the garbage out, let alone take a picture of him."

I picked up a picture of Risa Longo with another man, fiftyish. It was one of those photos where you put on old-fashioned clothing so the picture looks ancient. I held it up for her but she was looking at me inquisitively.

"Did you say something?" I asked. I recognized that look.

"I just said I wish I knew what this was all about."

"Who's this?" I held up the picture again.

"My first husband. He died over a year ago."

I replaced the picture on the ornate shelf, thanked Risa Longo for her time, and promised to get back to her if I learned anything of interest or found her wedding picture. I walked back to my car more than a little confused.

Lacy Penzance must have made up the adoption story as a way of finding the Longo woman. A woman after my own heart. And she had apparently succeeded—except that Risa wasn't her sister. So what was the real reason behind her search?

Lacy had paid Risa Longo a visit the night before she died. Something about Risa's husband had upset her enough to cause her to become hysterical, push her way into the house, and steal the photograph.

What was it? A tie to some kind of archeological work he was doing? Did it have anything to do with Risa Longo herself? And why had Lacy requested secrecy concerning her search for Risa?

Whatever it was, I was certain it had something to do with her death. But what? I didn't have a whole helluva lot of options.

Except one.

"Business is business," some businessman once said. I guess it's the conservative version of "All's fair in love and war." And death, I might add.

At least, that seemed to be the way French McClusky saw things. He owned Memory Kingdom, a chain of mortuaries in the California Mother Lode. "The next generation of the final frontier," he once called his investment when he stopped by to proof a series of ads for the *Eureka!* A Trekkie, too, no doubt.

French had chosen the fastest-growing retirement area in the state—the gold country—for his thriving funeral business. Shrewd and visionary, this was no Ichabod Crane look-alike in a black suit from an old Vincent Price horror film. French, who is half Asian, half Irish, was a descendant of one of the many hardworking Chinese who dug in the gold mines for a new life in the West.

His Chinese maternal grandfather had run a gambling den in the back parlors of the Chinese settlement, while his Irish father had managed the Pioneer Cemetery for years, until the owners put it on the market fifteen years ago.

That's when French bought the first in a series of permanent rest stops, turning untended dirt into a gold mine.

French spared no expense in creating the latest in terminal services for the dear departed. Four years ago he
introduced the first twenty-four-hour drive-up window
service, allowing visitors to view the loved one on a wide-
screen TV. He offered tours of the mortuary to groups, by
appointment. And I understood Halloween around the
place was quite a thrill.

The Memory Kingdom funeral homes resembled cot-
tages from a Disney film. Actually, French hired an ex-
Disney architect to design the blueprints for all his
buildings. I felt like I needed a Magic Kingdom Adventure
Pass to enter the place.

My first stop was the Whiskey Slide branch of the
Memory Kingdom chain to check out the source of
the business card with Risa Longo's name on it. Business
was slow—there was only one saleperson available and he
couldn't tell me anything about Risa Longo, Lacy Penzance, or the mysterious business card. If I wanted to
know more, I'd have to talk with French McClusky or
Celeste Camborne at the Flat Skunk location. I hopped in
my like-new Chevy and headed back down Highway 49.

The front door of the Flat Skunk funeral home opened to a
spacious room filled with overstuffed antique furniture
and elegant decorator pieces. Air-conditioned, with just
the right amount of indirect lighting, the room featured
four large walls painted to look like a full sky—all bil-
lowing clouds with silvery streams of sunbeams breaking
through.

Along one side were two small offices with windows
that looked out, not at the real sky, but at the fake one
inside. French occupied the first office. The blinds covering
his window were drawn shut. I could see Celeste in the
second office through the open slits of her blinds. She was
talking on the phone. Alerted somehow by my presence,
she turned, peeked through the blinds and waved, then
continued her conversation.

She appeared agitated and upset, frowning and gesticulating at the invisible caller on the other end of the line. When she saw me her face flashed a momentary grin, but she quickly resumed her irritated expression. I filled the next few moments scanning the various works of art on the walls and looking over some brochures on the table near a brocade couch, then I sat down and watched Celeste.

She was facing the window now; I could see her lips moving between the slits in the blinds. She twisted a ring on her finger as she spoke, the phone receiver resting on her shoulder.

I couldn't keep myself from trying to read her lips, in spite of the additional challenge. With the distance, bad lighting, and obstructions, all I could make out were a few words.

". . . careful . . . shit . . . Sluice . . . fuck you . . . tonight . . . goddammit Wolf . . . funeral . . ."

At that point, catching my intense gaze, she waved again and closed the slits.

After a few more minutes she opened the door to her office and entered the foyer.

Celeste Camborne looked like a thirty-year-old fairy godmother in her silky pink dress and bouffant curls. She welcomed me with open arms, a big smile, and a coy tilt of her head.

"Connor Westphal!" Celeste said, clapping her hands together and moving her lips like Mick Jagger. Her demeanor had completely changed. She spoke mostly in exclamation points. "How wonderful to see you!"

"Hi, Celeste."

She clasped my hand warmly between both of hers, while giving me one of those you-poor-dear looks. I've seen the look many times on the faces of certain hearing people, whose reactions to my deafness range from horror to pity. Celeste seemed to think of it as some terrible disease. But deafness is not a problem until someone like Celeste makes it one.

"Oh, Connor! It's so good to see you. How are you doing, dear? Is everything all right?"

I didn't know whether this kind of gooey,

condescending sympathy came naturally to Celeste or if she had been trained that way when she became a grief counselor. Even though I sort of liked Celeste, her patronizing attitude drove me batty. If she stuck that bottom lip out at me one more time I just might have to push it back in for her.

"I'm fine, Celeste." I wanted to add, "There's no cure yet but we're still waiting for that ear transplant." Instead I did what lately I found I did best. I began to lie.

"Uh, my great-aunt ... Lulu, uh, well—I may be needing something in the way of, you know, this ..." I swept my arm around and realized I was indicating furniture, not funeral accoutrements. "I thought I'd stop by and take a look at what you have to offer. God, this place reminds me of Fantasyland."

Celeste nodded and her head of big hair shifted slightly. "Yes, it has a tremendously calming effect on most people. Death sometimes seems like a dream, don't you think?"

A nightmare, I wanted to say. I smiled instead. She was already working her magic here in the kingdom.

As part of French's ever-expanding plans for utopian death care, Celeste counseled bereaved loved ones into dissipating their grief, no doubt by buying outrageously expensive coffinware. She traveled from funeral home to funeral home as needed, to assist those who would benefit from her spiritual, psychological, and financial guidance.

"Well, I'm glad you caught me," she said. "I've been preparing for Lacy's funeral this afternoon. Would you like me to get you a Memorial Counselor? He can show you some of the special new products we're carrying."

I had to think fast. "Actually, I was hoping for a quick tour, if you have time. I was planning to do an article on Memory Kingdom for my newspaper. It's such an institution."

Celeste checked her watch. "French isn't here. But I think I've got time for a quick one. We can kill two birds with one stone, so to speak. Maybe you'll see something for your aunt Lulu while Memory Kingdom gets some publicity."

Taking my arm, Celeste led me through a heavy drape where, tastefully arranged and decorated with dry floral arrangements, Laura Ashley pillows, and "Apple Pie" pot-pourri scents, were nearly a dozen coffins. They formed a large circle of raised, downy-soft beds in a variety of styles, fabrics, colors, and prices. Each sported a bronze name tag attached to puffy lining.

I pulled out my tape recorder and switched it on, then held it up to catch Celeste's speech. "So this is the coffin room?" I said, trying not to get too close to a patriotic number in teak. The bronze plaque read: "The Presidential Suite."

"It's the Selection Room, hon. We call these caskets, not coffins," she said, tilting her head as she spoke. "Terminology has changed quite a lot since the pine box days. We're always striving to be politically correct—or rather, 'death sensitive.' "

"Really," I said, reflecting on the terminology for deafness, which has also changed over the years. What was once "deaf and dumb" and "deaf mute" became "aurally handicapped," then "hearing impaired," finally settling on "deaf." Some even prefer Deaf. I expect "sound deficient" or "listening deprived" may be next.

"And French isn't an undertaker anymore. He's a Funeral Designer. The loved ones, as we like to call them, ride in coaches or professional cars, not hearses." She actually shuddered when she said that last word. It was beginning to sound a little like *Brave New World*.

"Matthew, the man over there assisting the client with the 'Executive Office' casket? He's not a cemetery salesman, he's a Memorial Counselor. We like to think the bereaved overcome their grief more easily when we use less emotionally charged terms."

I pointed to a bouquet of flowers. "Don't tell me—a floral memory, right?"

"Close! A Floral Tribute." She held her hand over one side of her mouth and huddled close.

"Want to know one of my favorites?" She smiled a naughty kind of smile, like she was about to say something really shocking. "You know what they call cremated ashes now?"

I shook my head, mimicking her naughty smile.

"Cremains! 'Cremation' and 'remains' combined into 'cremains.' Isn't that cute?"

Cute.

Taking my hand, Celeste led me out of the Selection Room and into the Reposing Room, where a current loved one was reposing on a brown velvet-covered mattress in a dark mahogany casket. The room smelled of fresh pine needles. Floral Tributes.

"Is Lacy here somewhere?" I looked around, trying to bring the conversation to the matter at hand.

"We're getting there. But first, let me show you our selections. According to *Mortuary Management,* Americans spend more on funerals than on dentists, police protection, or even higher education. We want to offer our customers the best in quality and value—with innerspring mattresses, lead-coated steel caskets, and handmade fashions available in sixty color shades. Each casket is fully lined, with a Permaseal rubber gasket to prevent air seepage and, well, you know—to keep critters from getting in. And we only use Natur-Glo Products—the ultimate in cosmetic embalming."

I always thought knowledge was a good thing. But there were some things you could know too much about.

We passed by a loved one who looked like he belonged in Madame Tussaud's Chamber of Horrors. I felt myself drawn to look at him in a sort of peek-between-your-fingers kind of way.

The heavy layer of face makeup gave his skin a deeply tanned look, in contrast to his pale arms crossed and resting on his chest. Gold rings decorated each cold finger of both perfectly manicured hands. His lightly pinked mouth was drawn up in a mysterious smile, as if he were holding a humorous secret between his lips. One eye was closed and peaceful, the other looked as if it were trying to open, with a small slit between the lids.

And his hair was perfect.

"That's Leonard Swec, president of the Elks Club.

You remember him? He died Sunday. Heart attack. The funeral's tomorrow."

"Is Lacy here, too?" I tried again.

"Come with me."

I followed Celeste to the Calcination Room, where a "kindlier heat" would turn the loved ones into a kindlier ash. I'd offer a nice description of this room but I wasn't doing a whole lot of intensive eyeballing. Suffice it to say, the cremain-maker was big, metallic, and hot.

"But aren't people in mourning particularly vulnerable to guilt-buying at a time like this?" I said, trying to crack the facade a little.

"To tell you the truth, we've found—and *Mortuary Management* will back me up on this—the bereaved *need* to be steered toward those higher-priced caskets to assist in the guilt therapy. Yes, it's true, they often can't make those on-the-spot decisions as clearly as they might. But that's why we're here—to help them, by offering the best quality for their money. We have products and services for all budgets."

I glanced around, then wished I hadn't. I didn't know which was worse—watching her lips describe the details of the inner sanctum or seeing something that would give me nightmares for years to come. I looked back at Celeste.

". . . those who are on a lower or fixed income can get a reasonable casket and services for a nominal fee, around two thousand dollars. But most people want the best for their loved ones, with all the extras. Like a burial vault. Some cemeteries insist on them, in case the casket disintegrates and the whole thing caves in." She shuddered. It was a pleasant mental picture.

"Anyway, there's a lot that goes into this. You have to consider flowers, outfits, clergy, honorarium, musicians, soloist, professional cards, guest book, memory cards, and cemetery maintenance charges. Some spend as much as twenty thousand dollars or more."

It was my turn to shudder. "God, that's a lot of money to spend on relieving guilt. And it's not the kind of product where you can get your money back in ten days if you're not satisfied, is it? Did Lacy spend that much?" I was determined to bring the conversation around.

"That's why we're developing more preneed memorial estates for people—future grave sites that can be paid for over time and created from your own personal selections. You'd be surprised how many people nowadays want to choose the colors they'll be wearing for eternity. Lacy certainly did."

I wanted to laugh, but she looked so serious, I decided to stifle it. I knew I wouldn't want to be caught dead wearing puce when everyone else was wearing aquamarine that season.

"Come on. I'll take you to the Replenishing Room where we create the Beautiful Memory Picture."

"What's that? Snapshots of former customers?"

Celeste giggled like a high school girl. "Oh, no, silly. It's where they embalm the body."

I felt my breakfast do a body slam and wondered what I was thinking when I decided to come here.

"And you can get a peek at Lacy. I think you'll be surprised at how she turned out."

I couldn't wait.

But I'd have to. At that moment some guy in a lab coat burst into the room yelling, "Where the hell is it?"

"Where's what?" Celeste asked.

The man in the white lab coat, jeans, plastic gloves, and Dr. Scholl's looked so pale he could have benefited from a little shot of Natur-Glo embalming fluid. The hip embalmer looked at me, then spoke to Celeste.

"Could I see you in the hall, privately?"

Little did he know, if he just turned his head, I wouldn't hear a word he said.

Celeste gave me a tilted smile. "Why don't you wait over there by the Preservation Room for a minute Connor while I talk with Charlie. You can't go in—no one's allowed except the dermasurgeons—the embalmers. But you can see pretty well from the window. French had it installed just for tours."

I clicked off the tape recorder and bravely moved over to the window while Celeste and Charlie ducked into a room next door. I glanced down the hallway—no one coming. I pushed open the door, remembering what my teacher once said: "Connor, you never listen." Duh.

It's the smell that really gets you. Takes you right back to seventh-grade biology class. The frog-pithing lesson. I got a major whiff opening the door. Definitely medicinal. Formaldehyde? Kindergarten paste? A vodka gimlet? I backed up, closed the door, and returned to the viewing window where, unfortunately, I could still see just fine.

The room was tiled, with lots of stainless steel, porcelain, and sterile-looking stuff. It reminded me of the surgery unit at the hospital where I'd had my ear-tube surgery. I recognized a number of instruments—scalpels, scissors, augers, forceps, clamps, needles, pumps, tubes, bowls, and basins—and saw a bunch I couldn't identify.

But that was no pithed frog lying there on the steel table. It was a pithed stiff.

I jumped when I felt a tap on the shoulder.

"Sorry about that," Celeste said. "It's always something around here. So how do you like the Preservation Room?"

"Uh . . ." was all I managed to get out. I fumbled through my backpack for the tape recorder and switched it back on.

"This is where the loved one is transformed from a lifeless body to a Beautiful Memory Picture. The whole process takes about three hours to perform: spraying, slicing, piercing, pickling, trussing, trimming, creaming, waxing, painting, rouging, and, of course, dressing." Each time Celeste named a process, a razor-sharp painted fingernail flicked to attention.

She continued with rehearsed enthusiasm, as if she were a perky guide on her 150th winery tour. She moved into autopilot for the remaining details.

"Next they add all kinds of fluids, sprays, pastes, oils, powders, and creams to fix, soften, shrink, or distend the tissue. Embalming is really a restorative art."

Distending tissue a restorative art? Where had I been? I'd once read in a competitor's newspaper ad that "any high school graduate can learn to embalm in sixty days or your money back."

"Do you give this tour to everyone?" I said, wondering what the dropout rate was.

"Oh, no. Mainly other morticians from across the country who want to see French's state-of-the-art setup."

Celeste went on to list more fascinating procedures. My eyes blurred as she spoke. I had a choice of looking through that too-revealing window or watching her blather on about fluids, pumps, and God knows what. I tried to think about something else, anything else. If I didn't concentrate on some sort of distraction, my stomach contractions would be interrupting her speech at any moment.

"And that's about it. Fascinating, isn't it?"

"You sure know an awful lot about the mortuary business, Celeste. Did you have to learn all this for the job?"

"No, no. I learned most of this on my own."

"Does every dead . . . I mean, every loved one have to go through embalming?" I asked, not really sure I cared to know.

At that moment, Sluice Jackson came shuffling down the hallway, halfheartedly pushing a broom.

"Sluice! Not now!" She seemed to speak insistently, then changed her demeanor. "Wait until this evening, please. Go back out to the garden and finish your work."

Sluice gave her a watery-eyed look. "I din't take it. It wern't me. I—"

"Sluice, get back to work!" Celeste interrupted.

He turned around and shuffled down the hall, mumbling on.

"He's a lost soul, poor guy. We try to keep him busy, but he's still a few nuggets short of a mother lode, if you know what I mean. I'm afraid we're going to have to get someone else to do the backhoeing soon. Anyway, where was I? Oh, yes. Embalming the body—"

"What's missing?" I asked, veering her from continuing her lecture. I was suddenly curious about her urgent conference with the Charlie guy. What could be missing from a mortuary? "A body?" I said boldly.

Celeste giggled. "Heavens, no! Something from the embalming room. I'm sure it's just misplaced. Sluice probably went in there and, you know . . . Anyway, as I was saying. Embalming the body is not required by law or anything. It just makes the loved one more presentable for viewing. Look over there. See that man's mouth that Charlie's working on now?"

I looked in the general vicinity of the body lying on the steel table and found a nice shiny screw to stare at instead of the man's blank, empty face.

"Yeah," I lied.

"His mouth has actually been sewn shut with a needle and thread. The corners are slightly raised to give him the appearance of peace and contentment. Isn't that neat?" I gave her a tight smile, feeling like my own mouth had been sewn shut.

She went on relentlessly. "Now the eyes, they're cemented shut and covered with flesh-tinted eye caps. Then the face is creamed to prevent skin burns caused by leakage of the chemicals."

I pulled my lips apart to test them. They still worked. But I'd somehow lost the power of speech. All I could do was nod now and then. She thought I meant for her to continue.

"See that long skinny thing over there that looks like a giant ice pick? That's called a trocar. It's really a hollow needle the dermasurgeon uses to make an incision in the body so they can drain the blood."

We were having some fun now. I began some slow deep breathing to calm the uprising in the hull.

"Then the embalming fluid is pumped in through the arteries with that machine over there."

My morning toast curled into a solid ball of dough. I started a subtle abdominal massage as she continued.

"The embalming solution is made from dye, perfume, formaldehyde, glycerin, borax, phenol, alcohol, and water. Isn't that something? They use anywhere from three to six gallons, depending on the size of the person. That guy looks like about a fiver."

Breathe in, breathe out, breathe in, breathe out . . .

"Once the embalming is finished, we keep him on ice, so to speak, for about eight to ten hours, until the tissues become firm and dry. Then he goes next door to Restoration. That's where they use plaster and waxes and paints to fill and cover bad features or to repair damaged limbs. Come on, I'll show you my favorite part."

I couldn't wait. I followed her to the Beautiful Memory Room. Inside was a woman reclining on a table looking as if she were about to rise from a refreshing nap. But I knew better.

Another woman, with less color in her face than in the deceased's, was back-combing the peaceful woman's hair.

"This is where I used to work before I got into grief counseling. I was a desairologist. That's a fancy word for hairstylist to the dead. Now you talk about your problem hair. We had to deal with really bad hair days." She rolled her eyes and adjusted her own puffy 'do.

"That's Lacy. How do you like her?"

I took another look. "I didn't even recognize her! She looks so different!"

"The magic of Memory Kingdom. She's already had her manicure and makeup application. Didn't Jason make her look so much younger? After her hair's done, they'll add the final touches, such as a favorite stuffed animal, a book of poetry, a locket, a special memento, whatever the family wants."

I glanced at Lacy and wondered why the sheriff had already released the body.

"What did Lacy's family want?" I asked.

"She doesn't have any family. But she had mentioned a few things to me, in the event she should pass away. So I've included them."

"Like what?"

"Her gold jewelry collection and a special locket. Well, now, that's about it. How about lunch?"

I'd made plans to never eat again, and politely declined the invitation, citing urgent newspaper business. I snapped off the recorder and thanked her for the tour, promising it would make a great story on the new, improved mortuary of tomorrow. Then I asked, "Celeste, do you know a woman named Risa Longo? Her name was written on the back of a Memory Kingdom business card that Lacy had with her when she died."

Celeste paused for a moment, looked away, then

shook her curls. "Don't think so, but she might have stopped in for information or something."

"Did Lacy ever say anything about her, mention her name? Did she ever visit the mortuary in Whiskey Slide?"

"Not that I can remember. We had some long talks during those days after Reuben died. I counseled her quite a lot. But I don't think that name came up."

"What did you talk about with her?" I asked.

Celeste tilted her head. "I can't really say much about that, you know. Professional confidentiality."

Kind of an oxymoron to think a former hairdresser keeps her mouth shut at times.

"But let me know about your aunt. And the article!"

"I sure will." I thanked Celeste for her time and left the house of the dead for some fresh air.

I drove back to my office, trying to settle my stomach as I wondered about the connection Lacy Penzance had to the mortuary. Things weren't piecing together at all, and I was wasting a lot of time better spent at the paper. I wanted the story—for myself and for the newspaper—but I was running behind on my deadline. And I had a lot of other work to do.

I got into the office by one o'clock, changed into my 501's and rugby shirt, and checked the messages taken by Miah, who was apparently out to lunch. There was one from Sheriff Mercer, wondering when he should stop by to check out my "disturbed" diner. One from a group of concerned citizens called TOAD—Those Opposed to Amphibian Destruction—demanding an end to "frog exploitation." And three from Dan Smith since I'd left him this morning. No return number. But I wouldn't have been able to call him anyway.

The sheriff was out on a call when I phoned. I left a message for him through Mickey Arnold on the TTY. The deputy typed blessedly quickly, probably because he didn't bother with capitals and punctuation. In an attempt to sound more official, he used a vocabulary a little beyond his grasp. "Rendezvous." Couldn't he just have said "date" when he asked me to the Frog Jubilee Dance? I keyed off before giving him a reply. Chicken.

I tossed the message from TOAD into the trash and picked up the three messages from Dan Smith. I checked my watch. Lacy Penzance's funeral was set for four P.M. I'd have just enough time to get home, shower and change, swallow a bottle of Pepto, feed Casper, check my mail—to see if it had been tampered with—and find just the right thing to wear for the somber occasion.

This was one funeral I wouldn't miss. Other than my own, of course.

I'm not big on funerals. I've only been to one, when I was thirteen and my grandfather died. It was open casket and I got my first glimpse of a dead body. He looked like a delicate porcelain doll, heavy on the rouge, and not like himself at all. Everyone was crying, including my dad. I'd never seen him cry before. I decided then that I didn't want to have a funeral if it was going to make everyone so upset.

But solemn, depressing funerals were becoming a thing of the past, according to Celeste.

The event at the Memory Kingdom Memorial Park was shaping up to be more like a party than a burial ceremony. Of course, no one was drunk or laughing too loud or trying to pick up a date, as they might have been at a typical party.

The chapel looked the setting for a wedding rather than a funeral. Pink and black streamers had been twisted around the ends of each pew, topped with large pink velvety bows. A lavish pink floral display was mounted on a black drape over the casket, featuring dyed-to-match pink carnations, pink lilies, pink daisies, and pink roses. The room was filled with a sickly sweet scent. It smelled pink. It probably sounded pink.

Hanging from the ceiling were small stuffed birds that looked like mutant pink-dyed canaries. The tastefully printed program I had been handed as I entered was pink, of course, with black lettering, and a picture of a tiny gold bird in the upper right-hand corner just above Lacy Penzance's swirled and stylish name.

I took a seat in the far corner of the nearly full chapel and glanced around at the attending guests while waiting for the service to begin. Most of the town's citizenry had turned out, including the sheriff and deputy, who nodded soberly from across the aisle. Again I marveled at how quickly Lacy was being laid to rest.

I recognized several regulars from the café, and of course, the funeral home was well represented by French, Celeste—who stood by the door as if ready to flee—and a few of the staff. Celeste matched the decor in her long pink gown with black velvet trim.

I spotted Sluice Jackson, who stood mumbling in a corner, guarding his leather pouch. He had dressed for the occasion by removing his ragged, bead-covered cap. His sparse hair stood up in wisps, as if swirled by a tornado.

The funeral began with a song, performed by a woman I didn't recognize. I could tell it was a song because her mouth stayed open a long time. I watched the singer for a few minutes until I became bored, then gazed at the listeners as I waited patiently for the song to end.

I had made a mistake in coming, I realized shortly after the minister began his sermon. I hadn't brought an interpreter and I was too far away to lip-read him with any kind of accuracy. He had a pair of those thin, flat, lipless lips that make a mouth look like a gash across the face.

I occupied myself by watching the guests squirm, doodle, yawn, pick their teeth, scratch, and cough during his ten-minute monologue. After a middle-aged woman headed for the podium to say a few words, I sneaked out the back.

The Gathering Room next door was still in the

process of being set up for the postfuneral assembly. I peeked in to see more pink-and-black decorations that floated, hung, or draped the room. Tables were set with large bowls of pink punch, tiny pink sandwiches, and silver platters of salmon paté and cold cuts. One wall featured large posters of Lacy, obviously blown up from photographs, in a variety of formal and charitable poses.

I noticed Celeste standing across the room giving orders to a group of waitresses. She waved cheerily when she saw me, then directed a flower delivery man to a far table, a caterer to a melting ice sculpture, and a custodian to a glitch in the lighting ambiance.

"Did you do all this?" I asked when the frenzy died down. I made a sweeping gesture of the room. Celeste beamed with pride.

"Yes. Of course, it's all in accord with Lacy's wishes. We talked a lot about her own final plans during the days when I was counseling her about Reuben's passing. I've simply provided what she requested. We encourage all our guests to plan the details of their finales. Lacy's favorite colors were pink and black, so she chose them for her color scheme. Did you get a look at her casket? It's lined in pink velvet with black trim and tiny embroidered gold birds. It's really becoming. She picked the flowers, the music, the food, even the caterers."

"Wow," I said as I took it all in. "This was all Lacy's idea? Did she have some sort of premonition she was going to die soon?" I wondered if there might have been some hints made during the grief counseling sessions.

"Oh, no! At least not that I know of. She was bereaved, but she didn't seem suicidal."

Wolf Quick appeared at the door, a little out of his element among the pink puffery. He signaled Celeste with a look and she excused herself. I snatched a pink cookie from a passing platter. While I headed back to the main entrance, Wolf followed Celeste to a room behind another heavy curtain. He looked upset, but then he always seemed to have a scowl on his rugged face. I wondered what was up between the two of them. Secret lovers? You never knew.

I sneaked a couple of fancy crackers from the prepared banquet table and wondered what I would choose if it were time to plan my own funeral. Maybe a beer bust, with plenty of chips and dip, some of those little cheese toast things, and maybe a cake in the shape of a giant—

I felt a tap on my shoulder and whirled around.

"Shit! You scared me!" I said, sputtering cracker crumbs. It was Dan Smith, freshly groomed, wearing a casual leather jacket, long-sleeved tan cotton shirt, and khaki Dockers. "You've got to quit sneaking up on me like that without a warning!"

"Sorry," he said, trying to stifle a grin. I'm sure that's what he said. His mouth was full of pink stuff so I couldn't make out the exact word, but it had better have been an apology.

"But how am I supposed to warn you without tapping you?" he said.

I ignored his unanswerable question. "What are you doing here, anyway? You didn't know Lacy Penzance."

He shrugged. "I could say I was hungry and heard there was a great buffet here, but that would sound cold and heartless. Truthfully, I just wanted to see who her friends were. I think there's a connection between Lacy Penzance and my brother's disappearance. Thought I'd check it out."

"You expect to find a clue to your missing brother's whereabouts in the crackers and salsa?" I frowned.

He smiled. There was pink stuff on his lips. It looked good on him. For a second, I wondered how it tasted. I gave myself a mental slap on the face.

I suspected the funeral must have just ended, because a few people were beginning to appear in the entryway. Within moments the room was full of Lacy's friends and followers, all eating and drinking, if not making merry, at least enjoying one another's company. Dan and I were soon pushed into a far corner, away from the "grieving" crowd.

I noticed the sheriff huddled in an intense conversation with a man whose back was turned to me. They leaned into one another, glancing around as if discussing something they didn't want anyone else to hear.

That, of course, made me really curious. I watched the sheriff intently as he spoke.

"Prenuptial?" I was fairly certain he said that word. Then something like, "Do you think Lacy was planning to marry—" He turned his head.

The man said a few words and the sheriff responded, "Who was he?" The man said something and the sheriff said, "You're sure?" Then someone with big hair stood in my way and I couldn't see his lips anymore.

Dan was staring at me. "It's not polite to stare," he said.

"I wasn't staring. You're staring."

"I'm not staring. I'm waiting for a response. You've definitely been staring at those two over there. Are you reading their lips?"

"Of course not. That would be an invasion of privacy, wouldn't it. Now what were you saying?"

"I said, this funeral is really something. Don't think I've ever been to one like this before. Not in New Mexico, not in New York."

"Lacy planned it all," I said, waving my hand at the decorations and food.

"Her own funeral?" Dan asked, then stuck his bottom lip out. "I guess that's not a bad idea." He looked around and grinned. "Of course, it's not my style, all that pink frilly stuff."

"So what is your style?" I asked, grabbing a couple of glasses of pink champagne from another passing tray. I was getting good at eating and drinking on the run. I offered one to Dan and he took it.

"Well, let's see. First of all, I'd go for dark green or brown. And pictures of Clint Eastwood or Hemingway on the walls, not posters of me. The champagne's nice but I prefer beer. Bud. Some burgers, pizzas, Polish hot dogs, and a bunch of peanuts. And I'd get rid of that crap they're playing."

I looked puzzled.

"The music."

"You don't like Linda Ronstadt?" I asked.

"Hey, I thought you were . . ."

I stuck my finger in my ear, wiggled it around, then pulled it out. "Yep. Still deaf."

"Cute. So how do you know about Linda Ronstadt?"

"I know about music. Just because I can't hear it doesn't mean I'm not interested in what's going on in the music world. Ever see a black hole? No. But it's still interesting to read about. Besides, I like to impress my hearing friends with music trivia. They're always surprised when I tell them about the latest Pearl Jam cut or explain the difference between ska and reggae. Linda Ronstadt is kind of pop-country, right? With a side of salsa. I prefer those artists who aren't so mainstream. Morrissey. Boingo. R.E.M."

Dan laughed loudly. I could tell because he threw his head back and attracted the attention of a couple standing nearby.

"What's so funny?" I asked, a little annoyed.

"You can't judge a musical group by its look! I mean, that's like judging a book by its cover!"

"You'd be surprised. I can tell a lot about people by the music they listen to. Old hippies who are stuck in the sixties listen to the Grateful Dead and the Beatles. People who listen to hip hop and rap are still in their adolescence. The ones who listen to Mozart and Haydn are either very interesting or very boring. And people who are a little out of the mainstream listen to alternative music. I tend to like the people who listen to that stuff."

"What about Beausoleil, Stevie Ray Vaughan, Dwight Yoakam, Eric Clapton? Can you tell what kind of person I am by the music I listen to?"

I nodded.

"What?"

"Confused." I turned swiftly before he could hurt me, and bumped into a man who probably listened to Mantovani. He was the one I'd seen earlier talking with the sheriff.

"Hi, Sheriff," I said, raising my glass.

The sheriff raised his, then introduced me to his cohort of the moment. He was a stiff-looking man in a black suit, with a face creased like a weathered board and covered with age spots. "Connor, how you doing? This is Simon Wheeler, Lacy's attorney. We call him Croaky."

I stuck out a hand, still watching the sheriff in case he continued to talk. When he didn't I turned my attention to Croaky.

"You're the newspaper gal, aren't you?" he said, grasping my hand and shaking it gently. His hand felt as if it might break in my grasp.

I swallowed the "gal" in deference to his age, and tried to remember if I had had any legal dealings with him. Thankfully, none came to mind.

The sheriff leaned over to catch my attention. "Quite a funeral, isn't it?"

Small talk. Hate it. Let's get to the point.

"Mr. Wheeler, one of my newspaper sources mentioned that Lacy Penzance may have had a new man in her life lately. She was even asking around about prenuptial agreements. Did she come to you about anything like that?"

The two men looked at each other and tried to cover their reactions of surprise. But the dropped jaws were dead giveaways.

"How—how did you know that?" Croaky glanced around the room, as if there might have been a mole in our midst.

"Newspaper sources?" The sheriff mimicked.

"It's all over town. Was she really planning to get married soon?"

Croaky looked at the sheriff and seemed flustered. "I—I suppose I can talk about it, since she's gone. She didn't have any relatives to protect. Sheriff?"

The sheriff rubbed his temples. "It might help us figure out what happened to her."

"Well, I want to do what I can to help. Uh, yes, she did come to my office and ask about prenuptial agreements."

I downed the rest of my champagne in one swallow.

"Lacy's husband has only been dead about six

months, right? You really think she could have been seriously involved with someone else already?"

Croaky looked at the sheriff as if to confirm my
hunch. "Well, that's what's so puzzling about this. She
never mentioned anyone. No one has actually seen her
around town with anyone new. But she definitely asked
for prenuptial information. What did your source say?"

I ignored him. It was my game. "What about her
estate? Where will the money go?"

"It's been left to various charities in the county. You
know how dedicated she was to her causes. The Pioneer
Preservation Project. The Penzance Historical Society. The
restoration of the old Penzance Hotel. Except she did leave
a check in my office for the sum of five thousand dollars."

Five thousand dollars. "What for?" I asked, figuring it
would be confidential. Still, it was worth a try.

Croaky glanced at the sheriff again, then at me. "As a
matter of fact, I was going to call you this afternoon, after
the funeral."

"Me? Why?"

"The check was made out to you."

"What? Why? What for?" I stammered, truly stunned.

He kneaded his hands as he spoke. "She wrote the
check in my office and left it in an envelope for you. Said
to hold it until she returned. But she never did come back.
So I guess it's yours. You can stop by and pick it up
tomorrow if you like."

The sheriff gave me the eye. "Connor?"

I looked at him helplessly. "Sheriff, I . . . really . . . I
don't know anything about it."

"Connor, who is this so-called source of—"

Someone tickled my back and I turned to find Deputy
Arnold. His touch gave me an uncontrolled shiver. I wasn't
used to being touched so lightly, not for a long time.

"Everyone's dancing, Connor. How about it? You can
follow my lead."

I glanced around the large room. It was true; people
were actually dancing near, if not on, her grave. I declined, claiming a deadline I had to work on, and used the

break in conversation to escape the sheriff and his pending interrogation.

I scooted away and searched the crowd for Dan. I found him flirting with some tart in a dress two sizes too small for her.

"Dan, darling," I said, batting my eyelashes the way I practiced in junior high. "The children will be wondering where we are. We'd better get home. Are you ready to go?"

"**F**ive thousand dollars!"

I was sure Dan was shouting.

We were standing in a corner at Lacy's funeral party collecting our things when I casually mentioned that a nominal sum of money was waiting for me at Croaky Wheeler's office. I thought it might distract him from my wicked interruption moments ago.

"Shhh!" I said, glancing around the room for reactions from mourners, but no one appeared to be concerned with anything other than their drinks, snacks, and personal conversations.

"I'm whispering!" he said.

"Well, your face is shouting. Try not to look so ... loud."

He closed his mouth, pulled his head back a little, and then took a sip of his pink drink. "All right. So why are you getting five thousand dollars from this Froggy Whositz guy? What did you do? A little extortion? Some blackmail? Were you in Lacy's will or something?"

"That's just it! I honestly don't know. She wanted to place an ad to locate her lost sister. I told her not to announce the amount of the reward in the paper because she'd get all kinds of kooks. But I didn't bill her for five thousand dollars—the ad only cost about ten bucks. And she didn't ask me to hold onto the reward money for her."

"Maybe she wanted you to have it when it came time to deliver. That way she wouldn't be directly associated with the ad. Maybe she wanted to keep the whole thing anonymous, even after finding her sister. Odd that it's the same amount that I found in Boone's office."

It was odd, her leaving me a check for five thousand dollars. Very odd. Now that she lay dead, what was to become of that money? It clearly didn't belong to me.

"Dan, there's a rumor going around that she was seeing someone. Did you know about that?" I still wondered if he knew more than he let on.

"Who—Lacy?"

"She was talking to her lawyer about a prenuptial agreement. That usually means a marriage is on the horizon. It's pretty common for people with a lot of money to write up these things. Maybe it was someone she didn't fully trust."

"Hey, I'm new in town. I don't know everything yet. I only hear the big news. If she was seeing someone, wouldn't everybody know about it? Have you asked around?"

"The sheriff didn't know anything about it. Lacy was apparently keeping it very quiet. I wonder why?"

"Maybe because her husband had only been dead six months. Maybe she thought people around here would talk, which of course they do. It's a small town. And she looked like a very proper lady from her picture in the paper."

"True. Maybe it wouldn't have looked good. But here's the big question. If she was about to marry someone else, suicide seems unlikely. Yet the alternative is even more puzzling. And what's the connection with her search for her sister? I don't get it."

We sat in silence for a few moments. Of course, I'm always sitting in silence, in a manner of speaking. But it seemed to be something new for Dan. He was getting squirmy.

"So, who do you think she was seeing?" Dan said finally.

"I don't suppose it was you?" I asked, trying to sound casual. But it had crossed my mind. Even though they didn't seem alike, opposites do attract.

He smiled and shook his head. "Not my type."

I was tempted to ask what his type was, but I didn't.

"You know, I think she'd been reupholstered recently."

"What?" Dan looked half puzzled and half amused.

"A face lift, you know. She had some fading bruises under her eyes and around her jaw. I thought for a moment someone might have hit her or she'd been in a car accident or something. But the bruises were symmetrical. When she pulled her hair back, there were tiny scars along her hairline."

"What's that go to do with this?"

I ran a finger lightly under my eyes. "She was getting older. Maybe she was worried about her looks. Or maybe having a new man in her life made her to want to be more attractive and youthful again. I don't know. She had the money. The sheriff said she'd spent a few weeks in Europe a couple of months after Reuben's death. She could have had it done there and no one would be the wiser. Unless you know where to look for the scars."

"Do you know where to look?"

I pulled my hair back. "Right here, see?" I made sure he saw the pristine, albeit slightly graying temples. I let my hair down. "Actually, you look pretty good, for your age," I said. "Boone looks a lot older—and a lot different. Sure you haven't gone under the knife?"

"Ha! No way. I told you, Boone is ten years older than me—and we have different fathers." He paused, then went on. "You know, I've got a funny feeling my brother got himself into some serious trouble this time. Sitting around doing nothing is driving me crazy. I can't just wait for him to show up—or not." He pulled on his leather jacket. "You staying a while?" he asked.

I nodded. "Got some thinking to do, so I might as well do it here."

"How can you think with all this racket—" he stopped, looked at me, blushed. "Sorry. I keep forgetting. You just don't seem . . ."

"Deaf. That's what I hear, so to speak. Keep in touch," I said, as he sipped the last of his champagne. He gave my shoulder a gentle squeeze. It was a disconcerting feeling.

I sat stirring my pink drink, watching the tiny bubbles appear and disappear. The stirrer was a little plastic arrow, about the length of a skinny pencil, with a tiny heart at the tip. I stuck the tip in my mouth and sucked off the drops of liquid.

As I held it up to read the fine print along one side, Mickey Arnold's face came into my line of vision. He was standing a few feet away talking with Sheriff Mercer, frowning, gesturing, and looking as if he was discussing something very important. I couldn't see the sheriff's face but his body language was clear. He alternately nodded and shook his head as he spoke and listened to the deputy.

I held up the funeral program and feigned reading it while I peeked around the side to read the deputy's lips.

"It just came in." The deputy was breathing hard. He had one hand on his radio, the other on his gun.

The sheriff said something and Mickey gave a sharp, official nod.

"Confirmed. Definitely a homicide. The body was completely—" He turned his head a fraction and I lost his words.

The sheriff rubbed his forehead and spoke.

Mickey replied with two "Yes, sirs" and one "No, sir."

The sheriff held him on the shoulder and said something up close and personal.

The deputy nearly saluted. "I'll check on it," I thought he said.

The sheriff massaged his temples with a clawed hand. I was worried he'd get a rug burn from all the rubbing. He walked over to talk with Lacy's attorney. Mickey took a half-empty pink drink from the table, downed it, and caught me looking at him. I waved the program at him.

He moved over solemnly, set his empty glass on my table, and plopped into a nearby chair as if he carried the weight of the funeral on his shoulders. "Hey, Connor."

"Hi, Mickey. You look tired. Long day?" I stirred my drink again. I hated myself for being coy. "Is something wrong?"

He looked around for the sheriff, who was busy with the attorney, then leaned in. "Well, it's definite. Lacy Penzance did not kill herself." He checked again for eavesdroppers.

"Really?" I said. Although the revelation was no longer a surprise to me, the thought that Lacy might have been murdered caused the little hairs on my body to prickle and stand at attention.

"Yep, she was killed, just like I figured. The M.E. confirmed it. I told the sheriff. He said keep it quiet until the funeral is over."

"What did the medical examiner say?"

"Well, here's what's really weird. He said Lacy was stabbed with that knife *after* another weapon was used to kill her. We haven't found the weapon yet, but it was definitely not the knife. The M.E. said it was something long and thin. And get this—during the autopsy, they discovered there was hardly any blood left in her body."

"Oh, my God. What happened?" I could feel my arms tingle with goose bumps.

Mickey folded his arms across his stomach. "We don't know much yet. Still checking on it. I have some ideas, but I can't say anything right now. I'll let you know later, but I gotta keep it quiet until the sheriff says it's okay to release to the public. You understand. Now don't go publishing this in your newspaper." He glanced again at the sheriff for a moment, then back at me. "Oops, Sheriff wants me. Hey, how about dinner tonight? Maybe we can thrash this thing through and come up with something."

I nodded vaguely but was so engrossed in my own thoughts I didn't even say good-bye. Lacy was murdered. Someone had actually killed her.

I swirled my drink again and pulled out the stirrer. This time, when I licked the tip, I stabbed myself in the tongue.

"Ouch!" I said, catching the attention of a few people standing nearby.

I looked at the weapon I had just poked myself with.

The weapon.

Something long, slim, sharp.

And, perhaps, missing from the mortuary? What was that thing they used to embalm the bodies? A trowel? A trucker? A trocar . . . that was it. The thing with a hollow needle. That pierces the flesh, then the artery. Then siphons out the blood.

It was long and slim and sharp. And missing.

I was jumping to conclusions. But what the hell. It made some sense. Still, why use a trocar? It wasn't exactly the kind of weapon available at your local Wal-Mart. Only a select few would be able to get hold of one—and know how to use it.

French knew how of course. He owned the mortuary. But why would he kill Lacy? Maybe he was Lacy's new secret lover, and he didn't want Jilda to find out. He and Jilda had been seeing each other ever since I'd arrived in Flat Skunk.

Celeste? She knew the place intimately. She'd probably know how to use one of those things. Maybe she was Lacy's new lover. You never could tell these days.

Any of the mortuary staff could have done it. Sluice Jackson cleaned up the grounds, did custodial work—he probably saw a lot. The guy was strange. And what was all that stuff he was mumbling at the mortuary this afternoon?

What about Wolf Quick? He seemed to have some kind of an association with Celeste. How easily could he get hold of a trocar?

Then there was Jilda. Maybe she was jealous. Maybe she—

Hell. I was jumping a little too far, even for a conclusion. I'd plotted too many mystery puzzles for my newspaper.

Still, a trocar would make a great weapon. There were no locked doors to the sterile room—I walked right in.

Anyone could have "borrowed" it for a while, if no one was around.

Maybe it wasn't such a select group after all.

I looked around. The once-crowded room was rapidly emptying. Most of the food was gone, some of the decorations had been pulled down, either stuffed in purses or trampled by the guests. I assumed the music was still playing—a few dancers were bobbing their heads and moving their bodies to a silent rhythm.

Lacy had been murdered. There was a check for five thousand dollars waiting for me at her lawyer's office. I had to find out what happened, not just for the newspaper, but because I still felt an obligation to her. After all, she'd essentially made her last request for help to me.

It wouldn't be difficult to think up reasons for talking with people who might have had a motive, or a special interest in Lacy Penzance—or even an opportunity to take the trocar. And most folks would probably overlook me if I snooped around a little. That's the way it is being deaf. Because we're sometimes silent, we're often invisible.

The whole thing was a long shot. Maybe Lacy wasn't murdered with an embalming tool. Nevertheless it gave me the creeps to think a killer was lurking around our little town. That, coupled with the fact that someone had been poking around in my diner, made my skin crawl.

Surely, I thought, it wouldn't take a whole lot of investigating to find out the whys and then the who. Not in a small town like Skunk.

Naïveté can be a wonderful thing. I didn't know half of what was in store for me.

But the key, I was certain, was Risa Longo.

There's nothing lonelier than a funeral party with no live guests. At the end, it was just me and the corpse, commiserating in silence in the chapel. Lacy looked peaceful, lying there with her hands crossed on her chest—ironically, they were posed in the ASL sign for "rest." I wished that peaceful feeling would brush off on me, but my anxiety wouldn't abate.

I recalled the photographs of Lacy's body on the grave, spread-eagle. It wasn't the kind of body language she would present willingly, even in death. She looked more composed after her fall than in those snapshots. I scanned her emotionless face. The tiny face-lift scars had been covered expertly with makeup.

I glanced down at her hands, her fingers laden with ornate gold rings, three on each hand. The wedding ring was intricately molded, and featured a large diamond. I reached over to straighten the ring, which had twisted slightly, and felt the chill of her lifeless finger. And the dampness. I looked at my fingertips; a residue of creamy beige liquid.

Makeup, even on her hands. I guess it wasn't so

strange, except that it was so thick, it hadn't dried completely. I touched her finger again and gently rubbed the knuckle, removing the layer of makeup. Rough, jagged scratches appeared on the knuckle ridges.

I lifted her icy hand, examined the fingers closely, and replaced the hand, tucking it beneath the other one to hide the discovery I'd made. I wiped the excess makeup from my fingertips on the inside of her skirt. Puzzled, I stood there looking at her for several more minutes before I left the chapel.

Hoping he'd gone straight back to the office, I stopped by the sheriff's on my way home from the funeral. I'd seen him leave soon after his talk with Mickey, and I wondered what his next step would be in the investigation.

I found him hunched over a pink paper plate filled with pinkish-brown appetizers from the funeral party, studying a sheet of pink paper.

"Hi, Sheriff," I said, plopping into a chair near the desk. He nodded with his mouth full. He may have even said something. Tough to tell with that wad in his mouth.

"Some funeral, eh?" I said. "More like a nice cocktail party. Maybe the mortuary business would pick up a little if funerals were more festive and less depressing. Of course, you probably don't want business to pick up too much, eh? You've already got your hands full."

The sheriff nodded again. He seemed uncharacteristically quiet. Maybe there was still too much food in his mouth.

"So what's new?" I waited for a response. He lifted his eyes briefly from the sheet of paper, not really looking at me, but acknowledging my presence. He swallowed what looked like something whole.

"It's a curious case, Connor. And it gets curiouser by the moment."

I picked a slightly squished canapé from the pink plate and popped it into my mouth. "What do you think happened to her?"

"I don't know. I keep reading her note over and over. And the more I read it, the more cryptic it becomes. I know she wrote it—I verified her handwriting. And the contents fit the notion of suicide. She was unhappy about losing her husband, and that's pretty much what she wrote. But there's something missing here. I just can't put my finger on what it is."

"What do you mean, something's missing?"

"I don't know. I don't mean just the jewelry. I mean some part of the puzzle."

I perked up. "Some of her jewelry is missing?"

He popped three puffy-looking things into his mouth and nodded.

"Yeah, a few things," he said with some difficulty. "A couple of gold necklaces, a few bracelets, some rings, and a gold pin. The maid called this morning. Said she checked Lacy's jewelry box and noticed the stuff was gone. She's coming down to fill out a report."

"Any chance the maid took them and is claiming theft after the fact?"

The sheriff shrugged. "It's possible. But if she did, she's a fool. We'll be watching her closely and we'll catch her quickly if she did."

The sheriff was right. This Lacy Penzance thing was becoming curiouser by the minute. A check for five thousand dollars for a missing sister. A visit to a sister who wasn't a sister. A faked suicide. A bizarre murder with a strange weapon and an odd murder site. And now missing jewelry?

"Sheriff, could I read the note?" I thought it might be a good time to ask. He seemed in the mood to share. After a moment's hesitation, he handed it over.

"This doesn't go in the paper, Connor, understand?"

I nodded absently, already absorbed in the haunting document.

The message was written on a pink sheet of paper decorated with little hearts. It appeared to have been cropped with a smooth but slightly uneven edge along one side. The script was curly, careful, and romantic. The paper was expensive, scented, and unsigned. It read:

"I've been having a hard time lately. Thank goodness for Celeste and all her help in dealing with

Reuben's death. She's been through a lot with me, and has proved to be a great confidante. I appreciated the support so much. But I don't think I'll ever recover from the death of my husband. Even with all his faults, he kept me from being lonely."

That was all.

Inconclusive, to say the least. But perhaps significant when connected to the night of her death.

"Sheriff, do you know yet what kind of weapon killed her? It wasn't the knife?" I knew it wasn't. Mickey had blabbed. But I didn't want to get my source in trouble.

"The M.E. says it was something long and sharp. That's all he can tell us."

"Could it be something like one of those instruments they use at the mortuary? You know, like a trocar?" I asked innocently.

He looked at me, definitely surprised. "Yeah, a trocar could do it. How do you know about that?"

"Oh, I took a tour of the mortuary with Celeste this morning. They have all kinds of embalming tools on view for the public. Some of them would make great murder weapons."

The sheriff raised one eyebrow. "You took a tour of the mortuary? Now why is that, C.W.?"

I ignored his innuendo. "Sheriff, no other weapon besides the knife was found in or near the body, was it?"

He blinked; the eyebrow arched a little higher.

"And you're fairly certain she didn't kill herself with the knife even though there was a note, right?"

"So."

"So what do you think happened?"

The eyebrows fell, along with his shoulders. "All's I can figure is, this thing, whatever it was, was probably inserted into the body first, then removed. Why, I don't know. Then most likely the knife was stuck in her. She lost a lot of blood, that's for sure. There wasn't much left."

"So someone may have killed her with this thing, let's say this trocar or something like it, then stuck in the knife to make it look like she killed herself. Is that a possible explanation?"

That eyebrow again. It was getting a workout.

I continued before he could think beyond my suppositions. "And they moved her to the cemetery and planted that note?"

He pressed his lips together tightly. That face was a mask of growing tension.

"It just seems awfully . . . arranged, don't you think?"

He said nothing. At least I didn't see his lips move.

I went on. "Almost dramatized, really. Or ritualistic, because of the loss of blood?"

He still said nothing. His face did all the talking.

"Any idea why she was killed?" I asked.

He pushed the plate of leftovers away, leaned back in his chair, closed his eyes, and pinched the frown lines between his eyebrows.

After a moment I picked myself up out of the chair and said I had to be going. Newspaper to print and all that. When I reached the door, I caught a glimpse of movement in the corner of my eye. The sheriff was waving his arms, trying to get my attention.

"Connor, you're not snooping around on this thing, are you? Someone's been murdered, and that's nothing to make into a mystery puzzle for your paper."

"No, Sheriff. I'm just trying to do a story for my newspaper, that's all. I want it to be a thorough job. Which reminds me, did you ever get over to my place to check it out? With this Lacy thing—"

The sheriff held up his hands to stop me. "Yeah, yeah, I looked over your place. Found the key under the dog dish like you told me. Couldn't find anything. Tried to take a few prints but your diner is covered in them, probably all yours. I had Mickey brush the doors and windows but he hasn't come up with much. Did you ever find anything missing?"

"No. Wait—yes! In my medicine chest."

"What'd they take? Drugs of some kind?"

Now I was really going to look like a flake. "I'm not

sure. I can't remember what was there. Something I never use, I guess."

"Then how do you know anything's missing?"

"I just know."

"You know, Connor, you might not be as safe as you thought you were around here, what with the murder and all. You might want to get some new locks on your doors and make sure your windows are secured. I'll have Mickey cruise your house for the next few days. But lock up."

"I always do," I said, then waved him thanks and left the office feeling more than a little uncomfortable about the goings on in quiet old Flat Skunk.

The sounds of darkness were approaching. I don't really know what sounds of darkness are, but the impending blackness of night must make some kind of sound. After all, you can see it, smell it, feel it, nearly taste it. I'll bet you can hear it, too.

I swung by my office to whip up new phony letterheads and business cards, since "Arson Investigation," "Amway Distributor," and "Census Taker" wouldn't do, then hopped back in my slightly injured Chevy and headed the two miles out of town to a Spanish-style villa up on the hill. Parking my car in the driveway, I took the clay tile path to the front entrance of the house and knocked on the metal-covered door.

The porch light came on and the door was opened by the maid, her dark eyes red-rimmed and her mascara smeared. She was dressed in a black polyester dress with a matching shawl, and was wearing black nylons without shoes. I guessed she had recently returned from the funeral and hadn't yet changed.

"Yes?" She smoothed her cheeks with her fingertips and held the door open cautiously.

"Excuse me. I'm sorry to bother you so late. I'm Lana Lang. I'm an insurance adjuster for the Smallville Insurance Company. I'm here to take a report regarding some missing jewelry from Ms. . . ." I checked my notebook, ". . . Lacy Penzance's estate. You are the one who called, are you not?" I handed her my business card. Perry

White would have been proud. I figured the timing was right. The real agents would be there in the morning.

She nodded and opened the door fully. I followed her past the Spanish marble foyer into a sitting room on the right. The area was filled with objects of Spanish art, crafts, and culture. I sat on a wrought iron chair covered with a bright woven pillow that looked Peruvian or Guatemalan. I'd seen similar ones at the import store.

"I understand some of Ms. Penzance's jewelry is missing." I flipped open my clipboard and showed off my new letterhead. The Tiffany font was impressive.

"Some jewelry is gone, yes," she said, in slightly altered syntax. The "Yes," looked like "Ches" or "Jes," but I could understand her well enough. She spoke slowly and simply, which made up for the differences in pronunciation.

"A pin, you know, that look like a golden sun. Three bracelets, all gold, kind of chunky, like little gold nuggets. And three necklaces that matched the bracelets. Oh, and four gold rings, big ones. They were kind of, how you say, curvy and not matching?"

"Free-form?" I said.

She nodded. "Yes, free-form. You want to see?"

I followed her up the tile stairs to Lacy's bedroom. It was pink, of course, with large rose-colored flower wallpaper and green accents. Tiny golden birds were carved into the four posts of the bed. The woman, who had introduced herself as Carmen, unlocked a cosmetic vanity, using a key on a ring that contained numerous other keys of varying sizes and shapes. She pulled a jewelry box from its hiding place.

"I did not take them, you know. That's why I reported it right away. Do I still have to go talk with the sheriff *mañana* . . . tomorrow?"

"Yes, my investigation is separate from his. I think he just wants you to fill out a report." I was beginning to feel a little guilty about taking advantage of the maid's naïveté. But I had my own agenda to serve. And I wasn't doing anything terribly wrong.

I opened the box and fingered through the items. A few silver pieces were left, and other miscellaneous jewelry, some with gems, pearls, or other stones embedded in them. But according to Carmen, most of the gold items were gone.

"Do you mind if I look around for a moment?" I asked. She shook her head and shrugged simultaneously, then sat down on the end of the bed, ostensibly to make sure I didn't take anything while I snooped. I didn't mind having her there. If I got caught investigating, at least I wouldn't be accused of stealing something myself.

Carmen switched on the small bedside television while I dug around in the drawers of Lacy's bureau, looking for something of value that the thief might have overlooked. I was especially puzzled as to why he had only taken the gold.

There were lots of used cosmetics tucked away in the drawers; a half-empty container of Retin-A, skin peelers, cover-ups, collagen creams, and vials of expensive makeup from the cosmetic boutiques at the better department stores. Bottles of antiseptics were the only odd items grouped with the makeup. I wondered what she needed antiseptics for. To keep germs out of her recent incisions, perhaps?

Underneath the dresser I found a drawer filled with boxes of Maxi pads. Odd. This woman should have been menopausal, unless she was on hormones. There was always the occasional need, I supposed. I pulled a box out to check behind it and realized it was heavier than I expected. I opened the floppy lid and removed the contents.

Journals. I checked the other three boxes. There were four journals in each box, the kind of notebooks that are covered in flowered fabric and sold at the stationery stores to make your writing seem more important, or at least prettier. I glanced at Carmen, engrossed in a *Roseanne* rerun. Spreading the four most recent journals on the floor, I opened the first one and read a few lines.

The book dated back to Lacy's marriage fifteen years earlier. The entries were made every few days, and were brief, with only the highlights of her life detailed. Very little emotion was revealed in the writing—just the facts, ma'am.

I flipped through the second, the third, and finally the fourth journal, each one of a different shade of pink, purple, or lavender, to see if there was something of interest that could put some light on her death. The fourth one—and most recent—began with Reuben's death. This time, the writing was more emotional. Although it seemed she had loved and missed her less-than-perfect husband, her fear or loneliness—and of being alone—was more evident than her sorrow of losing her partner.

"I miss Reuben. He could be a dear man, even though he had his flaws. It was comfortable, secure. That's what I needed most from him, having missed it as a child. His death is still a mystery to me and I try not to feel sorry for myself, but oftentimes I do. I try to fill my time with charities, but the loneliness is unbearable and I find myself angry at him for leaving me this way. I let him live his own life. I never complained about his other needs. Why did he have to go and die? Why did he leave me all alone? I'll never find another man at my age, no matter what Celeste says."

The paper in this last journal was pale pink, scented, and flowery, like the stationery Lacy had used to write her assumed suicide note. But all the pages seemed intact. The entries ended about six weeks earlier. I wondered if she could have started one more volume—a journal that would explain the more recent events in her life.

I checked the drawer. No more boxes.

I returned the journals to their hiding place, all but the last one, which I tucked into my notebook while the maid was engaged in a feminine hygiene commercial. As I got up to thank Carmen, I noticed that the light was blinking on the answering machine next to the bedroom phone.

"Did someone call?" I asked.

She shrugged.

"Have you listened to any of her messages since she died?"

"Uh, no. I . . . I don't know. Some. The sheriff took

the tape when he came here yesterday. I put another one in but I haven't checked it. I just haven't been thinking right, you know. I don't like to listen to her messages. It seems not good."

"So these calls came in after her death?"

Carmen pulled at her hair. "Yes. When Mrs. Penzance was alive, she didn't want me to answer her personal phone or take the messages from the machine in here. I always left it alone, like she said. But I guess I should listen now, and call them back and tell them Mrs. Penzance is not . . . here any more." Her eyes welled.

I pulled out my tape recorder. "Listen, why don't you play them now, and I'll record them. You never know. There may be something important on the machine."

"I don't know . . . maybe I should wait for the sheriff . . ." she said, hesitating.

"Well, it can't hurt. And if there is something important, you can tell him tomorrow. I'm sure he would appreciate that."

She paused for another moment, then let go of her hair and pushed the playback button. I turned on my tape recorder and held it next to the speaker. I would get Miah to translate it when I got back to the office. But if Carmen's expression was any indication, there was something significant on that tape.

My scabbed knees ached as I climbed the stairs to my
office. My right arm itched from what appeared to be
poison oak. And my head throbbed from the strain of constant lipreading. I needed some peace along with the quiet.

Although it was late, Miah was at his small desk in the
corner of my office, working away on the assignment I'd
given him to wrap the upcoming frog festival. Something
to do with a frog costume contest. If we were to get the
paper out by Saturday, we needed to wind up most of the
contents by tomorrow. And I had been neglecting my
share of the work trying to get this front-page story.

"What-doing?" I signed, after waving to catch his
attention. The simple sign, index and thumb making little
pincher movements, palm up, meant more like "What's
up?" than "What are you doing?"

He signed back the ASL version of "I'm trying to
make fun of this story." I think he meant he was trying to
put some fun into the story. Either way it didn't really
matter. I was beyond sweating the small stuff. I just
wanted to get it done.

"Favor, please?" I said, more with my face than my

hands. He nodded. His hair fell over his face and he threw it back with a sharp twist of his head. It was kind of a sexy move, if you tended to have thoughts like that about twenty-five-year-old guys.

"Interpret? Tape, Lacy Penzance answer machine. Maybe important, don't-know," I signed. He followed my signs, nodding occasionally and frowning intently. I can always tell when he's not understanding me. He gets this glazed look over his eyes, his mouth falls open, and he just nods his head reflectively. At the moment he was looking pretty sharp.

"You take from house, you?" he asked, eyebrows raised.

I made a negative face and shook my head. "Me? No. My tape. Just copied. Left it there. OK?"

He looked relieved that I hadn't stolen some important evidence from Lacy's home, like Exhibit A.

I cleaned up my desk while he listened and typed, listened and typed.

About the time I tossed out the last of the See's candy papers, old sticky notes, pizza coupons, computer catalogs, and creatively bent paper clips, he handed the completed copy to me. I had even recorded her outgoing message, just in case. It read:

"This is Lacy Penzance. I can't come to the phone, but I'd like to talk with you, so please leave a message. Your call is important, and I'll get back to you as soon as I can. Have a nice day."

First message: 'Hi Lacy, this is Dr. Ellington. That scarring you mentioned is not unusual and should disappear in a few weeks. If it thickens or seems to spread, give me a call. Otherwise, everything is normal, as I mentioned at your checkup. As for scheduling the second procedure, my nurse will call you to set up a time.'

Message #2: 'This is Melanie at Dr. Ellington's office? Doctor said you wanted to make an appointment for the next procedure? We have an opening next week, Wednesday, at

10:30? Give me a call at 837-7089 if you want that one, OK? Byee!'

Message #3: 'This is Barbara, from the committee. Your donation was very much appreciated. Many thanks, dear. We now have enough to decorate the Veteran's Hall again this year. Hope you like Frog Green. Frankly, I'm sick to death of it! (Giggle). Talk to you later, hon.'

Message #4, 5 & 6: All hang-ups.

Message #7: 'This is Wentling Portrait Studios and we're having a special on family portrait sittings this week . . .'

The sales pitch went on. I skimmed down to the next message.

Message #8: 'Lacy Penzance, this is Arden Morris. I received your letter today, but I'm still not exactly sure what you want. Uh, I'd be happy to meet you if you want to come to Rio Vista, but like I said, I don't think I can help. Anyway, you can call me at 916-644-1500 if you want to arrange a time. Uh, bye.'

I looked up at Miah. He figuratively signed, "There were four more hang-ups. That was it. What do you think?"

"I think we'd better get down to Wentling right away if we want to take advantage of that portrait offer." I winked and underlined the name Arden Morris on his notes.

"Think that's something?" Miah signed.

I gave him the universal sign for how-the-hell-should-I-know—shoulders up and down—thought for a moment, then handed him the phone.

"Let's call him. He sounds interesting—"

"It's a she," Miah interrupted.

"What?"

"She. Arden Morris is a she."

"How do you know?"

"Her voice."

"Oh, yeah, okay. Tell her you're Lacy's secretary and
. . . you're phoning to set up that appointment, whatever it
is. Maybe she hasn't heard the news about Lacy, since Rio
Vista's out of the area. And get her address."

Miah dialed, indicated a busy tone, redialed. The second
time he nodded. He gave the voice on the line his name and
spiel. Suddenly, his contrived smile drooped out of sight. He
hung up the phone without saying another word.

"She said she doesn't think I'm funny. She said I'm
some sort of sick human being and if I call there again
she'll call the police."

I guess she'd heard the news.

We had touched a nerve, I thought on my way to the tiny
Flat Skunk Library, which was open until nine P.M. on
Wednesday nights. I wanted to know more, and I had fif-
teen minutes until closing.

Despite the fact that the Flat Skunk Library reference
section is about as small as the paperback section at the
grocery store and the whole thing is housed in a double
trailer, I located Arden Morris's address in the ragged
Delta Valley phone book. The "A. Morris" on River Road
matched the phone number we'd received from Lacy's
answering machine tape.

After returning to the office and finishing up the
layout on three ads—one for the Who Did Your Hair
salon, one for Ernest N. Deavor Real Estate, and one for
the Mark Twain Look-Alike Contest at the Frog Jubilee, I
decided to make a last-minute trip to Rio Vista to meet the
mystery woman. Armed with more bogus business cards
and letterhead, I said good night to Miah as he headed
home, and closed the door to my office.

Dan was just coming around the stairway corner
when I turned around, a bag of cat food in one arm and a
bag of burgers in the other. The smell of the food
reminded me I hadn't had anything decent to eat all day
except for some pink stuff.

"Where are you off to?" Dan said, fumbling for the
keys to Boone's office.

"I have a lead," I said, conjuring up the Whopper and fries emanating from the steaming bag. I hoped I wouldn't actually drool down the front of my top.

Dan handed me the people food bag to hold while he stuck the key in the lock and opened the door. I followed him into the office and set the burgers on Boone's desk.

"Hungry?" he asked, ripping open the cat food bag and pouring a small amount of hard colorful chunks into a plastic bowl near the window. The cat came creeping out from behind the filing cabinet in search of a simulated mouse dinner.

"A little," I said, hoping my stomach wasn't speaking louder than I was. Even the cat food was beginning to look good.

"So what's up?"

I told him about the message on Lacy's machine and my plans to visit Arden Morris. He looked up at the mention of her name.

"Arden Morris?"

I nodded. "You know her?"

He moved to the filing cabinet and pulled out a drawer. After a little rifling, he triumphantly extracted a file with "Arden Morris" scrawled across the top.

"I thought I remembered that name from one of the files I cleaned up in the mess. Shall we have a look?"

He set the file down on the desk next to the aromatic bag of greasy meat and fries and flipped it open.

Nothing inside.

"Shit! Somebody's cleaned it out. What's going on around here?"

He pulled out a burger and set it on the desk absentmindedly. I swallowed the Pavlovian collection of saliva in my mouth. Tasted like a burger in a strange way.

After a moment Dan seemed to come back to the planet. He tore the burger in half and offered me the smaller chunk. I took it, trying to seem nonchalant, and finished it in three bites and forty-five seconds.

"You planning to go see Arden Morris tonight?" he said, after finishing his half. I looked at my watch. It was getting late for the long drive to Rio Vista to confront a mystery woman about a dead woman.

"To tell you the truth, Connor, I'd like to go, too. I think there's a connection to my brother in all this. If you want to wait until morning I'll join you, but it's kind of late now and I've got a few things I need to do."

I watched him pull another wrapper out of the bag. A chicken sandwich. He broke it apart and this time gave me the bigger half. I tried not to wolf it and my restraint was remarkable, considering my condition. I boldly helped myself to the fries.

"Yeah, okay, you're right," I said when I could talk again. "It's late. Tomorrow, then. After I send up the paper. I've really been neglecting my work and I could use the time to catch up. I don't know who Arden Morris is or what her connection to Lacy is, but I do think she's a part of this, whatever this is."

We finished our food in silence, gazing out the window at the lighted street as we watched the town activity die down. After the last of the fries was gone, I thanked Dan for the meal, told him I owed him one, and said I'd see him in the morning. I, too, had a few things I still needed to do.

As I left his office and started to return to my own, I had a thought. I reversed my steps, headed down the hotel stairs, and hopped in my car, heading for Memory Kingdom.

Outside it was already starry, with a sliver of moon, but the cloud-filled blue sky painted on the walls of the mortuary's reception room gave the feeling of midafternoon. To my surprise, the main entrance door was unlocked at the late hour. "Our doors never close," I thought would make a good motto.

I found French McClusky at his desk. He appeared to be the only soul in the place at that time of night. At least the only soul I could see. No telling what phantasms were lurking around the bodies back in the Morgatorium Room, or whatever it was called.

Celeste's office was dark, and I could see no other staff.

Knocking on French's half-shut door, I inched it open with each rap. French looked up, put his pencil down, and offered his salesman smile. He was holding up well for a man in his midfifties. Been sipping some of that embalming fluid?

"Hi, French," I said, entering slowly. "Sorry to bother you so late, but the front door was open, I saw your light on, and I had a few questions. Have you got a minute?" I closed the door behind me.

French removed his bifocals, leaving an imprint on the bridge of his nose, and set them carefully on his neat desk. His Wal-Mart suit was wrinkled from the day's work, his hairpiece slightly disheveled, and there were a few crumbs of food on the side of his mouth. I licked my lips in response, but he didn't get the hint.

"Come on in, Connor. Have a seat. I heard you stopped by and took the tour. Celeste mentioned you might have an aunt who may be needing our services soon. The counselors are all gone for the night. Can I help you with anything?"

I nodded and sat down in the leather chair opposite him. "Yes, uh, Aunt . . ." Oh, my God. I had forgotten my fictional aunt's name! Well, how about ". . . Lotta. I'm afraid she's . . ." I shook my head to avoid lying too excessively.

After a dramatic pause, I pushed on. "It's hard to talk about, you know. But I was really impressed by the way you and Celeste handled Lacy Penzance's arrangement. The funeral was so . . . unique. All that pink and those birds. God, it's so hard to believe she's dead."

French nodded. "She was quite a lady. What a shocker to learn it was murder. Who would want to kill a nice old gal like that? She was quite a contributor to this community."

She would have loved the "nice old gal," I was sure. "I didn't know her very well. But you did, didn't you? I think she mentioned you were friends when I last talked with her."

French shrugged. "You know how that is in a small town. We dated a while when we were in high school, but I wanted to be a mortician, like my father, and she had higher aspirations for her future husband. It didn't work out. We went our separate ways."

"What about after Reuben's death? I suppose you could have tried again. You're a single man."

He gave me a sharp look that quickly softened into a smile. "I'm kind of involved with Jilda down at the Nugget. She wouldn't have liked it much if I'd started fooling around with Lacy, that's for sure. She's got a bit of a jealous streak. No, the timing wasn't right for me and Lacy. Now about your aunt—"

"French, I've been thinking a lot about Lacy. I saw her the day before she died and something seemed to be bothering her. Do you know anything about a secret she might have been hiding?"

"A secret?"

I pressed on. "I think she was seeing someone. Recently. In fact, she might have been contemplating remarrying."

French stuck out his lower lip and frowned. "Really?" He paused, picked up his glasses, and wiped the lenses with the front of his shirt. "Well, I guess it's possible, her being a widow and all. But I never heard a thing about it. Funny." He paused again.

"It wasn't you?"

"Good grief, no! Hell, I met her a couple of times for dinner after Reuben died. Like I said, we were old friends. But Jilda would have killed me if she'd caught me, even though it didn't mean anything. I mean, Lacy's a very attractive woman and all. Even better looking than she was a few years ago. But I—"

He stopped, looking somewhat alarmed that he may have said something he shouldn't have. Quickly he picked up his glasses and replaced them on his nose.

"You won't say anything to Jilda, will you?" he said, frowning.

I shook my head and went on. "French, there's something else. When I was here taking the tour, one of the embalmers mentioned something about an instrument missing from the embalming room."

He frowned again and the glasses slipped down his nose. He pushed them back up with his middle finger, making an unconscious obscene gesture. "What? No! We're very careful . . ."

"I think it was a trocar . . ." I bluffed.

His eyes narrowed. "Connor, what exactly do you want? I thought you were interested in some services for your aunt. This talk about Lacy and embalming tools and stuff isn't really relevant."

He stood. I stood.

"I was just curious. You know, everyone's talking about Lacy's death. I thought you might know something about the weapon that was used to kill her."

"Weapon? You think a trocar was used to kill Lacy? One of Memory Kingdom's? Connor, you're way off the track here. I think—"

I turned around and headed for the door. Missed that last part. Bummer. I opened the door, then faced him once again.

"Thanks for your time, French. I'll get back to you on my aunt . . . Lana."

He closed his mouth and nodded. Nothing was worth losing a future customer. Then came that salesman smile again that had been missing for the last several minutes.

"Just let me know when I can be of service, Connor. Your aunt—now what did you say her name was—"

The phone apparently rang because French looked down at it, picked it up, and said hello. He listened for a few seconds, then said, "Oh, shit!" or maybe "Holy shit!" as his eyes shifted back and forth frantically. He dropped the phone down, grabbed his suit jacket off the hook, and headed for the door.

"Something wrong?" I asked. He looked pale, even for a mortician.

"It's Sluice."

"What? Is he—"

"There's been an accident. Sluice apparently fell into an open grave he'd been digging."

"Shall I call an ambulance?"

French didn't respond to my question. Instead he replied, "They think he's dead."

I hesitated before following French out the door. The sheriff would have to be notified if he hadn't been already, and French didn't appear to be thinking clearly. Still, someone had had the presence of mind to call French at least. Who? And from where?

French had no TTY, so I dialed the sheriff's number on the regular phone and started talking when I thought someone would have had time to pick up the receiver. I repeated over and over the phrase, "This is Connor West-phal. Sluice Jackson's fallen into an open grave at the Pioneer Cemetery," and hoped someone was listening. Otherwise I'd feel like a fool.

After five or six repetitions, I left the office and headed for the cemetery, adjacent to the mortuary. The smell of the town mascot filled the air, a constant reminder of my new community. Across the dimly lighted expanse of lawn, I spotted a backhoe and made my way over.

As I approached, I saw French and Wolf Quick hovering over a freshly dug grave next to the backhoe. The monstrous, threatening machine cast long, jagged shadows over the scene. The two men alternately gazed into the six-foot hole and glanced around the nearby area as if anxiously awaiting assistance. Wolf pointed to the backhoe, while French scratched his ear, and spit. I couldn't tell what they were saying from that distance.

By the time I arrived at the grave, a little out of breath from the run, I saw Sheriff Mercer hiking up the hill at a rapid pace to join us. That was fast. In fact, too fast to take my call and respond. Someone else must have alerted him first. Wolf?

"What's going on?" the sheriff said, as he got down on one knee and peered into the pit. "Goddammit! What happened? Is he alive? Where are the EMT's? We gotta get a look at him." The sheriff turned around and eased himself into the grave.

While French went in search of a flashlight in the sheriff's car, Wolf recounted the story in mumbled speech. He wasn't easy to read with the overgrown beard and mustache that curled over his lip, but I caught bits here and there. He had happened upon Sluice while walking through the cemetery, which to me sounded odd in itself, but I said nothing. He heard a noise coming from the open grave, stopped to look in, and saw Sluice. He figured Sluice must have fallen off the backhoe he'd been operating—the engine was still running. At that point Wolf had pulled out his cellular phone and called the sheriff, then French.

"He doesn't look like he's breathing," Wolf said, shining the retrieved flashlight into the hole. The sheriff had opened Sluice's jacket and was preparing to give him CPR.

French gave Wolf a horrified look. "He can't be dead. Not another one. Oh, God. Jesus. We've gotta get him out of there!"

"Just hold tight," Wolf said. "Sheriff's with him. The EMT's are on their way. They'll take care of him. We better not move him, in case—" I missed the rest as he turned toward the roadway. I followed his gaze. The ambulance had arrived, as well as Deputy Arnold and a couple of curious onlookers.

"Stand aside!" The two paramedics took charge

instantly. Ropes were pulled from the back of the ambulance. Stretchers were propped nearby. Medical bags were opened. While the male paramedic prepared his equipment, the female paramedic procured a ladder from the side of the nearby landscape shed. With Mickey's help, she lowered it into the grave and climbed down into the claustrophobic pit to join the sheriff.

Mickey shined a flashlight into the open hole and we watched as the woman took Sluice's pulse, assisted by a small mouth-held flashlight. After a few moments the sheriff came clambering out of the pit and said something.

"What did he say?" I asked Mickey who was standing next to me, his arm on my shoulder.

"He's still alive!"

It was after midnight when I finally left the sheriff's office and returned to my home-sweet-diner. I had hung around to watch the paramedics lift Sluice Jackson out of the grave and transport him to the ambulance, for a code blue ride to the Mother Lode Memorial Hospital in Sonora. I waited a while at the sheriff's office creating suppositions with the deputy until we heard from the hospital, a little past eleven. Sluice Jackson was stable. I'd gone home when there was nothing more to learn.

Was it an accident? Or could he have been pushed? Those were the two questions Mickey and I had debated the most throughout the remainder of the evening. At first I had wondered what Sluice was doing out in the cemetery with the backhoe so late at night, but French had explained it was routine to do the digging at night, so as not to disturb folks in the daytime. People don't like to see actual graves being dug in broad daylight. But another question remained: What was Wolf doing roaming around the cemetery at night?

Sheriff Mercer had been the one who called in around eleven-thirty P.M., reporting on Sluice's condition: lacerations to the head, various bruises, and a broken finger. Sluice was still semiconscious, but he was expected to recover. He had lost some blood from a head wound, but his blood pressure had stabilized and his heartbeat was nearly normal.

"What's the story with Sluice anyway?" I said to Mickey as I packed up my notebook and backpack to head home. "Does anyone really know anything about him? All I ever get are rumors."

Mickey stuck a wad of gum in his mouth, which didn't help the lipreading. I had to strain to understand him at that late hour.

"All I know is, he's an old prospector who's been in Flat Skunk forever, and he's still searching for his pot of gold. He's not quite all there, you know." Mickey tapped his temple. "Probably alcohol poisoning. But he's harmless."

The deputy chewed his gum solemnly for a few seconds before pushing it back into the dark crevices of his cheek like a squirrel.

"Sluice used to be employed by Reuben Penzance, who was mayor before you came here, you know. Sluice worked for him part-time, doing odd jobs, helping out around their ranch, much like he does at the mortuary. I think the Penzances felt sorry for him. He was with Reuben at the time of the mayor's accident, what—six months ago, was it?"

"The boating accident?" I'd read something about it when I'd first arrived, but I didn't know all the details.

Mickey looked down at the floor in thought and swung his feet at the base of the sheriff's desk in an alternating pattern. His once shiny shoes, now encrusted with red dirt from the walk in the cemetery, spun in small circles. He took a moment to scratch an inflamed rash on his arm, then continued.

"About six months ago Reuben was out fishing over at Miwok Reservoir. Sluice was there, caddying his fishing gear. The way Sluice tells it—when he's somewhat coherent—they'd gone out to the middle of the lake, and suddenly Reuben latched onto something big. Apparently he overcompensated and leaned too far out of the boat. They both fell into the water as the boat tipped over."

"Was there no one else around?"

The deputy shrugged. "Apparently not. Anyway, Sluice had a life jacket on at Reuben's insistence 'cause he couldn't swim. Reuben could swim, so he wasn't wearing one, but he'd been drinking. He must have got tangled up on his line or something and couldn't break free. We found him floating the next day, the fishing line wrapped around his legs. The hook was caught in his nose."

Yeech. "What happened to Sluice?"

"He got hold of a rock in the middle of the lake and held on all night, pretty terrified. It's a big lake, you know, and it took a while before he was found."

"Wasn't Lacy frantic when she realized her husband was missing? Didn't anyone go looking for him?"

"Lacy did call the sheriff eventually, when Reuben didn't come home that night. But by the time we got out there, it was too dark to do much searching. Truthfully, nobody was too worried, not even Lacy. Reuben didn't always make a regular habit of coming straight home from work. When we got to the spot, there was no sign of the boat. We figured he probably stopped off somewhere. He often did." Mickey glanced at me with a know-what-I-mean look. "When we finally found Sluice at dawn, wearing his life jacket and holding onto the rock, we knew something was up."

"How awful," I said. "What about the boat?"

"Divers went looking for it early that morning. Found it at the bottom of the lake after a few hours."

"How did Lacy take it?"

"Not good. Seemed to think it really didn't happen and kept waiting for Reuben to come driving up in his Cherokee. Celeste was a big help for her then. Got her to accept the fact that Reuben was gone and then helped her deal with it. She worked a miracle really."

"What happened to Sluice? Was he all right?"

"Apart from being cold, waterlogged, and terrified, he was, how shall I put it, shy a few more nuggets. Started muttering all the time. Now he walks around guarding his backpack like it's some kind of priceless artifact. Nobody pays much attention to him. Some folks think he might have been responsible for Reuben's death. Who knows? I doubt we'll ever know the truth. He hasn't been very coherent since then."

I started to head out the door, then paused and turned around. "Mickey, did Wolf say why he happened to be at the cemetery at that time of night?"

"Nope. Maybe he has a relative buried there. Don't know. I'm sure the sheriff will be asking him about that. Why?"

"Just curious about why a person walks around in a cemetery late at night."

I said good-bye to the deputy and drove home, taking in the scented air of our skunk population, my knees creaking with residual pain from the bike crash.

Something seemed to be haunting Sluice. Was he involved some way in Reuben's death? Lacy's murder? He was certainly familiar with the cemetery since he worked there. And he'd probably have access to all the instruments. But what would be his motive? Maybe you didn't need one if you were crazy.

Too many questions, not enough beer, I decided, as I put my key in the diner's lock. I hesitated before opening the door, and called Casper before setting foot inside. When I saw her behaving normally, I moved in cautiously, still uneasy about the earlier break-in. After a thorough search of the place, I flopped on the couch and distracted myself by catching the late movie once again. This one wasn't captioned, so I watched a bunch of screaming kids running from a schoolhouse in Bodega Bay. A flock of birds was chasing them, trying to peck out their eyes and make nests from their hair. Cool stuff.

I lay down on the couch, kicked off my black, baby-doll Doc Marten's that seemed to weigh ten pounds, and fluffed the throw pillows, too tired to change, wash up, or eat. The lone beer was enough to put me out. I never did see what happened to those poor little kids after the birds attacked the schoolteacher. But they didn't give me bad dreams. I had plenty else to give me nightmares.

Early the next morning I put my visit to Arden Morris on hold. Showered and dressed in maroon jeans and a matching ribbed cotton knit sweater, I fixed up my bike, then rode it back to the cemetery to have a look around. I was no detective; sinister footprints or trampled flower beds were not my forte. But I still wanted to be there, to try to visualize what had happened to Sluice.

The brightness of the day made the cemetery cheery and inviting rather than morose and forbidding, as on the previous evening. A few children were once again at play on the park playground structures, and a young couple sat cuddling on a bench next to a lone man reading a book.

I walked over to the open grave where warning signs were tacked to a pair of sawhorses that now blocked entry to the area. The backhoe was still parked beside the pit, parts of it highlighted with a white powdery film. Dusted for prints? I wondered.

I ducked under the plastic banner that connected the sawhorses and moved closer to the open grave. Peering inside, I saw something glinting in the morning light. Tiny, half-buried, but sparkly, apparently it had been over-looked in last night's darkness and confusion.

I looked around for something to hook or catch the shiny object but found nothing. I wasn't about to leap into the six-foot hole and retrieve it—I might never get out again. I pushed away a scene from Edgar Allan Poe and I thought for a few minutes. That led me to the ladder the paramedics had used last night to retrieve Sluice Jackson. Where was it? The landscape shed.

I found the ladder propped sideways against the side of the dilapidated building. In a matter of minutes I had lowered it into the pit and was climbing slowly down inside, checking first to see if anyone might be watching. The coast was clear.

Digging around the crumbly red clay, I picked up the shiny object, dusted it off, and slipped it on my finger reflexively. A ring—large, gold and ornate. Obviously cre-ated for a man. A worm sticking out of the sides of the dirt wall reminded me where I was. I quickly climbed back up the ladder.

Replacing the ladder where I found it, I scanned the area near the backhoe on a hunch. After several minutes of bending and swiping, I found what I was looking for hidden beneath a nearby bush.

Sluice's backpack. He never went anywhere without it. Except maybe the hospital.

He'd apparently set it aside when he went to work on the backhoe. I thought he might have done as much. It wouldn't have been easy to hold onto the bag while operating the big machinery. But I'd never known him to let it out of his sight. The backpack had been passed over last night in the dark. No one had even thought to look for it.

I sat down on a nearby cement bench and opened one of the zippered compartments. Two Cornish pastie meat pies, still in their wrappers, slightly squished, and smelling pungent. A pencil engraved "dom," which I took to be what was left of the name of the mortuary, knife-sharpened nearly to the nub. Four Q-Tips. A small tube of Vaseline. A set of dentures. A postcard from a country western singer, well known on the Mother Lode circuit, with the inscription: "To Sluice Jackson. Keep the fuck away from me. Stacey." A gold locket with a picture of a young girl inside. His sweetheart? His daughter? And at the bottom a crumpled piece of paper.

I unfolded the paper and smoothed it in my fingers. The name "Leonard Swec" was written in smeared pencil.

I returned the items to the bag and closed the flap. Nothing of any particular interest that I could see. The name Swec rang a tiny bell—I'd have to check it out.

I pulled the backpack's leather strap over my shoulder, hopped on my bike, and rode on to the sheriff's office. He'd want to see the pack and the ring, I was certain. No one was in the office except the dispatcher, who was busy taking a call. As I waited to explain my find, I watched her animated lips as she spoke into the tiny microphone attached to the headgear.

"Yes, French. Three? Uh-huh. Uh-huh. And you don't know where they could have gone to? Uh-huh. Uh-huh. Can you describe them? Uh-huh. Uh-huh. Uh-huh. Okay. I'll send Deputy Arnold over as soon as he gets back from another call. Try not to touch anything in the area. I understand, French. Uh-huh. Uh-huh. Yes, French."

She pulled the earphone from her head and shook her bouncy dyed-brown permed curls. "If it isn't one thing, it's another. Hi, Connor. Whatcha got there?"

Rebecca Matthews was an old pro on the dispatch circuit. And when I say old, I mean seventy-four and proud of it, still feisty, alert, and reminiscently beautiful, with a pink little smile, a creamy albeit crinkled complexion, and sparking green eyes, slightly bloodshot. She smoothed her sundress as she spoke.

I explained my find to Rebecca and asked her to keep the backpack for the sheriff until he returned. She promised she would.

"But it'll probably be awhile before he can take a look at it. He's out to the hospital where Sluice Jackson was admitted and I'm sure he'll be there a bit. I could give it to Deputy Arnold when he gets back from a domestic, but first I need to send him to the mortuary on a five-oh-one."

"Five-oh-one?"

"Suspected burglary. French claims one of his client's jewelry is gone and the family is having a nit-fit, making all kinds of accusations. They've threatened to sue him if he doesn't get it back. He says nothing like this has ever happened before. Says it will ruin his business. You know how he is, so quick to panic."

Jewelry. "Did he say what's missing?" I asked, my heart beginning to pound out a rap beat.

"Some rings. Three of them. Gold."

"What's the name of the family?"

"Sweat. Or something like that."

I pulled the loose ring from my finger and examined the inside. In tiny script the letters L.F.S. were engraved.

Swec. L.F.S. Leonard Swec. I thought, as I spun the ring around on my finger.

After talking with the dispatcher, once again I postponed my visit to Arden Morris in Rio Vista. Something more interesting had come up and Arden Morris could wait.

I parked my bike in front of Wolf's Gold Expeditions and Jewelry at the corner of Main and Church streets and smiled at the incongruous shop, located between the Naughty Lingerie boutique and Liquid Gold Cappuccino Café.

The jewelry shop was faced in weather-distressed wood made to look like an old mine. The logo had been hand-lettered in black paint with a large brush, reinforcing the image of a fortunate prospector who had just set up shop.

Once inside the swinging saloon doors, I moved over to the display case, which featured sparkling gold rings, necklaces, bracelets, watches, and the like. They were nestled on a bed of soft river sand and interspersed with large faux nuggets I suspected were iron pyrite. The jewelry, however, looked real, and had prices to match. Wolf did excellent work and his ornate pieces were unique.

When I first visited the store to have my ex-boyfriend's

gold bracelet melted down and returned to a nugget, Wolf had been accommodating but not overly friendly. Perhaps the gruff demeanor was part of the gold country show.

Wolf was attractive in a grungy sort of way, a kind of aging hippie, probably in his forties or fifties—it was tough to tell from the outdoorsy exterior. He wore his long, unkempt hair in a ponytail tied with a leather strap. His body, tall, thin, but muscular, was usually displayed under motorcycle-emblazoned tank tops and cutoff jeans. He probably kept a few women's eyes averted from the jewelry case for longer than necessary. His knit brows seemed never to relax over his dark eyes, and he hid his mottled, uneven teeth beneath a bushy mustache and a closed mouth.

Wolf was waiting on a customer at the back of the store where he promoted and sold gold-panning tours. A family of five, in Hawaiian shirts, Bermuda shorts, and straw cowboy hats, was signing up for the Gold Star Excursion, which would take them to three mines and guarantee them a few grains of ore from the streams. All that starting at $19.95 per person.

The family seemed eager to start buying the equipment that was de rigueur for the trip: picks, pans, vials to hold all that sifted loot, compasses, knives, the works. Their investment would be nearly two hundred dollars; the gold-dust payoff would be more like fifty cents.

I looked over the jewelry case while I waited for the transaction to be completed and wondered about the quiet, unobtrusive Wolf Quick. What had he been doing at the cemetery so late last night? How did he happen upon Sluice Jackson?

A murder mystery in the rough-and-ready gold country would be great for business, especially Wolf's business, I thought. Tourists would flock to the town out of morbid curiosity and vicarious thrills, and while visiting, might opt for a tour of the depleted gold mines and dry creeks. They might even buy a few pieces of expensive gold jewelry while they were at it.

I scanned the glittery rings beneath the clear glass.

Some with jewels, some randomly shaped, some smooth and shiny, some rugged and nuggetlike. Each was detailed and costly. A small hand-lettered sign read: *No Two Alike.*

I looked up from my sparkling daydream and noticed the tourists had vanished. Wolf sat perched on a stool in the back corner, talking on a cellular phone while polishing a bracelet. I watched his lips move but couldn't make out any of the words, his mouth obscured by the receiver and his thick mustache. I waited for him to hang up, then I moved over casually.

"Hi, Wolf. Business seems good today, huh?"

He glanced up to acknowledge me and went back to his work.

"I was looking for a ring for my uncle . . . Remus. The ones in the cabinet are nice, but do you have anything else that's more, I don't know, something different?"

Wolf finished polishing the bracelet and slipped it into his pocket. With a side nod of his head, he indicated I was to follow him into the back room.

We passed behind a tie-dyed curtain and entered Wolf's workroom. The small, cramped space was taken up by three massive, distressed-wood tables, each covered with a jumble of tools, molds, pots of melted wax, knives, chunks of gold, and other jewelry-making supplies I couldn't identify. A couple of bracelets and a necklace rested in molds, waiting to be set free. Underneath one of the wooden benches, Wolf pulled open a drawer to reveal a scatter of rings of varying shapes and sizes.

"Wow! You have so many," I said, fingering the collection. There must have been several thousand dollars' worth of jewelry in the drawer. "Don't you worry about theft?"

He looked at me, then called out what looked like, "Bitch!" snapping his finger. Unseen until that moment, a Great Dane emerged from under the table. The dog stretched, stood erect, and either smiled or snarled, depending on your attitude. I chose to call it a smile.

I smiled back. "Down, killer—uh," I said. "Nice doggy. Sit. Roll over. Play dead." The dog continued to smile/snarl. "You call her Bitch?"

Wolf said "Butch," then something I didn't catch, mainly because I was looking at his dog. The hound relaxed, circled me and sniffed Casper on me before returning to his spot under the bench. Then Wolf nodded toward a security system panel on a far wall. I got the picture. Fort Knox.

I nodded. "Butch! Good. Yes. Well." I went back to rifling through the rings until I found one that looked oddly familiar. "This one . . ." I held it up.

Wolf shook his head. "Not for sale. Sorry." He took it from my hand and slipped it into his pocket. That pocket was filling up.

I had seen that ring before. I made mental pictures of people's hands—Celeste, French, Sluice, Jilda, Dan . . .

Lacy. She was wearing it—or one like it—when she'd come to my office. And again at her funeral. In fact, hadn't she been buried with it? Odd—had Wolf made a copy of it? I supposed with all the jewelry-making equipment in the shop, Wolf could duplicate just about any gold jewelry pieces he fancied.

I sifted through a few more, said I didn't see anything just right, then thanked Wolf and told him I'd be back with my uncle so he could choose something for himself. Wolf nodded, but didn't follow me out of the back room and into the main part of the store. As I left the double swinging doors, a young couple was headed inside.

I swung by the Nugget Café to think, and sipped a toxic coffee and ate a blueberry bagel with strawberry cream cheese. As I glanced around the restaurant, it seemed as if everyone sported fancy gold rings. Were all of them from Wolf's store?

They all looked real. But you could tell the real thing from the imitations easily, if you took a moment to examine them. The weight and feel of real gold is something you cannot duplicate. You'd have to be dead not to know you weren't really wearing the authentic ore.

You'd have to be dead.

Like Lacy. I thought about Lacy's fingers and the scraped knuckle covered with makeup. I thought about Sluice's gold ring with the initials, "L.F.S." Had Wolf "borrowed" her ring, made a copy, and then replaced it? I thought another moment. Maybe he didn't replace it with the original. Maybe he made a copy in faux gold and replaced that on Lacy's dead finger. Who would know the difference?

If he'd done this to Lacy, had he done it with others? Was Wolf somehow removing the deceaseds' jewelry, copying it, then replacing the real thing with gold-plated phonies? If that were true, he could sell the real gold to the tourists at a tremendous profit with no one the wiser—except the inside person helping with the exchange.

Sluice Jackson?

Sluice could have done the switching. He had full access to the mortuary and cemetery grounds. He was there at all hours. And he had that gold ring with him when he fell into the open grave. French had reported the loss of someone's rings this morning.

But if any of this was true, and not just my imagination, what did it have to do with Lacy Penzance?

Nothing that I could figure. I was getting off track. But I couldn't shake the feeling that there had to be some connection.

"God, Connor, so much coffee isn't good for you, you know. You should switch to, like, herbal tea or something," Jilda said, as she cleared away the boneyard of bagel remnants I hadn't managed to squeeze in.

I didn't think so much mascara was good for her either, or so much nail glue or hair color, but what did I know? I wasn't the Surgeon General and if Jilda Renfrew wanted to risk her health, it was her business. Coffee was mine. Sure, it tasted like poison, but I didn't figure it would actually kill me. For awhile.

I reached out and took Jilda's hand to get a close-up of her nails. They were painted in hot pink with silver moons and featured a tiny diamond at each tip, trimmed with two thin diagonal gold strips. She also wore two gold rings, free-form in shape, on both her middle fingers.

"Killer nails, Jilda. Did you do that?"

"Yeah. You should come by the shop some afternoon when I'm there, Con. I'd do you up so cool."

"You do a lot of nails around here, don't you."

"Oh, my God, yeah. Everyone in town practically. Women, that is. The guys haven't gotten into it yet, but you never know. Some people thought the cowboys would never wear earrings either and look at them all."

I tried to picture Dan Smith with red nail tips, enhanced with gold and diamonds. I preferred his nails the way they were: short, ragged, and bitten to the quick.

"Jilda, did you ever do Lacy's nails?"

Jilda shook her head, turned her back to me for a moment, then turned back. I caught the end of it.

". . . but she was a regular customer over at Nail It To You."

"How come she didn't go to you? People say you're the best." Vanity never questions veracity.

She blushed a little and shrugged a shoulder. "We didn't get along that well, you know? When her husband died, she like started flirting with all the men in town. Even my Frenchy. A friend of mine caught them out to dinner one night over in Whiskey Slide, and I was totally pissed. But he said they used to go together, you know, back in high school, and it was for old times. He said she was real lonely and he was just trying to help her and all. But I know she was totally on the make."

"So he didn't see her after that? As far as you know?" I prodded.

Jilda sat down across from me and looked me in the eye. I could see dots of makeup shadowing beneath her eyes from excessive mascara coupled with repeated blinking.

She leaned in when she spoke. "Look, she was kinda desperate after Reuben died. It's understandable. But she had some therapy with Celeste. You know she got her face done, her boobs lifted, her tummy tucked, and then had a liposuction, a few months after Reuben died. No one was supposed to know, but she didn't fool me. I'm training to be an esthetician, after all."

"Esthe-what?"

"A beauty expert."

"So Lacy had cosmetic surgery?"

Jilda bit her lip and nodded. "It was like she was a new woman. She started going out with a bunch of guys. Actually, only the ones who had some sort of status in the town, like lawyers, doctors, even the sheriff, and of course she tried Frenchy, but not for long."

The sheriff. He'd never mentioned it. "What about Wolf?" I asked, sipping on the coffee and blinking back the tears in my eyes from the taste.

"No way! They didn't get along at all."

"But he made a ring for her, didn't he?"

Jilda cleaned out her nails. "I don't know anything about that. All I know is, she thought he was a loser. She used to walk out of a room when he entered and make rude comments under her breath about him. I don't know what her problem was, not that Wolf is the easiest person to get along with. Then again, neither was she when you really got to know her. She didn't like me that much, either."

"So you don't think anything really happened between French and Lacy those times they got together?" I remembered what French had said about going out more than once.

Jilda blinked. Uh-oh. Had I gone too far? Maybe she only knew about one meeting. Jilda looked away, didn't speak for a few moments, then worked on her nails again, a little more urgently.

"I remember French was kind of weird for a couple of weeks there, when she was coming onto him. But he snapped out of it. I saw to that."

"Jilda, do you have any idea who Lacy might have been dating right before she died? Apparently she was involved with someone, but nobody seems to know who." I figured if anyone would know, it would be the town waitress/manicurist.

Jilda put a nail in her mouth for a moment. "No. Could have been anyone. Just as long as it wasn't French, that's all I care. French would never cheat on me, I know that now. Celeste even says so."

"Celeste? How would she know?"

Jilda giggled into her hand. "You know, I thought she might have been a lesbian or something for a while there. She never dates or anything. Never seemed to be interested in men. But I figure she's just real dedicated to her job. She's real good at helping people overcome their sadness and stuff when a relative dies. She really helped Mrs. Penzance. I hope she's there for me someday."

"How do you know she doesn't date anyone?"

"It's a small town. French told me he asked her out when she first came to the mortuary—before we got involved. But Celeste wasn't interested, thank God. French is no slacker, you know. She's pretty and all, for her age, you know. She told me once that French was a good catch. But I guess they just didn't hit it off that way."

"Anyone else?"

"Well, I know Wolf has hit on her, too, but she fanned him. That's why I thought she might be gay. Wolf's a stud, you know, even for an old guy. I wouldn't kick him out of the covers. But Celeste wasn't interested. Then when Lacy's husband died, Celeste spent so much time with her, I thought there might be something more between them, you know? Oh, God, I shouldn't be saying this! It'll be in your paper tomorrow!"

I smiled reassuringly. "No, no. I just want to know more about her so I can write a good story. I won't put any of that personal stuff in it. The information I print has to be fact, not opinion. You don't think Celeste and Lacy were, uh, more than friends?"

She held her nails up for scrutiny. "Nah. But even if they were, it really doesn't matter, you know, just so it doesn't involve me. Gross. I'd die if some woman came onto me. God." She giggled again behind her hand, her nails forming a kind of glittery fan.

"Jilda, do you have any idea what happened to Lacy? Do you think someone around here might have had a reason to kill her?"

Jilda rubbed the imaginary lipstick off her teeth, ran her tongue over them, and smacked her lips. "I really don't know. I wish I did. I'm totally dying to find out who did it. God, what if it *is* someone in town? If she was messing with someone's husband or boyfriend, I wouldn't blame them, you know, if they got even. I might have done it myself if French hadn't come back. Well, maybe not killed her exactly. But I would have been real, real mad."

After phoning the locksmith to order a new set of locks for my diner, I thought about stopping by Croaky Wheeler's to see about Lacy's five-thousand-dollar check. I could use a few more megs for the computer and the Chevy would look a lot cherrier with some body work. But I decided to hold off. The money wasn't really mine. And it might obscure my reasons for trying to figure out what happened to Lacy.

I headed for the mortuary. The place was beginning to feel like my home away from home. Not a good feeling.

Celeste was conferring with an elderly woman when I entered. The woman looked distraught, forcing a brave smile through tear-rimmed eyes. Celeste caressed the back of the woman's hand, working her magic. Gazing intently into the grief counselor's eyes, the woman seemed to pour out her heart to the nurturing friend of the bereaved. No wonder Celeste was so good at her job. She knew how to listen.

Celeste caught sight of me, dipped her head slightly in my direction and gently pulled back from the distressed woman. I watched her give the woman's hand a couple of let's-wrap-it-up pats, then write something down on her business card. In a few moments Celeste walked the grieving client to the door of Memory Kingdom, arm around her as if she were a grown daughter comforting her aging mother.

Celeste closed the door and wiped what might have been a tear—or a dust particle—from her eye. "Poor Mrs. Kossow. She's lost without Allen. Just lost. I hope I can help her. No family to speak of. She's going to be so lonely. That's the worst part for most of these women."

Celeste seemed genuinely concerned. Or maybe she was using skills garnered from years of working in Hollywood. After all, wasn't everyone in L.A. trying to become an actor, working the restaurants and beauty salons and morgues on the side until that all-important call came from the studio?

"She lost her husband?" I asked.

Celeste smoothed the front of her silk blouse, as if brushing away all contact with the woman who had just left. "Cancer. He was seventy-eight years old. She's only sixty-nine. She's still got lots of life left in her. I hope we can spend a few hours together. I really think I can help her."

"Through counseling?"

"I hope so. Many widowed people are without friends or loved ones at that age. They can always use someone to talk to." Celeste sighed. "So what are you doing here, Connor? I hope you haven't had bad news."

"What? Oh, my aunt. No, thank goodness. I'm here on another matter, Celeste. It's about Lacy Penzance."

Celeste looked puzzled. She crossed her arms in front of her.

"I wondered, since you knew Lacy so well, if you could tell me more about her. I'd really like to write a thorough story about her. You two were fairly close before she died, weren't you? All I know is she did volunteer work, she was a pillar of the community. Then recently, she began to make herself more attractive. She may have been dating someone these past few weeks."

Celeste turned abruptly and motioned for me to

follow her. Once inside her office, she closed the door and offered me the chair across from her desk. She pulled up her own chair and sat down.

"Listen, Connor, I can't say too much. You understand. I did speak with her as a counselor, so what we shared is confidential. Although Lacy and I were friends until recently, I really didn't know that much about her either. She was a very private person."

"What do you mean, until recently? Did something happen?"

Celeste picked delicately at her bangs. "Not really. We just stopped getting together after a while. She . . . said she was . . . ready to handle things on her own. It was for the best. I had done all I could, really."

"There wasn't a problem between you two? A falling-out?" I asked, boldly going where I had no business.

Celeste's eyes locked on mine, her expression a mixture of hurt and anger. "No! Of course not! Look, these things just come to an end eventually. It's not a permanent relationship. I simply help people through some hard times. When a client feels she doesn't need counseling anymore, she moves on. Lacy was ready to face the world again, and I encouraged her. There was nothing more to it than that." Celeste rose briskly from her chair. "Now, if there isn't anything else—"

At that moment a phone line lit up and Celeste picked up the receiver, irritation crossing her face. "Hello?"

I tried not to stare openly at her, but I did steal surreptitious glances at her mouth from time to time. I caught "When did he get out?" "Are you sure?" "Where?" and "When the monkey spanked four wrestlers," which I'm fairly certain isn't what she said, but it sure looked like it.

She hung up the phone and gave me a blank stare. "Where were we? Oh, yes. You were about to leave."

I pushed on. "What about French? Wasn't he seeing Lacy recently?"

Celeste looked stunned. "What? Heavens, no! At least, not to my knowledge. French has a thing for that little waitress over at the café. Everybody knows that."

She resumed her seat. "Besides, Lacy wouldn't have been interested in him. He's not her type."

"Who was her type?"

Celeste began to respond, then caught herself. She flushed and glanced away. "Someone like Reuben, I guess."

"Celeste, did you know she'd had facial surgery recently?"

Celeste shrugged. "What's that got to do with—"

"She was planning to have a prenuptial agreement drawn up by her attorney. I think she had met someone special in the past few weeks. Someone she may have planned to marry. And no one seems to know anything about it."

Celeste looked down at her blouse and brushed more invisible lint from the front. "Look, Connor, I told you. I really don't know that much about the woman. Sure, she changed a little after Reuben's death. She took more interest in her appearance. She wanted to be attractive again. She started seeing some men. That's normal, even healthy. I don't know anyone she was specifically involved with, but I don't think it was important. Frankly, it was none of my business. And it's really none of yours."

She was getting a little touchy. I decided to change tack.

"Sorry for all the questions, Celeste. Just trying to do my job. I guess I'm getting a little frantic about my dead-line. And I'm tired of all the speculation. It would be nice to know the truth, you know?"

Celeste nodded almost grudgingly.

I looked at my watch. "God, I'm exhausted. I don't know where you get all the energy to do everything you do, Celeste. You never look tired. Even your hair is always perfect."

Celeste became self-conscious and gave her curls a shake. Today her hair sported a lovely cast of magenta that nearly matched her outfit.

"Well, I don't have as much time as I'd like, but . . ." Celeste left the words hanging and tucked her hair behind her ears.

I went on. "Of course, your hair is always perfect

because you're a trained stylist. I bet you did a lot of actors' hair while you were in Hollywood."

Celeste visibly perked up at the question. She sat up taller, grinned, and resumed her friendly demeanor.

"Yeah, lots! Alec Baldwin was a regular customer of mine. He has really thick, straight hair. I did Angela Lansbury for a while, until she won that Emmy for *Murder, She Wrote*. Then she started going to José Eber. I guess she wanted to look more like Fabio. I did Cher a couple of times, Bruce Willis—not much to work with. And a bunch of actors you probably wouldn't know by name but you'd recognize their faces."

"Did you ever do any acting yourself, Celeste?"

"Oh, a little, not much. Got a cereal commercial once. And a bit part in a Steve Martin film. I was a hooker. I did some stage work at small theaters in the Valley, but I really wanted to be in films. I gave up after a while, though. Too much competition. I made more money doing hair."

"Do you miss hairstyling?"

Celeste looked out through the half-open blinds of her office, thought a moment, then said, "Sometimes. But I really love grief counseling, helping others through their difficult times. To tell you the truth, I'd love to have my own funeral business someday. I'm saving my money. I think I really have a knack for making people feel better."

"You want your own business?" I must have looked more than just surprised.

"Why not? A woman can do as well, if not better, in this business. I thought I'd start with one, maybe somewhere on the coast, and try to franchise after that. There are a lot of older people retiring to the Mendocino area. Or maybe Carmel. Very popular with retirees."

"Will Wolf be involved in your plans?" I tried to sound casual. I guess I needed to work on nuances.

She looked at me, astonished. "Wolf?"

"I saw you talking with him the other day, at the funeral. And in the office when I stopped by for the tour— wasn't that him on the phone? You two seem to be friends. I was just curious."

She appraised me with an up-and-down look, as if seeing me for the first time. She seemed to gather her thoughts before she spoke.

"Truthfully, Wolf is a pain in the you-know-what. And no, he will not be a part of my future business. The guy is such a . . . such a gold digger."

I sat waiting for her to continue. She finally did, weighted by the uncomfortable silence. Me, I'm used to it.

"Well, if that's all—"

"It's odd, you know, how he found Sluice in that grave just after the old guy fell in. I wonder why Wolf was at the cemetery at that hour. Does he have relatives buried there?"

"Honestly, Connor, you ask very strange questions. I don't know anything about Wolf Quick. All he ever thinks about is that gold business of his. It's really becoming a bore. And frankly, so is this conversation. Now if—"

"I like your ring," I said quickly. She had begun twisting and turning the gold ring on her finger as she spoke about Wolf. She stopped when I made the comment. "It's so different. Did Wolf create that one?"

She let go of the ring and picked up some loose papers on her desk, as if to hide her hands. "Yes, I guess so. I can't remember. I have a lot of jewelry. Hard to keep track of where it all comes from."

"You know, that day I saw you talking on the phone, I think you were talking about a ring."

Celeste's hands stopped fiddling. "You're quite the little lip-reader, aren't you? That was a private conversation, you know, and it's rude to eavesdrop, even if you are . . . well . . ."

"Deaf?"

"Wolf and I were just having a little argument over a some jewelry he wanted to sell me. I wasn't interested, but he is a very pushy salesman. You want some advice? Get your jewelry at Goldie's in Whiskey Slide. They aren't so hard-sell there. More like us here at the funeral home—soft and unobtrusive, yet informative and supportive. Stay away from Wolf if you want a good deal. In fact, stay away from him period, if you want my advice."

Wolf, the used-car salesman type? I didn't see it. He didn't even get off his stool for the first five minutes I was in his store.

"Did Wolf know Lacy—"

She cut me off. "You know, Connor, you don't act like you're trying to find out more about Lacy for your newspaper. You act like you're trying to find out the dirt on her, or maybe who killed her. And I'm beginning to get the feeling you think I fit in the picture somewhere. So if you're implying—"

I laughed, probably too loud, and shook my head. "No, no, I'm just trying to fit a few loose puzzle pieces together. I—"

"Listen, I didn't have anything to do with Lacy Penzance's death, if that's what you think. I came to love her like a sister. I did all I could to help make her feel better. When I accomplished that, we went our separate ways. For you to think I might have been involved in her death somehow is just—"

"I wasn't implying—"

"Connor, I have work to do." She stood up again and walked to the door, waiting for me to follow. It gave me a moment to think. I wondered what Celeste's motive might be if she really were a suspect. Blackmail? Did Lacy know something about her that Celeste didn't want revealed? Jealousy? Money? Did Celeste want more than her share for the grief counseling and funeral services?

I stood up and met her at the door. "Celeste, do you have idea who might have wanted Lacy dead?"

"No! Of course not! But it certainly wasn't me. If you must know, I have an alibi, if I need it, which of course I don't. I was with someone that night. When, and if, the sheriff decides to question me, I'll tell him all about it. As for you, none of this is your business. So why don't you leave this investigation up to the police, Connor. Stick with what you know best. Writing obituaries."

She closed the door in my face.

"Celeste Camborne, aged thirty-two but looking much older, passed away this afternoon, a victim of excessive cellulite and chronic split ends. She was mourned by a couple of people who didn't know her that well. Her funeral will be held at the mall, pending—"

The door opened and Dan appeared in the doorway.
"What are you working on?"
"Oh, nothing. Just an obituary."
"Somebody else die?"
"Not yet."
He looked puzzled. I changed the subject. It wasn't worth explaining my technique for blowing off steam.

"Ready to go?" I shut off the computer screen and stood up. Enough wasting time. I hoisted my backpack onto my shoulder.

"I'm ready." He held up a file folder. On the cover was the name "Rio Vista."

"Where did you get that?"

"It was in Boone's filing cabinet, in the back where he keeps the discontinued files."

"Is there anything inside?" I took it from him and flipped it open. Nothing.

Dan combed his beard with his fingertips. "Empty when I found it."

I looked at him and said nothing.

"So, you don't mind if I come along?" Dan asked.

I had a moment of second thoughts about sharing the ride with him to Rio Vista. After all, we had different agendas. Maybe very different. And he might be in the way. Or at the very least, distracting. I didn't want to be distracted, especially after the other night.

"It's fine. But I'm kind of curious as to why you want to go there."

"Like I said, I think there's a connection to my brother in all this. These empty file folders are related to Lacy Penzance in some way. Her file was empty. Risa Longo's file was empty. Arden Morris. Now this one. I want to check it out."

I didn't have a good reason not to take him. Just some vague feeling of discomfort. And I couldn't identify the source. We seemed to be following parallel paths—was it all part of the Lacy Penzance puzzle? Or did Dan have something else going on?

I rode my bike home, checked on Casper, then got into the Chevy and drove back to the office to pick up Dan, waited a few moments while he grabbed some things, then he followed me to my Chevy. I drove the two or so hours southwest to the Sacramento Delta, an area composed of a thousand miles of waterways connecting fifty-five tiny islands. Dan listened to the radio while I watched the scenery change from dry brush and volcanic rock to cattails and river moss. I turned off Route 160 at the central valley river town of Rio Vista and pulled out a map.

The town hadn't changed much since the gold rush days. Levees along the two-lane, meandering roadside were built to control the flow of the Sacramento and San Joaquin rivers. They were the work of Chinese laborers who had come to work the railroads, then turned to fishing and canning when the tracks were complete. Most people traveled by boat, up and down the waterways where Humphrey the Whale once made his historic appearance. Restaurants like Sid's, Doc's, and Al's sold a lot more beer than wine.

Arden Morris's three-story Victorian home jutted out from the river, surrounded by lush lawn and colorful snapdragons, roses, and California poppies. As we drove down the narrow driveway, I spotted a couple of gardeners trimming shrubs and pulling weeds along one side of the landscaped yard.

Sitting on the verandah, reading what looked like a Danielle Steele novel and sipping a drink that matched her raspberry outfit, sat the woman I presumed to be Arden Morris.

She looked up when we stopped the car. Setting down her book and drink, she stood, placing a hand over her brow to shade the sun, and greeted us cautiously as we let ourselves through the gate of the white picket fence.

"Yes?"

We climbed the three white steps to the porch. I introduced myself and Dan. Arden Morris brushed her fluffy red hair back from her face with raspberry tinted fingernails, and offered a stiff, raspberry smile. Although she was still slim and shapely in the tight jumpsuit, I judged by the tiny lines on her face and hands that she must be in her late fifties, early sixties. I gave her one of my extremely vague, all-purpose business cards and began my spiel, hoping we weren't breaking too many laws for impersonating Nancy Drew and Joe Hardy.

"Ms. Morris, we're investigating a homicide that occurred in Flat Skunk recently. The victim received a message from you on her answering machine sometime after her death. We'd like to ask you a few questions if you don't mind. Did you know Lacy Penzance?"

Arden Morris's brow pinched a little. It might have been the sun. "No, I didn't. Why?"

"Did you telephone her earlier this week?"

"Well, yes. I got a letter from her, then she called me a few days ago and left a very strange message on my machine. I called her back because I was curious. But apparently I was too late. I read about her death in the newspaper after I left the message."

"What was her message?"

"She said she knew something about my husband and wanted to meet with me. She sounded so odd. I was kind of afraid to call her."

"You never spoke to her?"

"No. No one answered when I called so I left a message. Then I found out she had died."

"Exactly what time did you call, Mrs. Morris?" Dan asked.

"Uh, Tuesday night. I didn't hear about her death until the evening news. I was out all day boating on the Delta."

"When did she call you?" Dan continued.

"Uh, Monday afternoon, I believe it was."

She sat down in her white wicker chair and guzzled the rest of her drink. Dan and I helped ourselves to seats nearby.

"Is your husband home, Ms. Morris?" I said.

"No. He's . . ." She looked us over before she continued. ". . . at work."

"Do you know if he knew Lacy Penzance?"

"I . . . I don't know. I don't think so."

"I'd like to give him a call. Do you have his work number?"

She hesitated. "He's away. I don't have the number where he is . . ."

I looked at Dan, then back at her. "Are you and your husband . . . separated?" I said gently.

"Oh, no. Nothing like that. He's just not home very much. I don't like people to know I'm home alone a lot. We just moved here a couple of months ago and I don't know that many people. My husband works as a foreign correspondent for *National Geographic* and right now he's in a politically sensitive area in Latin America. He's gone for long periods of time. It's not easy, but we make it work."

"Do you happen to have a picture of him, Ms. Morris?"

Arden Morris didn't speak for a few minutes, as if trying to puzzle things out in her head. She looked up. "I'd sure like to know what this is all about. Is my husband . . ."

"We're just checking everything we can. Do you have a photograph of him that I could see?" I persisted.

"What for?" she said slowly. "Is he . . . involved in this somehow?"

"To be honest, we don't know. But if you could show us a picture, we might be able to tell you more," Dan added.

Arden got up and went into the house, returning a few moments later with her purse. She opened the wallet and pulled out a photograph of a couple, standing at the side of a road, arm in arm. The picture was fuzzy and the features were difficult to make out. I could barely distinguish Arden Morris, only that the woman had red hair like hers. The man next to her looked like a zillion other men on the planet.

I passed the picture to Dan who gave it a once-over and returned it to me. On second glance I noticed something I hadn't spotted when I'd been trying to make out the features of the couple. They were leaning against the side of a small car.

A red Miata. Just like the one that had run me off the road.

"Do you have a better picture of him, Ms. Morris?" I asked. "This one is difficult to make out."

"That's all I've got. He doesn't like to have his picture taken much. He prefers to be behind the camera."

"No wedding picture?"

She shook her head. "We just went to Vegas. He didn't want to make a big deal of it. It was a second marriage for both of us."

"How long have you been married?" Dan asked.

"Eight months next Saturday."

"You were divorced before?" I asked.

"Widowed. Both of us."

"You said you recently moved here? Where did you live before?"

"Angel's Camp. It's a small town in the gold country."

I glanced at Dan then looked back at Arden Morris. "What's your husband's name, Ms. Morris?" I asked, scratching a growing patch of poison oak on my wrist that seemed to irritate me more when I was under stress.

"Del."

I returned the photograph to Arden Morris and thanked her for her time. Dan and I left her sitting bewildered, sipping what was left of her drink on the front porch. "We'll keep in touch," I called back, but she didn't respond. She was staring at the photograph.

"What do you think?" Dan asked, after we got back in the car and headed away from the expensive spread.

"I don't know. Both Risa and Arden have husbands whose jobs keep them away for long periods of time. They've both been married only a short time. And they were both widows. They lived in the gold country. And both women have money, just like Lacy. I wonder if Risa Longo's husband drives a red Miata."

"Why do you say that?"

"Just a hunch." I smiled mysteriously. "Now then, Lacy contacted both of those women, inquiring about their husbands. Why?"

Dan turned toward me as I drove through the main part of town. I could tell he was saying something but I couldn't take my eyes off the winding road long enough to read his lips. I pulled the car over at a turnout. "Here, you drive."

"Why?"

"I can read your lips better if I don't have to watch the road too."

I slid over the red-and-white tuck-and-roll as he walked around and got into the driver's side.

"Okay, what did you say a moment ago?" I sat facing him and watched his mouth as he spoke. Sideways made it challenging, but not impossible.

"I said, you're squeaking." He tapped his ear.

I touched my hearing aid. It had come loose from its tight tuck inside my ear. This causes a high-pitched squeal that apparently annoys hearing people. I pushed it back in. He said something I couldn't make out.

"What?" I said, puzzled by the way his lips were moving.

He glanced at me and smiled. "Nothing."

"What? Tell me!"

"Nothing. I was just . . . singing."

I looked at the radio. The light was on again.

"Oh." My thoughts returned to Lacy. "Okay. How about this. How about Lacy, for some unknown reason, suspected her new boyfriend might already be involved— or married. To Risa Longo. It wasn't her sister she was looking for. It was the other woman. That's why Lacy went up to Whiskey Slide and demanded to see a photograph of Risa's husband. A husband who doesn't spend much time at home."

Dan didn't exactly nod in agreement, but he did comb his beard with his fingers, which made me think he was considering this.

"And what if, through her own investigation—or with the help of Boone—Lacy found out there was yet another wife, Arden Morris. A woman, also well-to-do, who also lives with a man who doesn't spend much time at home."

The beard combing turned into a vigorous brushing. I was onto something.

"What if Arden and Risa are married to the same man. The same man, in fact, who was courting Lacy Penzance, a recent widow—and also very wealthy. Both Risa and Arden, also widows, were well-off financially. So was Lacy. What if he were your ordinary con man, romancing lonely wealthy women for his best interest."

Dan pressed his lips together.

I went on. "The question is, who is this guy?"

"The man in the red Miata?"

I raised an eyebrow. "I think we'd better stop by the Mark Twain and check out the guest who's driving the red

Miata. He may very well be the one who'd been seeing Lacy while trying to keep a low profile."

Dan stopped the beard grooming and placed both hands on the steering wheel. "If all this is true, isn't it possible that one of the other wives might have killed Lacy when it was discovered Lacy might have been 'the other woman'? "

I paused, sorting it out. "Well, then, why wouldn't she kill both of the other women?"

Dan shrugged one shoulder. "Maybe because she doesn't know about the other one. Maybe she only knew about Lacy, because of Lacy's visit or phone message."

"Or maybe she, whoever she is, simply hasn't had time to kill off the other one. Killing people takes time and planning. Maybe Risa is planning to kill Arden or Arden is plotting the same thing about Risa, as we speak." A sick feeling filled my stomach as I imagined the possibilities.

Dan interrupted my thoughts. "Maybe this mysterious husband is the killer. After all, he probably inherits once the wives are dead."

My stomach tightened. I could feel my heart beat double time. "But then, why kill Lacy before he marries her? And why hasn't he killed his other wives?"

I sat scratching my poison oak and consciously trying to keep my stomach from flipping over. I was going to make myself sore and sick if I didn't stop.

"Do you think Sluice Jackson has anything to do with all this?" I asked, taking a deep breath and slumping against the back of the seat.

Dan turned his head to be sure I could see his lips move. "And what about my brother? Where does he fit into all this? Where the hell is he?"

"Mind if we stop off here for a few minutes?" Dan asked. He was pulling up to a rustic, windowless tavern in the middle of Rio Vista.

"You want a drink *now*?"

"Just want to see if maybe Boone stopped off while he was in town looking for Arden Morris. He did have a file folder with her name on it. Maybe somebody around here remembers him."

I followed Dan into the dark country-western-style den of smoke and spirits. This was not one of the many California towns where smoking had become illegal. I inhaled two cigarettes worth as we headed for the polished oak bar. After questioning the bartender for a few moments, we returned to the car and fresh air.

"Nothing?" I asked, fanning my cotton top to get the smoke out.

Dan shook his head. "Mind if we check a few more?"

I didn't, and we did. We hit several other saloons along the main street until we got to the far end of town. The Alibi Saloon greeted us with yet another "No

Weapons, No Spitting, No Tank Tops," sign as we entered. I hoped I could control my spitting.

The bartender wore a T-shirt with the words "Elvis Is My Personal Savior" written across the front, stretched to capacity over his straining gut. Once again Dan asked about his brother. The bartender glanced down at the picture of Boone.

"I think so. Yeah. Yeah, I think he might'a been in here. Had a double vodka on the rocks. Yeah. In fact, he had several. I never forget a drink. You can tell a lot about a man by his drink. Bet he was a cop, or an accountant. This guy was serious about his booze. Sat over there. Didn't say much, until that other fellow arrived."

"There was someone else?" Dan asked.

The bartender looked at Dan and smiled, revealing crooked, smoke-stained teeth. "What can I get you?"

I started to say "nothing," but Dan interrupted. "Two beers. Red Dog." He placed a ten-dollar bill on the counter. The bartender snatched it up and returned with two frosty bottles featuring an ugly red bulldog on the label, opened and ready to drink. He didn't offer mugs. And he didn't return the change.

"Yeah, there was another guy. But I don't remember much about him 'cause he didn't order nothin' to drink. I always remember that, too."

"Can you describe him at all?" Dan asked intently.

The bartender scrunched his eyebrows, rubbed his prickly chin, cleaned out an ear, and wiped his diggings on the front of his shirt.

"Nah. Looked regular, you know? Got a picture of him, too?"

Dan said no. The bartender thought another moment. Dan pulled out another ten and asked for a couple of bags of chips. Once again the bartender kept the change.

"Well, let's see. I don't think the other guy stayed very long. Bought your friend a drink but didn't have nothin' himself. They talked awhile, then the two of them took off. I do remember one thing. When he paid for your friend's drink, he pulled out a fancy gold ring with the money. I remember 'cause he dropped it and swore when it rolled under the bar. He was almost panicky about losing it. Must have been real valuable. Too bad he found it."

We'd had enough smoke to take five years off our lives. It was time to depart or get oxygen masks. We thanked the bartender for the half-drunk beers and unopened chips and left in search of a place to take a real food break. The bartender had recommended a restaurant called Al the Wop's, located in the neighboring ghost town of Locke. Once a Chinese camp for the railroad workers, Locke now featured little more than the restaurant, a couple of Chinese museums, and a handful of antique stores.

"Mind if I make a couple of phone calls before we eat?" Dan asked. "I don't want to leave Rio Vista without checking the hospital and sheriff's office."

I waited in the car while Dan stopped at an antique-looking pay phone and made the calls. I watched his lips repeat the same questions to the phone receiver; he seemed to get the same responses to each call.

Until the last one. Dan's body language changed dramatically after he asked if there had been any unidentified men who had turned up recently. He stiffened abruptly, placed his finger in his other ear, and turned away so I couldn't see his lips.

I got out of the car.

"What is it?" I mouthed the words through the glass when I caught Dan's attention. He turned away from me again. I sat down on the fender of my car and waited, my stomach in knots.

After a few minutes Dan hung up the phone, then paused a moment before leaving the booth, his hand still on the receiver. I got to my feet and moved to the door. Dan slowly pulled open the shattered shatterproof glass door and stepped out.

"That was the local sheriff. They've got a floater, a John Doe, pulled from the Delta a few days ago. Sheriff says he's pretty far gone, but I think we ought to take a look. Are you up for it?"

How do you get up for something like that? I got into the car.

We drove to the next town of Isleton and located the sheriff's office between a secondhand thrift store and a video parlor. It was definitely a small-town operation, with a main room for greeting the public, a couple of offices, and a one-body morgue located at the back, where we were led.

"You think this might be your brother, huh?" Sheriff Cosetti asked matter-of-factly. "He doesn't look like much, so prepare yourselves. A body floating in water for a few days can really be a mess. Putrefaction, it's called. They get kind of bloated, and their skin turns a yellowish white and pasty, and it's hard to make out the features . . ." I stopped watching his lips at that point and fell in behind the two men as we walked to the end of the building.

"Well, here we are. Take your time, now. There's an emesis basin over yonder if you feel queasy, little lady."

The sheriff opened the door and swept his hand forward, gesturing for us to lead the way. He followed us in, opened up the small refrigerated compartment, and pulled out a body, covered in a translucent plastic body bag. The sheriff unzipped the bag. The blurred features were indistinct.

I almost lost it at the smell, a reek of chemicals and decay forming a sickly sweet odor. I had smelled a variation of it when a mouse had died in my diner and I couldn't locate it for days. Where was that emesis basin?

The sheriff spread the bag open to reveal the rest of the dead man's mottled body. "He didn't have a wallet or anything else that could help us identify him. We figured he must have been a drifter, 'cause nobody in town reported anything. His clothing's in that bag over there. That's all that was left."

"He wore a gold ring—" I started to say, but the sheriff cut me off with a shake of his head.

"No jewelry. The guy was cleaned out, except for his clothes. They even took the earring out of his ear. And his shoes."

I watched Dan as he braced himself for a thorough viewing. I didn't want to look anymore than I already had.

But I almost couldn't help myself. It was like peeking through fingers at a horror movie climax.

The face looked like it had been shaped from gray clay, soft, moist-looking, and mostly colorless. The body was bloated, bluish-white at the top of the chest and abdomen, and dark purplish underneath, where the blood had collected. There was a small bruise above his right nipple. I'd have nightmares for weeks. I started to turn away when Dan grabbed my arm for support.

"It's him," he said. I knew.

I could feel nearly the whole of Dan's weight on my shoulder. I put my arm around his back in my feeble attempt to hold him up.

"It's him," he repeated. He lowered his head and covered his eyes.

The sheriff gave him a moment before he spoke. "The tattoo?" He was pointing to the bruise, which on closer inspection was actually a small black-and-red engraving of a heart pierced by a knife.

Dan pressed his eyes.

"I didn't know he had a tattoo," I said, surprised. "He never showed it to me. I guess I never saw him without his shirt."

Dan dropped his hands to his side. His eyes were red-rimmed and welling. "He got it right after . . . his father died . . ." I thought he was going to continue but he turned abruptly and walked out of the room.

I met him in the hallway, took his arm, and walked with him to a chair in the main office. He pressed his eyes again with his fingertips, then raised his head. "I'm all right. Sheriff, I'll . . . make arrangements for him when I get back to his, uh, the office."

The sheriff pulled out a clipboard of paperwork Dan needed to complete before we left. At Dan's insistence, I waited outside in the late afternoon sunlight and thought of old Boone Joslin. He'd had a tough life. And now he was dead. Drowned. Nobody knew why or how. Had he been drunk and fallen into the water? Or had he been drowned deliberately? By a man with the gold ring? I suppressed a wave of nausea. . . .

Forty-five minutes later Dan and I entered the restaurant recommended by the bartender. Although neither of us had much of an appetite for lunch, we needed a place to think, and a cool beer sounded soothing.

From the outside, Al the Wop's looked condemned. The small one-lane main street was flanked on either side by rickety, distressed buildings that didn't appear as if they'd last through the next rainstorm. Locke truly looked like a ghost town, in every sense of the word.

But inside, the restaurant brimmed with energy and life. The restored teak-and-mirrored bar was choked with patrons, most of whom seemed to know one another. The place was filled with the usual country-western bar decor—a stuffed moose, velvet paintings, burl clocks, and silly signs. Dan pointed upward with his thumb and I followed the direction of the gesture; hundreds of dollar bills were glued to the ceiling.

We were seated in the restaurant area away from the bar, in wooden booths painted so thick with layers of lime green paint and Verathane, they might one day be studied by a geologist. We pulled menus from between bookends made from jars of crunchy peanut butter and grape jelly.

Only two choices were listed for lunch and dinner: steak or chicken. If you didn't like either, you could make yourself a peanut butter and jelly sandwich with the slices of fluffy white bread the waitress brought to your table. The food smelled good, reminding us we hadn't eaten for hours—it was nearly two o'clock. I ordered the chicken, Dan had the steak. We split a peanut butter and jelly sandwich on the side.

"I'm . . . sorry about Boone," I said after awhile, not knowing what else to say. "I didn't know him all that well, but we were becoming friends. He was always there to help me if I had a problem."

Dan half smiled. "I didn't know him that well either, to tell you the truth. He was so much older than me and we didn't always get along. We had different ways of viewing the world, I guess. I thought maybe this time we'd find something in common, maybe be able to work together. But I guess he'd gone back to drinking."

"That surprises me, too. He's been sober since I've known him. I think he attended A.A. meetings on a pretty regular basis. He had one of those 'One Day at a Time' stickers on his desk. I asked him about it once and he told me he went to meetings. He didn't share a lot more, though."

"He always had a drinking problem," Dan said. "I was hoping he'd licked it for good, but maybe you never beat something like that. He had a few ghosts he probably wanted to keep at bay. I guess he thought vodka was one way to do it. Unfortunately, it just makes the ghost greater—and more dangerous."

I wondered if there was something more personal beneath that last statement. It wasn't the time to ask.

"What do you think happened to him?" I asked, when my mouth wasn't too sticky from the peanut butter.

"I don't know. Maybe he was drunk, fell in, couldn't get out. But what puzzles me is, who was the guy Boone left with?"

"And what about the missing jewelry and shoes? A looter of some kind who preys on drunks?" I took another bite of peanut butter and jelly. I hadn't had white bread since fifth grade. I wished I could taste it, but right now it was just filling the hole in my upset stomach.

After a few minutes of sitting in silence, the waitress brought the order. I halfheartedly cut up my chicken, while Dan poked his steak around as if it were alive.

"Tell me about Boone," Dan said, laying his fork down and folding his arms on the table.

I swallowed the piece of chicken I had in my mouth, and took a drink of the beer, composing my reply.

"He was . . . interesting. Unpredictable. I liked him, but not many people did. He had strange, irritating habits that bothered people. Boone could be loud, I guess, from what people said. Never bothered me of course. He said 'fuck' a lot. Used it as an adjective, an adverb, a noun, whatever. Your brother didn't seem very happy, didn't laugh much. Never saw any women that I know of. Didn't have any close friends. Once a week we'd share a pizza and watch *Murder, She Wrote* on his little TV. We'd both try to guess whodunnit. He never did."

"How about you?"

"Always. Made him madder than hell. We had a bet going. Whoever guessed the right person didn't have to pay for the pizza. I never had to pay. But other than that I didn't see him a lot. We both had our work to do."

Dan sipped his beer and stabbed the steak distractedly with his fork.

"And you?" I asked. "You were his brother. What was he like for you?"

"Like I said, I didn't see him a lot. He grew up with a different father, who took off after a while. Then when he was ten, father number two came along, and I arrived soon after. I think both those events kind of displaced him. He started rebelling, getting into trouble, drinking. The drinking seemed to numb a pain he carried with him. I found out later he had beaten pretty regularly by his real father. When his dad finally left, I think Boone was relieved. But when Mom married again, Boone never gave the guy a chance. He left home around fifteen or sixteen, when I was five or six years old."

"Where did he go? What did he do?"

"We didn't know for a long time. Heard he joined the service eventually."

"So you pretty much grew up without him."

"Yeah. I went to school, got a degree in Administration of Justice, then became a cop for the City of New York. Classic, huh?"

"Wow. You were actually a cop? Why'd you quit?"

"Long story."

"I've got time."

He chugged his beer and ordered another. I followed suit.

"Boone changed after he got out of the army. I used to get an occasional phone call or letter, depending on whether he was drunk or sober. He seemed to settle down after Vietnam. Went back to school and got his degree, then went on to law school. Kind of ironic. While I was sending the guys to jail, he was getting them out. Anyway, his drinking was still a problem. He'd attend A.A. for a while, then go for weeks, months, without taking a drink, thinking he had it conquered. Then something would happen, like he'd lose a case or a girlfriend, and he'd go into a three-day binge, complete with blackouts."

"Could that have happened to him this time?"

"Possibly. When he's having a blackout he has no idea where he is or what's happening. He can't remember anything the next day. He's done some pretty crazy stuff. Used to strip all his clothes off and run around the hills naked, fall asleep when the booze ran its course, then come to and not know where he was, how he got there, or what he had done."

"How frightening."

"Tell me about it. So one day he came by our house. He'd been drinking. I don't think he knew what he was doing."

"What happened?"

"By then my father had died. Mom was alone again. I was out on a homicide when Boone dropped by and found Mom with his real father. I guess the old guy had been showing up again. Anyway, he'd been beating on her."

"What did Boone do?"

"Neighbors called the police when they heard my mom screaming. I was sent on a domestic and it turned out to be my mom's address. I got there and found Boone's father. He'd been shot to death."

"Oh, my God."

Dan hesitated, took another sip of beer, and stared down at the fork protruding like a sword from the middle of his untouched steak. He spoke slowly and with some difficulty.

"Boone had shot him with the gun Mom kept in the house. The gun I gave her to protect herself. When I got there Boone was delirious, drunk, crying, out of his mind. Mom was hysterical. I knew they'd throw the book at Boone, even though his dad had been beating on Mom and probably would have killed her. I figured if I stepped in, claimed the shooting myself, I could keep him from going to jail and ruining his life. After all, I'm a cop. Cops shoot people."

"So you took the blame."

He pressed his lips together for a moment. "Boone never even knew what he had done. He woke up the next day with no memory of anything, and I made Mom swear not to tell him. He promised to go to A.A. again, and this time he sounded like he meant it. He left town, moved as far away as he could—'out west' he used to say—and became a private investigator. We heard from him now and then over the years, but I never saw him again . . . until today."

"What happened to you? Did you get off?"

Dan shrugged. "Not exactly. There were some holes in the story. They took me before Internal Affairs and decided it wasn't a justified killing, that I could have done more to stop the guy, arrest him, or get him out of the situation. They asked me why I hadn't used my own gun, why I had used the gun in the house—which was registered to me. I'm not a very good liar, I guess. I couldn't make it work. They knew there was more to it, but I stopped talking at that point."

"Were you arrested?"

"Nope. 'Reassigned.' They promised me a teaching job over at the correctional facility if I resigned. But by then I needed a change. Things were falling apart. I left the state and got a job teaching Administration of Justice at the University of New Mexico and at the C.F. My degree came in handy for all those guys who didn't get good lawyers and wanted to pursue their cases in appeals courts."

"But you were terminated there, too."

He looked at me. "How did you know?"

"I . . . I thought you told me."

"You're a lousy liar, too," Dan said with a half-grin.

"I am not. I'm a good liar!"

"Your body language gave you away. You blushed, you stammered, you couldn't meet my eyes."

"Where did you learn all that about body language?"

"Part of the police academy instruction. Know your opponent."

"I'm not your opponent. Although I'm not so sure about you."

He gave me a look that set a few hairs at attention, then downed the rest of his beer. "Okay, so I got fired. Actually I quit, but that's a technicality. I was working with this one guy who said he was not Mirandized. So I helped him get a new trial. Turns out he was accused of raping the police chief's daughter. They didn't appreciate my butting in. So I was canned."

"Did he rape her?"

"Not according to six other men who had dated her in the past. She used this rape scam with every one of them. It was apparently part of her foreplay. But my guy got caught—and was screwed, so to speak."

"So you came out here to what—work with your big brother?"

"I don't know. I wanted to see him. See what California was like. Spend some time figuring out what to do next. I've been a cop who's put criminals in jail and a teacher who's helped them get out. What's left? Become a criminal myself?" He laughed.

I didn't. There was still something he wasn't telling me. Whatever it was was lurking right behind those dark eyes.

Dan and I shared the bill at my insistence—twenty bucks for two peanut butter sandwiches and two slightly mutilated but mostly untouched beef and chicken orders— and left the restaurant. We rode back to Flat Skunk in silence. At least I did. Dan played the radio and kept punching the buttons to find new music stations. He asked me why I had a radio. I said it came with the car.

When we arrived back at my office, there was a flashing light on my message machine.

"Dan, could you listen to my messages for me? My regular machine is broken, Miah's not around, and I'm waiting for a call from the sheriff about—" I started to say the break-in at my diner but decided not to mention it. I still didn't know who was responsible, and at this point, everyone was a possibility.

Dan didn't press it. He punched the play button, picked up a pencil, and began to write down the first message.

"Connor—Mickey. Call me—another . . ."

Dan put the pencil down slowly, punched the rewind button and listened to the message again, combing his beard as the tape played. Then he looked at me with wide eyes.

"What?" I said, feeling those butterflies collecting in my stomach again.

"There's been another one."

"Another what?" I said, trying to read his face.

"Another . . . murder. Some guy staying at the bed-and-breakfast inn over on Front Street. He's been stabbed."

Beau was standing outside the Mark Twain B & B, talking with half a dozen onlookers, rubberneckers, and ambulance-chasers, even though the ambulance was already gone. And along with it, the body of the man in the red Miata, according to Beau.

It was late afternoon by the time we arrived, and growing cool again, a reminder that spring was fickle. The sheriff and Mickey stood among a group of inn guests, taking statements, while television crews packed up their gear into minivans.

Dan and I had apparently missed most of the action.

I couldn't get to the sheriff or Mickey immediately. They both seemed engrossed in official business, pointing and nodding and readjusting their belt buckles. But Beau looked as if he wouldn't mind being torn away from the murder groupies. He waved halfheartedly as we approached.

"Excuse me," he said to a couple of elderly women who were "tsking" and "oohing" and making a bunch of other mouth noises I couldn't recognize. He made his way over and clasped my hand. "Connor! Did you hear what happened?"

I said I had, then introduced Dan to Beau. "So what are the details?"

Beau took my hand and pulled me over to the side of the inn near the garden pond he had put in last weekend. Dan followed hesitantly, as if he wasn't sure he was invited. We sat in white wrought-iron chairs that were supposed to create a serene retreat.

"Oh, my God, Connor. I just don't believe it! That guy, the one who ran you off the road the other day—"

Dan looked at me curiously. I rubbed my knees in memory of my fall.

"He was killed! Sometime last night! Right here in my beautiful bed-and-breakfast inn! Oh, God. It's awful."

Beau's lips quivered. His lashes flashed.

"Were you the one who found him, Beau?" I asked, putting my hand on his knee and giving it a comforting pat.

He nodded vigorously, bit his lip, then turned away for a moment to look at a frog that had hopped out of its watery home. When Beau had composed himself, he continued.

"It was terrible. I knocked on the door with breakfast—cranberry scones and kiwi jam. He always took his breakfast in the room, never came out to join the other guests at the dining table. Anyway, I knocked, no answer, so I thought he was still asleep. I took the tray back to the kitchen, figuring I could reheat the scones when he was ready—although they wouldn't be as good. Anyway, about an hour later he got a phone call, so I went back to tell him about it and offer him his breakfast again. But there was still no answer."

He paused to check on the adventurous frog for a moment. The slimy amphibian had filled its neck with air and was opening and closing its mouth. I found myself trying to read its lips. Beau resumed his story with a renewed look of concern.

"I was a little worried, so I used my key to check on him. That's when I found him, lying on my great-grandmother's crazy quilt. One of the antique mining picks from the wall was sticking out of his chest! The killer just took it right down and—God!" He shuddered. "I called the sheriff right then and there."

Someone tapped me on the shoulder. I looked around to see the deputy.

"I see you got my message," Mickey said, flipping his notebook closed.

I stood up to face him, feeling almost angry. "What's going on around here, Mickey? Things are getting way out of hand! Another death? Jesus! What happened?"

Mickey bent his head to the side. "We don't know much more than what Beau here told us." Beau sat up straighter, acknowledging the reference. "The victim was stabbed with an old gold-mining pick. Looks like it went right through the heart."

I thought about Lacy Penzance's stab wound. Wasn't it much the same? "A pick? How odd."

"Lacy wasn't stabbed with a pick, was she?" Beau asked.

Mickey shook his head. "No. We're fairly certain Lacy was stabbed with an instrument used in embalming cadavers. The mortuary recently reported a theft."

"An embalming tool! A mining pick! We've got some kind of lunatic running around town!" Beau said dramatically, rubbing his hands on his legs. His flashing eyelashes punctuated his statements.

Mickey shook his head. "He's not a lunatic, that's for sure. In my opinion, this guy is very intelligent, very cautious, and extremely calculating. We don't know who it is yet, but we'll find him—or her, for that matter. We picked up a few hairs, some clothing threads, and we have a partial print on a sheet of paper found in the room that doesn't seem to belong to the victim. We'll find him. It's only a matter of time, believe me. And I've got a pretty good idea where to look." Mickey glanced at Dan and rubbed the butt of his holstered gun as he spoke.

Dan seemed preoccupied, not attending to the conversation any longer. I glanced over at Beau who appeared terrified. The deputy, in contrast, seemed confident and in control, even if he did look kind of goofy with his hair sticking out.

"Do you have an ID on the dead guy?" Dan asked, coming out of his trance.

The deputy nodded. "Yep. Found his wallet, license, something called a Screen Actor's Guild card—expired— some credit cards, and a business log. He's an actor, formerly of Santa Monica. Name's James Russell. Ring any bells?"

"Doesn't sound familiar," Dan said.

"How about Chad Anderson?" He paused.

I blinked.

"Larry Longo?"

I frowned. "Risa Longo's husband?"

"And Del Morris."

I gasped. "Oh, my God!"

"And Jeff Knight. His wife, Gail, over in Volcano, has just been notified of his death."

At that point, I sat down.

Dan and I drove to the tiny former mining camp called Volcano in silence for a few minutes, then Dan hit the steering wheel hard with his hand. "Goddamn it!"

"What? Flat tire? What's wrong?"

"Stupid!"

"Who? Me?"

"No! Me! Didn't what's-his-name say the guy was from southern California somewhere? An actor?"

I bit the inside of my cheek for a moment. "Yeah. He said the guy was married to Risa Longo in Whiskey Slide and Arden Morris in Rio Vista. And now he's got another wife in Volcano named Gail Knight."

"Sounds like Hollywood to me." Dan ran his fingers through his hair.

"So you think maybe he 'acted' like he loved these women, married them, and what—took their money? It wouldn't be the first time someone's done something like this."

"Didn't your deputy say the guy had four other ID's and an address book full of women's names and addresses?"

"Including Lacy Penzance. How does someone get so

many fake ID's? Is it really that easy?" I thought for a moment then added, "And he's not my deputy."

Dan nodded. "Extremely easy. All you have to do is to go to another state, check out the microfilm at the library for an obituary of a child who was born about the same time you were, and died before the age of two. Use the name of the dead infant to write to the Bureau of Vital Statistics and request a copy of the birth certificate. Then use that to get a driver's license and social security number, saying you've been out of the country for several years and haven't applied for one before. That's it."

"You know a lot about this stuff." I got a tickle at the back of my neck when I thought about Dan's own identification. I pushed the thought away and continued. "So, he must have been the mystery man Lacy'd been seeing. She figured out the guy was a bigamist and she started searching for his other wives to confirm her suspicions. She managed to find Risa Longo. Then she was about to meet Arden Morris when she was killed."

"By him?"

I didn't know. But he was dead now, too. So what did that mean? The parts just weren't coming together like they did on *Murder, She Wrote*.

"That business ledger Mickey said they found in the guy's room. If it was full of incriminating information, why didn't the killer take it with him ... or her?" Dan asked.

"You think it could be a her? An ex-wife who found out about his past, then killed him? And killed Lacy first to get her out of the way?"

"Could be," Dan said. "Maybe it was Risa or Arden who killed Lacy, then she got rid of the two-timer for fooling around on her."

"If that's the case, whoever did it might be after the other women on the ledger list. The sheriff said one of the pages had been torn out."

"The possibilities are endless," Dan said.

I thought a minute. "The weapons aren't your everyday murder weapons.

Dan frowned, turned off the radio, and gripped the wheel.

"What were you listening to?" I asked.

"I don't know. I wasn't paying attention. Uh—" he seemed to be trying to recall something. "I think it was Pearl Jam."

Music is so invisible to me. I try to make shapes and colors out of it, but it's not easy. It's a puzzle, elusive, and yet I know it's there because other people react to it. They dance. They sing. Their moods change all of a sudden. To me, the answer to this puzzle was kind of like music. I knew it was there, but I just couldn't hear it. Because I can't hear things, I try to figure out solutions in other ways. I try to see it, taste it, smell it, touch it. And finally, I'm able, in my own way, to hear it.

"Look, Dan, it's possible that whoever killed Lacy with that trocar killed what's-his-name at the bed-and-breakfast with the mining pick. Someone connected to the mortuary? Someone who had a connection to Lacy Penzance and the dead man, and wanted both of them dead."

We made good time to Volcano, arriving at nearly eight-thirty P.M. but the trip turned out to be a waste of time. Gail Knight wasn't seeing anyone, which was made very plain to us by a burly man who called himself her brother. I tried what I thought were a couple of unusually creative and believable approaches, but he wasn't buying.

"She isn't seeing anyone," the big guy said firmly.

"But I have important information about—"

"I said, she isn't seeing anyone. Are you deaf, lady?"

I said, as a matter of fact I was, at which point he closed the door in my face. I pitied the poor Girl Scouts who tried to sell cookies to this man. Dan and I headed home.

We pulled up to the hotel building once again and headed up the stairs. Although it was late, I desperately needed to catch up on some work. The deadline loomed ahead relentlessly. Dan wanted to sort things out about Boone, in Boone's surroundings, so we said good night and went our separate ways. I unlocked the office door and stepped into the chaos I'd left behind.

After an hour of trying to think straight but unable to

keep my mind on work, I called it a night, exhausted from the stressful day. Too many things had happened and I doubted whether I could even get to sleep, but it was worth a try. I switched out the light, secured the door, and walked past Boone's office. The light was still on.

I knocked. I opened the door, not waiting for an invitation. I wouldn't hear it anyway.

Dan was sitting in Boone's chair, hunched over, his forearms resting on his knees. He looked tired and worn.

"You okay?" I asked. He nodded without looking up. I moved in closer and could see his eyes were rimmed with tears. He sniffed and wiped his nose with the back of his hand. I put a hand on his shoulder and gave it a rub. I'm not good at this comforting stuff. I've always kept my distance from people, both physically and emotionally. It was part of the problem I'd had with my ex-boyfriend.

Dan reached up and placed his hand over mine. I massaged his shoulder, and after a few moments, pulled him up and led him to Boone's couch. Unfolding the sofa bed, I yanked open the covers and guided him onto the bumpy mattress. Before I could move away, he pulled me down next to him and I lay there, holding his head on my breast, until we both fell asleep.

I was going to have to stop sleeping on couches.

My arm had fallen asleep during the night sometime after the rest of me, and it felt as if a colony of bees had made their home inside. The kink in my neck was back, the poison oak patch had conquered new territory, and both knees were accented with crusty scabs the color of a bad red wine.

And I had pillow hair.

Dan was gone. In his place on the lumpy couch, next to his curled-up cat, was a note that read, "How about lunch at the Nugget around noon? Got a few things to take care of this morning. Dan. P.S. You snore."

I do not snore. It was probably his cat.

I rolled out of the couch bed, fluffed my flat hair, rubbed my numb arm, massaged my stiff neck, scratched all around my poison oak, and ignored my ugly knees.

A vision of the dead mystery man popped into my head. Things certainly could be worse.

After a quick stop at home to feed Casper and take a shower, change into fresh jeans and a Dr. Seuss T-shirt, I made a brief search for the calamine lotion. Not finding the bottle, I made a mental note to pick up a refill, then taped new bandages over my knees. Patched together temporarily, I rode my bike to the Mark Twain Slept Here Inn.

Looking a little less anxious than the previous day, Beau was sitting on the verandah with his mocha and reading my competition.

"Any dirt?" I called up as I parked the bike off to the side of the porch.

"In this rag? Are you kidding? Just another tabloid full of lies. Of course, that's why I read it. But it could use a few more stories about Sean Connery and not so many about Leviathan Smiley's latest grandchild. By the way, loved your mystery puzzle last week."

"Did you solve it?" I plopped down in a wicker chair next to him and eyed his drink.

"I would have, if you hadn't made the clues so obscure. How was I supposed to know it would take *two* bottles of rat poison to kill the IRS agent. I thought it was at least twice that. Did you read the story on 'The Bed-and-Breakfast Murder'?" He held up the front-page headline. It read: "Dead-and-Breakfast," with a by-line by Mary Meek. "They just *had* to call it that, didn't they. Oh, well. Business is booming. My phone hasn't stopped ringing. Everyone wants a crime scene with their blueberry scones and heirloom comforters, I guess. Want a mocha?"

"I would die for one of your mochas, pardon the expression. With cinnamon. And whipping cream. And chocolate sprinkles. In one of those oversized mugs with—"

"One Sanka, black, coming up."

Beau returned moments later with my coffee-and-chocolate drink, just the way I like it. The break gave me a chance to think about the previous night's tragedy.

"Get any sleep last night?" I asked, when Beau returned.

"Not a wink. Of course, I don't think the dead man got much sleep while he was here either, so I shouldn't complain. At least I woke up this morning. Can't say the same for him."

"What do you mean?" I asked, after licking the mocha mustache from my upper lip.

"He's dead."

"I *know* that! I mean, what do you mean about not getting much sleep?"

Beau pursed his lips. "Well, I'm not one to gossip," he said, then flushed when I rolled my eyes. "But our mystery man had a visitor practically every night he was here. And the two of them weren't exactly playing Yahtzee in there."

"Really! Who was it? Lacy?"

"I don't know. I don't spy on my guests, contrary to what you might suspect. But every morning when I cleaned the room I'd find evidence of a midnight guest."

"Like what?"

"Well, wine glasses and empty bottles. Cosmetic jars. All that women's stuff. You know."

I knew women's stuff.

"And that bottle of hair coloring the sheriff found. It wasn't a common brand, like Clairol. It was called 'Persistence' or 'Permanence,' or something like that. I think the shade was Cappuccino. Personally I prefer Cinnamon on mine. It's a little more subtle."

So the bigamist had a visitor who colored her hair. Lacy? I asked Beau if he'd saved any of the castaways but he hadn't. The sheriff had confiscated the hair-coloring bottle, and the rest of the discards were long gone. For another half hour we discussed all the possibilities of who the man might have entertained, but came up with nothing that resembled a solution. Beau hadn't seen a strange car, hadn't glimpsed a telltale silhouette on the window shade, hadn't found anything other than the "women's stuff."

I thanked Beau for the mocha and rode my bike to the office. Miah was keying in the obituary for yesterday's murder victim.

"It's like trying to make a mountain out of a mole-hill," Miah said. "We've got nothing on this guy." He leaned aside to let me read the bit of copy. An anthill was more like it.

"I've got an idea. Let's make a couple of phone calls."

Miah dialed the first phone number I gave him. I read his lips as he asked the questions I had written out, and watched him jot down the responses. He called the next number, and the next, using his obituary format to glean the information we needed.

"Great job!" I gave him two vigorous thumbs up. "Listen, I've got to go see someone. Can you hold things together for me while I'm out? I've got Barbara Libbey coming in with that report on the frog festival ticket sales in about an hour, and three more fillers to add. Will you cover those for me? I'll owe you."

"You always owe me," Miah said, sweeping his blond hair back. Nipple ring or no nipple ring, he was still the cutest young guy in Flat Skunk. I was grateful for his help. I hoped he was grateful for the paycheck.

My next stop was the mortuary. I hoped for another little chat with French and Celeste, but French wasn't in. I knocked on Celeste's door. She greeted me courteously but didn't seem to be her usual cheery self. Small puffy pillows framed her eyes. Her usually perfect hair was flat and droopy. She wore an extra layer of makeup, as if to mask her emotions rather than cover up her blemishes. She kept her hands fisted at her sides.

With slumped shoulders she led me into her office, promising attention for the next few minutes, until the expected prospective buyer arrived—a man who apparently knew the value of purchasing "pre-need."

"Sorry about all the questions the other day," I said. "I was just trying to get some information for the newspaper. This Lacy Penzance thing is a big story and I'd like to write the best possible report I can. I guess I pushed a little too far."

She gave a half-smile. The fists remained clenched. I went on.

"Pre-need, huh? It sure is popular. I guess that's what I should do for my aunt."

Celeste spoke with little animation or enthusiasm, almost as if by rote. "Most people don't want to leave the financial burden to their bereaved loved ones. How is your aunt?" Although facing me, she didn't look me in the eye.

"Fine, actually," I said quickly. "Couldn't be better."

Celeste appeared unimpressed. She looked past me and I wondered if someone had appeared at the door behind me. A quick turnaround revealed no one.

"Celeste, I was wondering. Are you handling the burial of the man who died last night?"

Celeste's lips tightened slightly. She looked at her watch, then rifled through some papers on her desk. "What man?"

"The man who was killed at the bed-and-breakfast last night. You did hear the news?"

She interrupted with a wave of her hand. "Oh—yeah. Uh, no, I don't think Memory Kingdom is going to be involved with the . . . resolution of the body. At least, I haven't heard anything yet. I'm sure he's—it's—still over at the coroner's office."

"You didn't happen to know him, did you, Celeste?"

Celeste stopped fiddling with the papers, pressed her hands on the desk, and met my eyes. "For God's sakes, Connor! Not this again. What is with you? No, I didn't know him! Why would you even think that?"

Definitely hit a nerve.

"Sorry. Guess I figured you knew everyone who comes to pass in this town, you being in the mortuary business and all. Pretty narrow-minded of me, huh?"

She just glared. I went on. "People are always thinking the same thing about me. Do I know this deaf person or that deaf person. They think we're all one big happy family, just because we're deaf." I laughed, then turned it into a cough. This was getting me nowhere.

I ran my fingers through my hair. "God, these murders are making me old before my time. I think I'm getting a few new gray hairs from all this stress."

She didn't take the hint, just narrowed her eyes as if trying to figure out what the hell I was talking about. I floundered on.

"That color you're using. It's really natural looking. I tried a new color a while back but it didn't do anything except turn my hair an unflattering shade of green. I guess you do your own coloring, being a former beautician and all."

"Stylist. We don't use 'beautician' anymore." Celeste absentmindedly pushed at her flat hair, picking strands from the bottom and twirling them in her manicured fingers.

"What color is it?"

She spoke listlessly. "I mix them. I could do yours for you sometime, if you want."

"That'd be great. Where do I buy the colors you use?"

"I can get them for you at the beauty supply shop. They give me a discount."

Still nowhere. I needed a name. Another tack.

"Is it Clairol? My mother used Clairol."

She shook her flat but shiny mane. "No, that's for housewives who prefer to do it themselves when they really shouldn't. I use professional coloring."

"What brand?"

Celeste looked at me, paused, frowned, then said, "I don't remember. I use all different kinds."

Right. "Beau says he uses a color called Cappuccino, I think. No, wait—Cinnamon. He—"

Celeste paled and her eyes flared open. I thought she was going to speak but she said nothing.

"Celeste, is anything wrong? You don't look very well."

She blinked and sat up straight. "No. Everything's fine. Just tired, I guess. Didn't get much sleep last night. I think I'm overdoing it."

Join the club. She got up to show me out. I didn't move but turned around in my chair and watched her walk toward the door. "Celeste, I have one more quick question."

"I do have this appointment, Connor. If you don't mind, could we make it some other time?"

"Do you know Risa Longo?"

Celeste blinked and started to shake her head. "I—"

"Arden Morris?"

Celeste closed her mouth and looked at me.

"Gail Knight?"

Celeste closed the door, turned around, and crossed her arms in front of her.

"No, I've never heard of them. What do you want, Connor?"

I was certain there was a connection, but I had to create the details. Being deaf, you learn how to bluff well, especially when you don't want to give away how little you sometimes understand.

"They all knew you . . . They met you when their first husbands died . . . They were all counseled by you in their time of grief . . . And they all thought you were a saint." I peeled out my fingers one at a time for each point. The phone calls Miah had made for me were paying off.

Celeste didn't smile at the compliment of being compared to a saint. "So? A lot of people come and go around here. I have many clients. Now, I really have to—"

"Celeste, I think you were at the bed-and-breakfast last night, with the man known occasionally as James Russell. There was a bottle of hair color found at the scene. I'll bet it was yours."

"What? You're crazy. Why on earth would I go there to color my hair? Besides, mine is Mahogany, not Cappuccino—" She stopped abruptly.

"How did you know it was Cappuccino they found at the B-and-B?"

Celeste's face drained of color, leaving the artificial glow of blush on her cheeks. She looked like a rag doll.

"You knew the man who was staying there. The man who was apparently married to at least three wealthy women. The man who was about to marry a fourth: Lacy Penzance."

"I . . . don't . . ."

"Do you know what happened to him, Celeste?"

"No, I . . ."

"Did you kill him, Celeste?" I asked impulsively, then suddenly realized I might be standing in front of a cold-blooded murderer, unarmed and defenseless. I glanced around for a protective weapon, but Celeste didn't whip out a trocar and try to shish-kebab me.

Instead, she burst into tears. Wild, physical sobs, tears streaming down her overly made-up face, giving a bizarre carnival look. She leaned back against the door and slid weakly to the floor.

All I could do was sit there and let the outburst run its course. After the big sobs subsided she spoke, her mouth wet from the copious tears.

"I . . . didn't . . . kill . . . Jim . . . I didn't . . . I loved him."

I knelt over her and took her hand, but she pulled it away. I moved down next to her on the floor, close, but not touching, so I could watch her lips.

"You were there last night."

She bit her lip, then said, "I went to see him, yes, for a while."

"Why?"

Celeste paused, bit her lip hard enough to make a mark, and wiped her running nose with the palm of her hand. "I helped him with his hair. And then I left. That's it. He was alive and perfectly fine—and now he's dead." She burst into tears again.

I waited a few moments. "He was your husband, wasn't he?"

She looked at me, her expression a mixture of panic and amazement.

"The ring." I nodded at the gold band she was twisting on her finger.

I waited for the next outburst of tears to subside as we sat on the floor, facing one another. "You found out about his relationship with Lacy, and you killed him? And her?"

"No! No! I told you! I didn't kill him—or her."

"But you know about the other women . . ."

Celeste nodded. It caused her nose to drip down onto her lip. She wiped it away with the back of her hand.

"What are you going to do?" she said, in jerky, hiccuping sentences. I had to strain my eyes to understand her altered speech.

"Nothing. I just want to know what this is all about. I'm sure you'll do the right thing."

"Are you going to tell the sheriff?"

"No, but you should. If you don't, he'll figure it out for himself. He found hairs and fingerprints—and that bottle of dye your husband used to change his appearance. It won't take him long."

Tears welled again in her eyes. "I didn't kill Jim. I met him a couple of years ago, when I was a hairdresser in Hollywood."

I nodded for her to continue.

"He was an actor, an aspiring one anyway. We hit it off and got married impulsively one night. Things went fine for a while, wonderful really. But then I lost my job and he wasn't getting much work as an actor. So I took the mortuary job up here while he stayed in L.A. trying to get parts."

Celeste took a deep breath and pinched her nose.

"Where'd you get the idea to introduce him to your clients?"

She looked away and wiped a tear that spilled down her splotchy cheeks. "I . . . I started working as a grief counselor for French. All these lonely rich widows would tell me their problems, just to have someone to talk to. I used to tell Jim about them. Some of the things they would tell me . . ."

She reached over to her desk, grabbed a tissue, and blew her nose.

"So, once you had the information on them, you introduced them to James?"

"He got the idea to meet them. He'd call them up and say he was an old army buddy or college friend of their dead husband's. Then he'd ask them out to dinner and share some of the information I'd learned about them. You know, to prove he was an old friend."

"So it was his idea to romance them?" I suggested.

Celeste laughed. "No one could resist Jimmy's charm. Not even me. He was a great actor."

She wiped the moist streaks under her eyes and took another breath.

"And then he married them?"

"Not at first. At first he just took what money he

could get. It didn't seem so bad. They were rich. They could spare it. And he gave them a wonderful fantasy life. But over time he got carried away."

"He didn't stop there?" I suggested.

Celeste pulled a tissue from the desk and kneaded it in her hands. "If things looked promising he'd propose, thinking that would get him even more—property deeds, wills, things like that. Then one day he said he was going to marry one of them."

"Then he'd what—take their money and run?"

Celeste smeared a tear off her cheek. "Sometimes he'd withdraw money from the bank, or liquidate their homes or cars, saying he needed the cash for a secret mission or journalism job or whatever. He was very creative at coming up with excuses for leaving for weeks at a time. And the money we—he made—it was phenomenal!"

She smiled wistfully. It seemed what she admired most about her man was his ability to lie so effectively.

"How did he get away with that? Didn't the women become suspicious?"

"Not until Lacy. He was very careful. These women wanted to believe in him so badly, they'd buy into almost anything he said. He'd take off for weeks at a time, saying he was on some kind of mission, then come back for a few days, give them a thrill, get some more money, then take off again."

"How could he keep that up? Especially with so many women?"

Celeste shrugged. "After a while he just wouldn't return to the earlier ones anymore. He'd send a fake telegram about his death without leaving any information they could trace. He took what he could and then moved on to the next one."

"And you set him up."

Celeste didn't answer. Her eyes welled with tears. "It wasn't supposed to be that way. But Jimmy was so persuasive. He said he didn't love any of them. Just me. I hated sharing him with those old women, but what could I do?"

"The two of you essentially ran a kind of polygamy ring," I said, summarizing her exploits into a clear ugly picture.

She sniffled and looked and me pleadingly. "We didn't really hurt anyone. The women were happy to find someone who loved them again. They didn't need all that money—they weren't going to live forever, and they had plenty. They loved having this exciting, elusive man in their fantasy lives, even when he was gone."

"How did he keep all the women separate? Wasn't he afraid they'd find out about each other?"

"He was careful. They were all in different towns. Since I travel from place to place working for the Memory Kingdom chain, it made it easy to find new prospects throughout the Mother Lode."

"And Arden Morris? What about her?"

"She moved to Rio Vista after they were married."

"Did he kill Lacy because she found out about the bigamy scam?" I asked.

"No! He didn't kill anyone! Neither of us did! He was just in it for the money. And I was in it for him mostly. Nobody got hurt—except Jimmy."

"You don't know that for sure. What about Lacy? She got hurt. She's dead. And I'm fairly certain she was onto him. And perhaps onto you, too."

"I know she was onto something. She found out about Risa Longo—I guess she went through Jim's wallet and found the business card or something. She went up to Whiskey Slide to see for herself. But it wasn't a big deal. Jimmy was just going to disappear for a while until things cooled off. They'd never find him because he had so many false identities."

"But Lacy died."

"Yes, she's dead. And I'm sorry, not that I particularly liked her. She was just another spoiled, rich lady. But we didn't have anything to do with her death."

"Somebody used a trocar, Celeste. From the mortuary."

"I know! I know! I don't know how they got it. But I swear to you, we didn't do it. That's way out of our league."

"You can't really speak for James Russell, can you?"

Celeste looked at me. A large tear collected in the corner of her eye, rolled under her nose and down to her lip, then dropped to the floor, making a tiny damp circle in the dark carpet.

"**W**hat's going on here?" French demanded, pushing his way into the room, face flushed and eyes surveying what little he could see inside the room. Celeste, leaning against the door, scooted a few inches to give him access. "Didn't you hear me knocking? Celeste, you've got a client! Celeste?"

Celeste sat huddled in an upright fetal position at his feet. French looked at me for an explanation.

"Guy troubles," I said, looking up at him. "She'll be all right. Just give us a few minutes, okay? Think you can take care of things?"

French, clearly out of his league when it came to "guy troubles," nodded dumbly and backed out of the room. I don't think he'd ever seen Celeste less than perky.

"Come on, Celeste. I'll get you a drink of water." I stood up and pulled her gently to her feet, then guided her around the desk to her chair. She snatched a wad of tissues from the decorated box next to her brass nameplate and smeared them around her face while I went down the hall in search of a water faucet. I filled a coffee-stained Universal Studios mug with water and returned to find her red-nosed, puffy-eyed, and subdued.

I set the mug on her desk. "Is French involved in any of this?" I asked.

She shook her head vigorously. "God, no. He hasn't got a clue about anything. Not even his own business. Hell, I practically run this place."

"Any chance he could have found out something, and maybe confronted James?"

Celeste sniffed. "I really don't think so. It's not in him. And if you're going to ask me if I think he killed anyone, forget it. There's no way. Sure, he dated Lacy a few times after Reuben died. But when she dumped him, he just sort of put his tail between his legs and went back to Jilda. He's a mouse."

"Well, if he wasn't involved in the deaths of James or Lacy, and you weren't, who's left?" I decided not to mention Boone for the time being.

"I don't know!"

I watched her rub the gold ring on her finger.

"That's a beautiful ring. It looks very expensive."

Celeste stopped the rubbing and folded her hands, obscuring the ring.

"Did you get it from Wolf?"

"Of course not. I got it from Jimmy."

"I mean, it looks like Wolf's work. It doesn't look like a copy."

Something snapped. Celeste stood up, brushed non-existent dirt from her skirt, and said: "Connor, I've had just about all I can take from you. You know, none of this is any of your business. Why don't you stick to what you do best—whatever that is—and stop accusing me of God knows what. Can't you see I'm upset. Now, please—"

At that moment French burst back in the door. "Celeste! They want to talk with you! They're not interested in what I have to say. Please, can you come out here now? We don't want to lose these people."

Celeste didn't give me another glance as she walked out the door. I left the mortuary a few minutes later, just as a bunch of yellow daisies was being delivered by a young man in a green jumpsuit.

I wasn't going to get away with using this confrontational approach with everyone, I thought, as I entered Wolf's shop. I would have to be a little more restrained. I had the excuse of publishing a newspaper, and I figured I ought to make use of it when questioning these people. That is, if I still had a newspaper and not a bunch of blank sheets, the way I was neglecting things. Besides, I was making accusations without any proof. What was I thinking?

Wolf came out from the back room wearing some kind of welding mask on his head. He lifted the plastic eye guard as he entered, then pulled off a pair of gloves and greeted me curtly without looking up.

"How did you know I was here?" I asked, scanning the room for some sort of signal bell. "You didn't even give me a chance to grab any jewels."

He didn't laugh. "The mat has a buzzer. It sounds in the back. You still looking for a ring for your uncle? Or are you ready to turn that lump of gold into something you can wear to that little office of yours?"

"Nah, I like the lump. It's a metaphor for my love life. Think I'll keep it that way."

"Yeah? I have a theory about love," Wolf said, placing the gloves on the countertop. "It's nothing more than a chemical dependency. Me, I don't like being addicted to anything. Except my work."

"So there's no Mrs. Wolf, I mean Quick?" I said teasingly. He didn't seem amused. We all handled our loneliness in different ways. I moved on. "Wolf, uh . . . I'm doing a story for my newspaper . . . on the first murder to take place in Flat Skunk in a hundred years. I wanted to ask you some questions, since you've been here, what— since you were born?"

Wolf perched on the stool behind the counter and examined a ring he'd pulled from his pocket. He said nothing. I took it as a go-ahead.

"You heard about that man who was killed at the bed-and-breakfast inn?"

Wolf continued examining the ring.

"Through my, uh, research, I found out he was married to someone in town."

No response. Not even a twitch of an eyelid.

"Celeste."

Wolf stopped and looked up. He seemed genuinely surprised. "You're kidding."

"Did you know the guy?"

Wolf shook his head without taking his eyes off me. A man of few words.

"Celeste was wearing a gold ring she says this guy gave her. Very ornate, free-form. It . . . well, it looks like your work."

Wolf shrugged. "A lot of people wear my jewelry."

"Do you remember selling a ring to a man called James Russell? Or Celeste?"

"I sell a lot of rings to a lot of people. I can't remember them all. What's this got to do with the article you're writing?" Wolf slipped the ring back in his pocket and picked up his gloves.

"Sluice Jackson had one of your rings, too, Wolf. That day he fell into the grave. I found it there the next day."

"So?" He looked blankly at me, his brown eyes cold and empty. I turned to the jewelry case and ran a finger along the middle of the glass, as if touching each of the rings. It was time for a long shot.

"That ring I found in the grave? It didn't belong to Sluice. It belonged to someone at the mortuary. One of the deceased. In fact, it was one of several that were stolen from a man named Leonard Swec."

I looked back at Wolf. He said nothing, but slipped on the gloves, slowly, taking his time with each finger as he pressed them into place. I kept talking—it was effective in keeping people distracted, at least for a while. I made it up as I went along.

"I have this theory. Someone removes jewelry from the deceased, probably during the night, and then gives it to someone else, who—"

"Who what?" Wolf asked, leveling his gaze at me.

I usually have no trouble making eye contact. It's a

necessity when you're deaf. But Wolf's piercing dark eyes almost seemed a physical assault. "Who, uh, well, copies them, and then returns the fakes to the mortuary, while keeping the originals. Then—"

Wolf laughed, folded his gloved hands, then stretched out the tension. I glanced peripherally at the front door for a clear getaway in case he suddenly reacted.

"You could copy them, couldn't you? In a few hours you could have duplicates ready to be replaced on the loved one's hands, while you melt down the originals and redesign them. Then you could sell the new designs to the gold-crazy tourists for a huge profit. Who's to know?"

"You're the one who's crazy," Wolf said, flexing his thick, strong, glove-covered fingers. I glanced at the door.

"Lacy's gold jewelry was missing from her home after she died, Wolf. Did she find out about your creative jewelry business, too?"

Wolf got up off the stool and turned toward his back room, his head bobbing slightly. After a few seconds he turned slowly back to face me, grinning strangely.

"Oh, yeah. I forgot. You can't hear me, can you? Well, let me repeat myself. You're not only deaf, you're dumb. And you're dangerous, spreading rumors like that. Rumors you can't possibly prove. Because they aren't true. That's not journalism. That's libel."

"Sluice may have something to say about that when he recovers from his fall. You were at the cemetery when he 'fell,' weren't you? Coincidence?"

Wolf gave another little laugh. "You really are nuts. Just like Sluice. And he's never going to recover, at least not mentally. The old guy's lost it. Ain't nobody gonna believe what he says anymore, so forget about it. Besides, I had nothing to do with his fall. Why would I? He was—" He cut himself off and glanced over my shoulder. "I've got work to do."

He turned around again and left the room, leaving me standing in the middle of the jewelry store. I thought about following him when I caught a glimpse of movement behind me. I whirled around to see two couples who had entered the store sometime during our conversation. All I could do was walk out the door.

I checked my watch. I still had a few minutes before I was to meet Dan for lunch at the Nugget. I decided to go early and have a chat with Jilda Renfrew, after a quick stop at the Black Bart Drugstore for a bottle of calamine lotion.

The cafe was packed at eleven-thirty in the morning. Everyone seemed to be buzzing about the latest death in Flat Skunk. I waved to Deputy Arnold and Sheriff Mercer, who were downing cheeseburgers in one corner. I nodded to French, who was chatting up clients in another booth. Celeste was absent from her customary seat next to him.

Lacy's attorney, Croaky Wheeler, sat alone in a window booth reading the *Mother Lode Monitor* and dining on what looked like a meat loaf sandwich. I ignored him, not ready to deal with the five-thousand-dollar check waiting for me in his office. The rest of the booths were filled, so I took a seat at the counter and ordered a glass of orange juice from Jilda.

"I guess you heard about that guy at the Mark Twain, huh, Connor? Whoa! Unbelievable!" She set down my juice, then leaned her elbows on the counter in front of me. "God, it's like there's some kind of serial killer loose around here or something. I'm getting totally paranoid."

"It's pretty scary. Did you happen to know the guy? James Russell?" I tried to sound casual.

"No way. But I heard he was married to a whole bunch of women. Must of been some kinda major stud."

"So you weren't one of his wives, huh?" I teased.

She laughed. "Naw, I'm a one-man woman. French is my honey." She glanced over at him but he was too engrossed in making a sale to notice.

"Well, I hope you were locked up safe in your room with the windows closed and the lights on last night."

"I was with Frenchy, thank God, although don't print that in your newspaper. He doesn't want anyone to know we actually sleep together. He's kind of old-fashioned that way, you know. Thinks people wouldn't understand 'cause I'm so young and he's older. Isn't that cool?"

Cool. I finished my juice and noticed the sheriff and deputy getting ready to leave their table. I moved over next to them.

"Mind if I grab this table?" I asked, as the sheriff pulled a couple of dollars from his pocket for a tip.

"It's all yours," he said with a toothpick in his mouth. He gestured toward the red leatherette seat. "I recommend the Pepto-Bismol today."

"Thanks. Hope it goes well with calamine lotion." I set the bottle on the table and gave my arm a scratch. "At least the colors match. Any news on that guy they found last night?"

The sheriff pulled the toothpick out of his mouth, which helped my comprehension a great deal.

"Yep."

I grinned. "Well, what? Tell me!"

The sheriff looked at Mickey, then back at me and made a zip-the-lip gesture.

"Come on, Sheriff! Don't hold out on me! The police and the press have to work together on these things. I want to do a serious story on this." I hoped I wasn't whining.

"You'll find out soon enough. Soon as the evidence comes back from the lab. Then everything will be P.I."

"Public information," Mickey explained.

"I suspect I'll be making an arrest sometime soon," the sheriff continued. "Yep. But I can't say anything more yet. If my suspicions are correct, everyone is in for a big surprise. Especially you, Connor Westphal. By the way, I don't suppose you're responsible for all this, just to build up circulation in that newspaper of yours, huh?"

"My paper hasn't even come out yet! Listen, Sheriff, I—"

Just then Dan entered the café. Both the sheriff and the deputy looked over at him, then at each other. While the sheriff paid the bill, Mickey mouthed the words, "See you tonight, Connor, and be careful," then followed Sheriff Mercer out the door.

"Hey," Dan said as he slid into the booth. "What was

that all about? They looked like they'd just seen the ghost of Elvis or something."

"I don't know. Sheriff says he's close to making an arrest in the death of James Russell, or whoever he is. But he won't say who or what he's got. He's being very mysterious. Why does everyone love the drama of this so much?"

Dan and I ordered Hangtown Fry, the oysters-egg-and-bacon dish new to Dan's palate, and relatively new to mine. As soon as we finished, we headed outside into the bright sunny afternoon, stuffed and satisfied.

"I need to walk," I said. "Wanna come?"

We chatted about our latest cache of information as we strolled toward the end of Main Street to the cemetery. Dan followed me up Pioneer Hill and we located Lacy's freshly filled grave. Dan started to sit down when I grabbed his arm.

"Poison oak. Right there. Be careful."

He stood back up.

"We can sit on those benches over there." I pointed to a cement seat about fifty feet away. Dan nodded and we walked slowly over. The cemetery offered a kind of relaxed ambiance in the daytime; it didn't seem to encourage hurry.

"Well, it looks as if everyone—and no one—has a reason to kill Lacy and James Russell," I said. "The folks around here sure have their little secrets, and they're working hard to protect them. Did you tell the sheriff about Boone?"

Dan nodded. "He already knew. Guess the sheriff from Rio Vista notified him after we left. He asked me a few questions. Said they're calling it accidental over there, but he seemed to think I might know more than I do."

"Really?" I said, hoping he'd continue. While waiting, I thought about the conversations I'd had with Celeste, Wolf, and Jilda. Dan chewed on a blade of grass.

"It sure looks as if someone from the mortuary is involved, what with the trocar being used, the missing jewelry, Sluice falling into the grave. But . . ."

"But what?" Dan asked.

"What about Boone? How does he fit into all this?"

He shook his head, then held the grass blade between his thumbs and held it up to his mouth. His cheeks puffed up.

"What are you doing?" I asked.

"Making a—" He looked at me, then dropped the blade of grass to the ground. "Nothing."

I didn't pursue it. "Boone must have discovered something important enough to be silenced. That's assuming he didn't drown on his own. Maybe he figured out the bigamy scam. Or maybe he knew about the jewelry exchanges."

We tried to hash it out for another half hour or so but the loose ends only became more entangled as the afternoon wore on. We walked back to the hotel building and entered our respective offices to do our respective chores. Dan had a brother's mysterious death to deal with. I still had a newspaper to publish—tomorrow, by God. I pushed the newspaper envelope the rest of the afternoon, promising no interruptions until all the copy was ready to go to print.

At five o'clock I got a call on the TTY.

"connor it's mickey we sort of had a date tonight do you remember for dinner are you still free GA."

Oh, my God, I had completely forgotten. I stared at the red letters trying to think up a plausible excuse. I just didn't feel like schmoozing tonight.

"Mickey! Hi. Sorry. I DID forget! It's been one of those days!! Will you ever forgive me? Could I have a raincheck? GA."

"no problem this case is getting to be very time consuming the sheriff is close to an arrest and i should hang around until things break GA."

"Great. Thanks for understanding. Don't suppose you know who he's going to arrest? GA."

"i really can't say but can tell you this the hair and clothing threads we found at the mark twain were celestes ! we also found some of lacys stolen jewelry there but the fingerprint belongs to someone else can't say who but connor you should be careful GA"

I thought for a moment, then typed, "Thanks,

Mickey. I will. Let me know what happens, will you? Can you call me at home later? I'll be working there most of the night. GA."

"sure enough ill check on you see ya later GA."

"Bye. GA. SK."

"i always forget that SK part GA. SK."

I hung up the phone.

I rode my bike home and cautiously entered my diner. Within seconds I was greeted by my faithful dog, Casper, who had a reassuring effect on my stress levels. I served her up a big bowl of doggy beef Stroganoff. I was glad to have a dog, and not just for the company. With all that was going on around town, she made me feel a whole lot safer.

I helped myself to the refrigerator leftovers—a bowl of rice, a couple of slices of cantaloupe, some dill-rye toast, and a chicken leg—and washed it all down with a light beer.

I was just about to go to bed when Casper started barking. I couldn't hear her but I saw her head snap several times and the snarled expression from her mouth was unmistakable.

"What is it, girl?" I asked, suddenly alert. The locks had been changed—but then locks hadn't stopped an intruder the other day.

The hair suddenly prickled on the back of my neck. I turned to recheck the front door when the lights throughout the diner went out.

I froze, tingling with sweat, not moving, not breathing. I couldn't see Casper in the darkness but I could feel the whisk of her tail as she backed up beside me. I reached down to touch her and felt her head still snapping wildly.

And then I didn't feel her any more.

I had to stop myself from calling "Casper!" I didn't want to give my location away in the dark if someone was there. I felt a bead of sweat trickle down my chest.

I had to move. If there was someone, they probably already knew where I was. Stifling a panic, I tried to grope my way to the front door. After two steps I tripped over an end table. It wasn't easy curbing the urge to yell "Fuck!"

Growing more frantic, I stumbled on in the direction of the door. Something moved next to me—I could feel the air swish by. Casper? I reached down to feel for her. Nothing.

Was someone there? Was someone—

My answer came as a jolting grab from behind.

I took in a quick breath—mint?—and tried to duck. Too late.

A cloth with something strong-smelling, like ammonia, covered my face. I felt as if I couldn't breathe. My lungs filled in a painful gasp as I thrashed and swung my arms and legs at the assailant behind me. My throat burned.

I grabbed at the stinging cloth, kicked—mostly at thin air—and tried to twist away. Cold, clammy hands held me tight at my head with a grip on my hair, holding the cloth against my face, suffocating me with the pungent odor.

Suddenly I was very, very dizzy.

I woke in darkness. Lying on my back, I couldn't make out anything but blackness. I could feel my own breath come back at me, but felt little else, except the raw burn in my throat and lungs, and a throbbing pain in my right leg. I tried to lift my head, but it ached so badly I lay back down, the effort and pain too great. I tried to lift my arms; they were leaden; they wouldn't move.

Oh, God, I was paralyzed!

I wiggled my fingers and toes. I bent my elbows slightly, and shrugged my shoulders. I moved my legs back and forth along a smooth velvety surface. No, not paralyzed. At least, not completely.

What then? I spread my fingers and felt the soft, velvety fabric once again. I followed the curve of the material slowly as it moved around to cover me. Completely.

Oh, my God. A casket.

I tried to sit up and bumped my head.

Some people might have screamed. That was not my first thought. Making a loud **noise** simply did not occur to a person like me, used to **soundlessness.** My first thought was, I'm going to suffocate in here—and suddenly I found I couldn't breathe.

Gasping for air, I tried to lift my arms and legs but they were immobilized between puffy pillows of softness. Feeling claustrophobic, I turned my head face up and was nearly smothered. With sweat dripping off my neck in rivulets, I turned my head sideways again. The back of my neck tickled and itched.

I tried kicking the top of my prison with both feet, but my legs didn't have much power or leverage with only inches of space in which to maneuver. I struck weakly a few more times for the hell of it.

I was still having trouble breathing, beyond the burning sensation.

I remembered Celeste saying something about the coffins being airtight, to keep the bugs out. Some kind of rubber gasket. It felt as if a weight were pressing on my chest. How long had I been here?

I wiggled my fingers on either side of the velvety smoothness, hoping to find some kind of inner latch. Ha! What was I thinking? A safety catch for those occasional premature burials?

Finally it occurred to me to scream. I'd seen it in the movies. It usually brought help. It was worth a try.

I screamed. At least it felt like I did. I screamed and kicked and pounded like hell, hoping someone might hear me. I screamed and kicked and pounded until I was hoarse, sore, and physically defeated.

Fuck, I thought. I've got to get out of here.

What were my chances of spending hours in this thing, undetected? I could suffocate in this airtight container in a matter of hours. Or maybe minutes. What was it my science teacher had said about the amount of air per cubic foot? I think I missed that question on the test.

I began to think about everything in life I still wanted to do: Make a proper go of the newspaper. Fix up the diner and maybe open it on weekends for cappuccino and croissants. Grow my hair long. Lose five pounds. Okay, ten pounds. See the home of my ancestors in Cornwall, England. Meet someone . . .

I thought about my old boyfriend. Suddenly I missed the bastard. He was better than nothing, wasn't he? I thought about Jilda and French. Celeste and her bigamist husband. I thought about Mickey. And Jeremiah. I thought about Dan.

Goddammit! I had to come up with something or I'd really lose it.

I took a deep breath, hoping there was still enough left to last me a while. All right, assuming I'm in the mortuary, surely someone—the night watchman—would be around. I had to assume eventually he would hear me if I screamed. What choice did I have?

I screamed and kicked and pounded again, for what seemed an interminably long time. I gasped in air as it grew warmer and stuffier and more difficult to breathe in the man-made womb. Tomb.

I screamed "Fuck!" until my throat felt even rougher, and dry and scratchy. I could feel droplets of sweat sliding down the sides of my face and pooling at the back of my neck. My back was drenched. What little air there was was stifling.

I kicked again, more angry than anything else. Tears filled my eyes at the hopeless feeling that was beginning to overtake me.

And then I had an idea. My first priority was an air hole. Not only would I be able to stay alive, but maybe someone would hear me if I could get the sound out. Could I make enough noise to raise the dead, so to speak?

Frustratingly slowly I worked the fingers of my right hand up my body, to my chest, up my neck, and around the side of my left shoulder like a contortionist, each movement increasingly painful as I maneuvered my arm into positions it did not naturally go. Near the top of the casket, just above my head, I felt the cool rectangle of metal I had been searching for.

I'd remembered from the tour that each casket had a bronze plaque with a name engraved on it, somehow secured to the puffy lining. Glue?

I grasped the metal name tag with my stubby fingernails and tugged awkwardly. After several minutes of clawing, the thing ripped away from the cushiony fabric. With the plaque in hand, I slowly inched my arm back down my body. The plate was small, about six inches by two inches. I hoped it would do.

I crept the fingers of my left hand along one side of the coffin, where I supposed the top and bottom met. After a few moments of prodding, poking, and pressing, I located the rubber gasket running along the juncture. Slipping the bronze plaque into the crevice, I pushed hard, attempting to use it as a wedge to create an opening.

The lid didn't move. I tried again. And again. I couldn't get any leverage. It was hopeless, and I was nearing true panic.

I took a slow, shallow breath, thought a moment, then tried another tack. Turning the plate on the diagonal, I jammed the sharp corner into the rubber lining where the two parts of the casket came together, and started digging like a frenzied prospector at a newly discovered gold mine.

After a few minutes that seemed hours, I could feel the rubber begin to give and tear. I was breaking through. More digging, gouging, and grinding in the interminable darkness, and the soft wood of the casket also began to chip away. How long had it taken before I'd dug the plaque into the wood about a fingernail's worth? It wasn't much, but it was a start. I had nothing better to do.

I twisted and dug the corner of the plaque around until I felt more of the soft wood give. Back and forth, back and forth, I twisted the piercing corner until my fingers were raw and scraped from the friction and pressure.

Finally I pulled the plaque out of the tiny crevice I had created. A glimmer of light winked at me.

I tried to crook my neck toward the air hole but didn't have much room to move. Still, I sucked in a few difficult breaths, then I let out a scream that I hoped was ear-piercingly loud. I screamed until I thought I might never be able to speak again. When I finally stopped screaming to take a breath, I felt the casket vibrate.

Someone had heard me! I felt the casket moving. Someone was opening it!

My elation was dampened with a sobering thought: Who was on the other side?

I broke out in another sweat, lying motionless as I waited for the lid to lift. After a few moments of unbearable stillness, I felt a rush of cool air sweep over me as the lid was lifted off.

I gulped down several deep breaths, then pushed myself up, dizzy and light-headed, and took in a few more deep breaths until my breathing became more regular. The lights although dim, hurt my eyes and it took a few moments to adjust.

Abruptly I jerked around to face whoever had come to my rescue.

Sluice Jackson stood there staring at me, wide-eyed, pale, and frozen with fear, as if he'd seen a ghost.

"Sluice! Thank God! I . . . I was trapped in there. Someone . . . if you hadn't . . ."

I knew I was rambling. Sluice was looking more and more confused. He backed away from me as I spoke. The purple bruises on his face and hands were evidence of his recent fall into the open grave. I climbed unsteadily out of the coffin, and was surprised to see that the hand holding the bronze plate was bloody. There were droplets of crimson on the pale blue fabric where I had been digging.

"Sluice, listen carefully," I said gently. "Someone shut me in there. Did you see anyone?" It hurt to talk from all the screaming I'd done.

Sluice shook his head. His mouth hung open, saliva lined his lower lip. He reeked of alcohol and cigar smoke.

"I din't do it! I din't do it! I heard the screamin'. I thought it was that damn cat. I din't do nothin'."

I looked at the terrified man, not knowing what to say. I hadn't had a lot of experience dealing with old mentally challenged prospectors.

"Sluice, it's okay," I reassured him. "Someone locked me in there and you got me out. You saved my life." I wiped the bloody hand on my pant leg and felt a new bruise on my thigh. My pants were missing a button and my top was disheveled and torn at the neck.

"I din't do nothin'." He turned away and shuffled quickly out of the Selection Room. I was left alone with a roomful of caskets.

And the memory of a lingering smell. Mints? Mouthwash? Or did chloroform smell like Tic Tacs?

I brushed myself off, and looked around for something to wrap my bleeding hand. The mortuary was dim, except for a few night-lights. Shadows seemed to dance in the empty room, and I shivered. Whoever it was that locked me in here could still be around. I headed for Celeste's office, wondering how—and when—Sluice had gotten out of the hospital.

Celeste's door was locked. I debated just leaving the damn place, but returned to the lobby where I located a pay phone in a far corner by the restrooms. I dialed a number using my credit card and waited a few seconds before speaking.

"This is Connor. If you can hear me, I need you to

come over to the mortuary as soon as possible. It's urgent. I'll be waiting outside. God, I hope you're listening. Please hurry!" I repeated the message two more times, then I hung up the phone.

I left a similar message at the sheriff's office, then hung up the phone again. I stumbled out the front door. My hands were shaking and I felt my heart still beating rapidly. Halfway down the mortuary driveway, I saw Dan Smith running up the slight incline. I guessed he was breathless by the way his chest heaved up and down rapidly.

"What's going on? I got your phone call! What the hell's up?"

I looked at him. "Dan, where have you been? What have you been doing the past—" I checked my watch— God, two hours "—the past two hours?"

"Your hands are shaking. You're bleeding! Connor, what's going on—"

"Please, Dan, just answer. Where were you?"

He shrugged his now familiar one-shouldered shrug. "I don't know. I . . . let's see. I cleaned up Boone's office, switched on his little TV and watched some Hitchcock movie. They've been running them all week. *North by Northwest*. Had some microwave popcorn. Started to doze off. Then you called."

I leaned into him, trying to smell his breath. But I must have given him the wrong impression, because he took my shoulders and pulled me closer. He kissed me.

The kiss lasted a little longer than strictly necessary for my scientific purposes. But you gotta do what you gotta do.

"Popcorn," I said, and smacked my lips.

Dan frowned. "That's all you can say?"

"You taste like popcorn. And you smell like popcorn."

"You got a problem with popcorn? I could change to potato chips. Chew some Dentyne. Gargle a little Brut."

I laughed. "No, you taste just fine. I mean—" I'm sure I blushed. I could feel the tingling on my chest and neck as heat fanned out like a spreading virus.

He tried to stifle a grin but couldn't quite manage it. I

took his hands and lifted them up to my face, then took a big whiff. They smelled like popcorn, too. With butter. And salt. And a hint of pine-scented soap. He must have thought I had some kind of hand fetish. He might have been right. Hands are as expressive as faces to me.

"So what's all this about?" he asked, not letting go of my hands when I tried to release him.

I explained my recent adventure, and the last thing I remembered before I awoke in the casket—the smell of mint and chemicals.

"God, Connor! So you thought I might have . . ." Dan let go of my hands as he trailed off.

"No, of course not," I said a bit too quickly. "But I had to rule you out, you know, just to be sure."

"Connor . . . don't you know me yet?" He lifted my scraped and bloody hand and stroked the back of it gently.

I said nothing. I didn't know him any better than I knew anyone else in this town. But he didn't smell like Tic Tacs or chloroform, so I figured he must not have been the one who locked me into Edgar Allan Poe's nightmare.

We stopped by the sheriff's office to make a report, but only the dispatcher was in. For some reason she hadn't received my message, so I left a note for the sheriff to call me at home. Dan and I walked back to the hotel. I washed off the blood in the hall bathroom while Dan waited in my office. When I returned, he was glancing around at my books and posters and comic books.

"Nice place you got here." He pulled out a copy of Robert Louis Stevenson's *The Strange Case of Dr. Jekyll and Mr. Hyde*.

I wasn't interested in small talk. "Whoever did this had to have had a key to my diner. It was locked up tight—I'm sure of it. The odd thing is, whoever it was could have killed me right away, but didn't. So why was I locked up in that coffin?"

"You probably would have suffocated in there eventually," Dan said.

I gathered my thoughts for a moment. "Everything points to the mortuary. The casket, the trocar, the death of a man married to three widows who used Memory Kingdom for their dead husbands' services."

Dan put the book back on the shelf and sat down in the chair opposite my desk.

"Maybe someone wanted to scare you."

"Why? What have I done?"

"Maybe they don't want you writing anything in your newspaper. Maybe you're too nosy. And maybe you're onto something and the killer knows it, even if you don't."

"But I'm not! I don't know anything! I don't know who killed Lacy or James Russell. I don't know who may have killed your brother, or who pushed Sluice into that hole, or who tried to suffocate me! I don't know a thing!" I was confused and angry, but also on the verge of tears.

To keep from crying—and to release some of my anger—I slammed my hand down on the desk, which was a mistake. The impact caused a newly formed scab to break open, and my hand started bleeding again. I grabbed a rumpled paper napkin lying on my desk and stanched the bleeding wound. At least my poison oak wasn't itching, I thought, as the porous paper filled with blood.

And then, watching the paper napkin slowly change from white to red, it came to me. I did know something after all. Actually, I knew plenty. All I had to do was come up with a way to prove it.

Memory Kingdom might have been a gold mine for some. The *Eureka!* was my gold mine of opportunity.

It was getting late—only a few hours until my newspaper deadline—when I opened the file to the lead story that was supposed to run in the morning and keyed in a fresh headline.

IDENTITY OF LACY PENZANCE'S KILLER REVEALED!

I should study the tabloids more. I began typing:

Lacy Penzance, found dead early Tuesday morning with a stab wound in her chest, was not a suicide as originally reported by the *Mother Lode Monitor.*

Sheriff Elvis Mercer is now calling Penzance's death a homicide. The murder weapon was discovered to be a trocar, a mortuary tool used in embalming the dead.

After a lengthy and thorough investigation by

the sheriff's department, the unidentified killer remains at large.

The suspect may also be responsible for the slaying of James Russell, a transient who resided temporarily at the Mark Twain Slept Here Bed-and-Breakfast Inn, owned by Beau Pascal. Russell was found Thursday, also dead from a chest wound, made by an antique mining pick. Further details are being withheld pending the investigation.

A recent anonymous note sent to the offices of the *Eureka!* late last night has provided important information regarding the killer's identity. A lost journal written by the late Ms. Penzance just before her death indicates—"

And that's all she wrote.

It was a cheap journalistic shot, but it just might work. I faxed the new edition to the printing office in Whiskey Slide and had them substitute it for the frog fluff that was about to go to press. The paper would be ready at the crack of dawn and all over town by breakfast. There was nothing left to do but go home to bed, and hope I didn't have any more unexpected company.

I thought about stopping by Dan's office to see if he wanted to sleep on my couch for a change, but decided I was being paranoid. I wasn't going to let the night stalker take over my life.

Then again, maybe that wasn't it at all. Maybe it had more to do with Dan than any intruder. Still, I wasn't ready for Dan's further intrusion either. I was used to my life the way it was—alone. I didn't want any entanglements. Attraction was nothing more than a hormonal imbalance—wasn't that what someone had recently said?

But Dan, either reading my mind—or hearing my footsteps—caught me as I headed for the stairs and insisted on escorting me home.

"Look, Connor. You've had two break-ins, an attempt on your life. You're either staying here with me tonight on the couch, or I'm going home with you to check the place out."

I didn't argue. In truth, I found myself surprisingly relieved. Dan drove me home in his Bronco. I unlocked the door to an exuberant Casper, who licked me and everything else she encountered in her excitement. I had been worried about her and was anxious to see if she was all right.

"Hi, girl!" I gave her the full welcome, letting her slurp the makeup, dirt, and sweat from my face. "You're okay, huh? What did they do to you, Casper girl? Huh? What happened?"

Casper said a bunch of things I couldn't understand. Her lips were extremely difficult to read. But I gathered from her body language that she was fine, damn glad to see me, and eager for a midnight snack.

While I searched the expansive short-order kitchen for something edible, Dan took a look around the diner and my living quarters in the back. "Find anything?" I called out, while locating my treasured but mismatched Fiesta bowls. I pulled down a rose, a yellow, and a turquoise.

"All clear," Dan said, after reentering the kitchen. He slid into one of the newly upholstered vinyl seats and rested his arms on the back of the booth. Casper leapt up next to him. I signaled for her to get down and set a bowl of cereal on the floor for her. I set one on the table for Dan and joined him at the booth.

Dan didn't comment on my unusual living quarters, just glanced at the decor between mouthfuls of Corn Pops. When we finished, he followed me into the back living space.

"Interesting place you have here," he finally said, rifling through a half-dozen comics that lay on one of the blond wood end tables. "*Crusader Rabbit. Heckle and Jeckle. Richie Rich.* I remember him. Got any *Green Hornet*?"

"No, that's a guy comic. I like girl comics. *Lulu, Little Audrey, Little Lotta, Katy Keene, Betty and Veronica.*"

"I used to read *Archie*, until I discovered *Slime Monsters from Planet Zero*, and *Pond Scum Man*, and *It Came From the Frozen Tundra*."

"You're joking, right? I never heard of them."

He smiled.

I yawned.

"Sorry. Am I keeping you up?"

"No, no. It's been a day, you know? I think it's catching up with me."

"Yeah, all right. I, uh, I better get going. I'll see you tomorrow." He looked at the couch then at me.

"Thanks for taking me home."

I walked him to the door. He hesitated for a moment, looking at his shoes, then glanced up at me, reached out, and took my brushed and swollen hand for a brief moment. "You going to be all right? I don't like leaving you alone."

I hoped to distract him from the full blush that had enveloped my body. He started to lean in but I turned away. He stepped back.

"I—" What could I say? I wasn't ready? I didn't want to get involved? I didn't know him well enough? What other excuses could I come up with?

He patted my hand. "I'll see you tomorrow."

I pressed my lips together as he stepped out. I closed the door behind him. My hands trembled as I reached out to bolt the new locks.

After securing the diner, I pulled off my rumpled clothes and lead-weight Doc Martens, slipped into silk boxers and my oversized T-shirt with a night sky that glowed in the dark, and tried to fall asleep. I tossed for over an hour before pirates—who all looked like Dan— carted me off to their island hideaway.

By eight A.M. the *Eureka!* was all over Flat Skunk and the rest of the Mother Lode chain like a bad odor. My lead story was the topic of conversation on everyone's lips at the Nugget—at least the lips I could read. And everyone was complaining.

"What happened to your newspaper?" French asked, as I entered the café. He held it up for me to see. "Printing problems?"

"What?" I asked, taking the paper from him. The lead

story and slug looked great. But the story ended abruptly with a recipe for frog's legs in pesto sauce.

"Oh, my God! They mixed up the stories! Where's the rest of the article?"

I scanned the front page frantically, looking for answers to the horrendous mistake.

I should have gotten an Oscar for that performance.

"Goddammit! Idiots. Great. Now I'm going to have to run the story again tomorrow, with the right copy. The biggest story of my career. Shit!"

French chuckled as he retrieved his paper from my hands. I sat down in an empty seat and read over a copy that had been left by the previous diner, pretending to steam over the ineptitude of my printer.

But it had turned out perfectly.

In a few minutes Dan entered the café and joined me. He barely managed not to laugh at the newspaper error.

"Goofed, huh?" he said simply while Jilda poured his coffee. I gave him a flat smile. I was about to order a bagel when Mickey burst in looking excited and flushed. "Connor! There you are!"

He came over to our table and sat down next to me, opposite Dan. He turned to face me. "Great headline! It sounds like you got a lead on who killed Lacy Penzance. What happened to the rest of the story?"

"The printer screwed up. I can't confirm it yet, but—" I leaned in toward Mickey. "Someone sent me an anonymous note about one of Lacy's journals that's been missing. I think it's the key to everything. I'm going to have to redo the paper and print another issue tomorrow with the corrections. And the new information. But it's going to cost me."

"What does it say about the journal? Does the sheriff know?"

"Actually I don't know. Not yet, anyway. I won't be able to get it until tonight. At least, that's what the note said. This was all supposed to be in the paper." I hoped I sounded exasperated.

"Connor, if you're withholding important evidence, you really need to turn it over to me or the sheriff."

I looked around the café to see if anyone was paying attention to us. Unlike myself, everyone was minding their own business. I spoke what I hoped was softly.

"I honestly don't have anything yet, Mickey. But I should, soon. The story was only a teaser. I was planning to do a follow-up tomorrow."

"Trying to sell newspapers, eh? Sounds risky, Connor." Mickey nodded slowly, putting the new pieces to the puzzle together while picking at the dried poison oak scab on his arm. It made me itch, and I rubbed at my own drying patch.

"So where did you get this latest information?" Mickey asked.

"Uh, it came in over the TTY. I don't even know who made the call."

"Damn!" he said.

Dan signaled Jilda for more coffee. I had almost forgotten he was there.

"Mickey, you know Dan Smith?"

Mickey puffed up his chest. "You're Boone's brother."

Dan glanced at me, then back at Mickey, who said nothing more about Boone. Had Dan not notified the sheriff of his brother's death as he said he had?

"You staying in town for a while?"

"Don't know yet."

The deputy narrowed his eyes. "Don't suppose you knew that fellow who was killed over at the Mark Twain? Name of Russell?"

Dan shook his head.

"Funny. We found a fingerprint there on a piece of paper. Identification just came back. Can't say much about it, but it might be a good idea if you didn't leave town for while, Mr. Smith." He emphasized the "Smith."

Before I could sputter anything coherent, Mickey stood.

"Well, I gotta run. Things are coming to a head on our side, too. How about that raincheck, Connor? See you tonight? Maybe we can figure all this out over pizza and beer."

I nodded vaguely. My mind had suddenly been distracted.

"I'll call you," he may have said before he left.

Dan and I were back at my office before we continued our conversation.

"Dan, I thought you told the sheriff about your brother," I said accusingly. I was getting tired of Dan's mystery.

"I said I called the sheriff. He already knew about Boone—at least, he knew about the floater in Rio Vista. I just didn't mention I knew the ID."

"Why in God's name not?"

He shrugged that now irritating shrug of his. "I wanted to see what played out. I didn't figure it would do any good at that point. Besides, I wanted to do some investigating on my own." Dan sat down across from my desk. I remained standing, arms crossed, brows knitted. It was my toughest look.

"And what about those prints Mickey was referring to?"

He leaned back in the chair and folded his hands across his chest. "I have no idea. I was never there. I didn't even know the guy."

"That first day I met you, I had a napkin with my mystery notes on it. I went next door to see Boone, but you were there instead. Do you remember it?"

"No."

I mentally retraced my steps. "I had it with me when I came back to the office. I remember stuffing it in my bag when I left the café. I brought it back here . . . and started to work on it . . . then Lacy came in . . ."

I had been talking to myself out loud. It surprised me when Dan responded, "Lacy took it?"

I didn't answer but bent over the trash can and retrieved a blood-soaked paper from the bottom. It wasn't the mystery napkin. But the pieces were slowly coming together. I had been wrong, very wrong, in my hunch about who murdered Lacy Penzance.

"Dan, I've got some work to do. Do you mind if we talk later?"

Dan picked up on the chill in the room and stood. He looked puzzled or maybe a little hurt, but said only, "All right. See you later, then."

I didn't like being rude, but I had some sorting out to do before I could pull off my new plan. I spent the whole day working on it, giving Miah the duty of taking phone calls from curious readers wanting to know more about the missing part of the article or the rest of the frog recipe that had been cut off. I didn't mention my plan to him either.

At around four-thirty P.M. the phone light lit up once again and blinked. This time Miah heard the white noise of the TTY and set the receiver on the intake cradle.

"TTY," he signed. I stopped what I was doing and waited for the log-on, but no name appeared. I watched the message move across the screen. It read simply:

"deadline"

The word flickered off as the line went dead.

I set down the receiver and chewed the inside of my cheek. My heart was racing as I pondered the message that had just flickered to darkness on my TTY screen. What was it supposed to mean? And who was the messenger?

A few more pieces fell into place.

I lifted the phone to dial the sheriff, then abruptly hung up.

"Miah, you listen to music. Do you ever make your own tapes?"

"All the time. Why?" he signed.

"Would you do me a favor?"

"What?"

"Make a tape for me?"

He looked puzzled. "Yeah, but why?"

In lieu of an answer I gave him instructions for what I wanted, then headed for the office next door.

"Sheriff? It's Connor. GA," I typed when I returned a few moments later.

"HEy Connor. WHat's up?"

I waited for the GA, then gave up.

"Did you get my message about the mortuary? GA."

"YEah, Connor. What's going on? WHat happened?"

"I don't know. Someone . . ." I paused. It seemed a little incredible retelling it. "Someone was in my house again. They knocked me out and locked me in a casket. At the mortuary. And just now I had a phone call. Someone's . . ." I thought for a moment, wondering how all this was coming across on the TTY. ". . . threatening me. I think they want me to butt out of the Lacy Penzance business. GA."

"A casket? You serious? Why didn't you call me?"

"I am! Now! GA."

"Maybe buting out is a graet idea, COnnor. YOu say were run off the road. YOur house was broken into—twice. NOw you say yuo were shut up in a casket and youre getting threatening phone calls. IM gettting complaints about you from the folks over at MEmory Kingdom, not to mention the penzance maid who says someone stopped by posing as an insurance agent—and it sounded a lot like you. I dont know what to do with you CONnnor? That newspaper story you wrote. Whta's that crap aabout? GA."

"Nothing, Sheriff. A mistake. I really don't know anything. Not yet anyway. GA."

"YOu must be involved somehow CW. And you could very well be in serious danger if you dont watch it. I CAn only doo so much you know."

"OK, Sheriff. Is Mickey there by any chance? I'm supposed to meet with him tonight. GA."

"HE tried to call you but yuor line was busy. SAid he was going to stop by your office on his way to the mortuary."

"Is he checking out that missing jewelry? GA."

"CoOnnor!"

"Sheriff, about that fingerprint on the paper you found at the inn. Whose was it? GA."

"SOrry Connor but I can't give you that information yet. Not until we're ready to make an arrest GA."

"Will you let me know as soon as you can? GA. SK."

"WAtch yourself, COnnor. I mean it. We got a killer

running around, and it looks like he's got your number. You got somewhere to sleep for the next few days, cause Id recommend it. GA. SK."

I lied and said I did, then hung up the phone and twirled around in my chair for a few moments until I made myself dizzy. I turned slowly to look out the window. Mickey was walking up the street toward my building, applying Chapstick to his lips.

I watched him until he reached the hotel and turned the corner toward the stairwell. Searching through a file folder, I found the journal I'd lifted from Lacy's stash and opened it on my desk.

The door light flashed. I yelled, "Come in," and Mickey opened the door, wearing one of those embarrassed grins he couldn't seem to shake when he was around me.

"Hi, Connor. Is this a good—"

He stopped and looked at the journal, his eyes widening. I closed it and rested my hand on top.

"Is that—" He didn't finish his sentence.

"No, it's one of her old ones, not the one that's been missing."

Mickey gave me a suspicious look. "Connor, did you steal that from Lacy's place?"

"No, I just borrowed it. It's given me an idea."

I explained part of my plan to the deputy. He nodded every few moments, encouraging me to go on. When I finished, he gave me a big open-mouthed grin.

"Go for it—only don't tell the sheriff I know anything about it if you get caught. I could get into big trouble if he finds out."

While Mickey waited for me downstairs, I locked up my office, and stopped first by Miah's shop to check on his progress with my request, and then Dan's office to see about a couple of things. I walked with Mickey across the street to the Nugget. The place was packed for the Saturday night special: meat loaf and gravy, peas, and raspberry Jell-O. We sat in a booth in the middle of the café, ordered a couple of BLT's and slices of boysenberry pie, and I pulled out the journal.

No one paid much attention.

"I think you may be interested in this, Mickey," I said a little too loudly. Heads begun to turn. "Someone dropped it by the newspaper office anonymously. I think it contains some information you might need."

"What is it?" Mickey said, feigning interest. He could have used a few acting lessons from Celeste, but his performance would do for our amateur production.

"It's Lacy Penzance's missing journal. It tells just about everything she was involved in right before she died."

The room went still. I assumed the phrase, "You could hear a pin drop," would have been appropriate.

Mickey pretended to read a few excerpts to himself, then looked up. "Whoa, there are a lot of familiar names in this thing." He glanced around the café at the patrons: Wolf, who sat alone; Beau, who was gossiping with Rebecca Matthews, the dispatcher; French, without Celeste; Croaky Wheeler with a client I didn't recognize; Sluice at the counter, and Jilda behind it.

"Even that guy who was killed at the Mark Twain is mentioned in here. Thanks, Connor. This looks like the break we've been waiting for!"

I glanced around at the attention Mickey had garnered; there was a mixture of reactions. Wolf looked angrier than his usual scowl. French just seemed dumbfounded. Beau blinked a few extra times. Croaky checked out everyone else. Jilda reacted with exaggerated surprise—you could tell by the eyebrows. And Sluice gave another one of his deer-caught-in-the-headlights stares.

Mickey slammed the journal shut, looking very official and serious. "I'm going to have to take this to the sheriff and—"

He stopped midsentence. I didn't know why for a second—I thought everything was going so well. But he looked abruptly at Jilda who seemed to have called his attention. I saw the object of his interest: Jilda was holding up the receiver of the café's telephone.

Mickey moved over to the phone, the journal clutched tightly in his hand, and took the call.

"Deputy Arnold," Mickey said. In a matter of seconds his face lost its color. Tiny beads of sweat glistened on his forehead like miniature diamonds. He hung up the phone, and, without saying another word, wiped his brow with the back of his hand. He glanced up at the diner patrons who were staring at him intently and began to stammer.

"There's ... been an emergency. I've got to go. Everyone—just stay put!"

Mickey carried the journal on his way toward the door. I jumped quickly to my feet.

"Mickey, what is it?"

Mickey stopped and pointed a finger at me like I was a little kid. "Stay here, Connor. I'll be right back. Do what you can to keep them all here. I'll explain later."

I'd never seen him looking so distressed.

Deputy Arnold fled the Nugget, leaving the meat-loaf gourmets with mouthfuls of half-eaten food.

"Okay, you heard the deputy. Just stay put," I repeated Mickey's words to the group of onlookers with the authority vested in me.

Then I followed right behind him out the door.

Not wanting to upset Mickey by deliberately disobeying him—at least, not wanting him to know—I kept my distance as he headed for the sheriff's office to get his patrol car. I backtracked to the Penzance Hotel, unlocked my bike, stepped just out of sight, and waited.

In a few moments Mickey was driving down Main, and I was more or less behind him, pedaling like an Olympic contender. I followed him at some distance to Gold Dust Street. He turned down a pockmarked road, which was difficult to maneuver on my bike in the dimming light of sunset. We passed by tiny clapboard homes built decades earlier, unfenced and unlandscaped, with postage-stamp lawns, overgrown flower gardens, relentless weeds, and rusted cars.

I had never been to Mickey's place, but I figured that's where we were headed. The cabin-sized house was located two blocks down the road, framed by an easy-care rock garden. On the front porch stood a disassembled Harley

Davidson motorcycle, apparently Mickey's hobby during his time off. It hardly fit his image, but maybe that's why it appealed to him. I watched as he leapt out of the car without closing the door. Jamming his key in the front door lock, he entered the house, again leaving the door wide open behind him.

The man was in a hurry.

I moved behind a nearby shed and waited for Mickey to return. It was growing dark and getting cool. I wouldn't be able to see him well or keep up with him if he went any great distance. And I was sure this wasn't his final destination. Otherwise he would have closed the doors.

What was he doing in there?

I propped up the bike, stepped over to the front window and peeked in. No Mickey. I scanned the tiny living room. The coffee table was filled with police journals, crime books, and gun magazines. On the wall hung a variety of weapons and police paraphernalia: antique handcuffs, a billy club, a collection of bullets, and a historic gun display.

On the mantel above the fireplace was a picture of Mickey fresh out of police academy, looking puffed and proud in his new khaki uniform. Next to his picture were framed snapshots of well-known police officers who had made names for themselves over the years: Serpico, Joseph McNamara, Daryl Gates, Napoleon Hendrix—all in uniform, and all signed "To Mickey."

I didn't want to get caught—I knew I wouldn't hear him coming—so I ducked out of the way and waited until he appeared at the door. After a few moments, panting and moving quickly, Mickey came through the door holding a key ring in one hand and the journal in the other. He quickly ran back to the car, tossing the journal onto the car seat.

I waited until he'd driven past me, then emerged from the growing darkness and rode the few blocks back to Main Street hoping I could keep up. If he was headed out of town, I wouldn't have a chance.

But he wasn't. Abruptly he turned into the driveway of Memory Kingdom Mortuary.

The mortuary. It had begun here. I had a feeling it would end here.

Mickey had already gone through the front doors when I arrived. Had French left the doors unlocked? Was Celeste working late? I slipped in cautiously, flashing for a moment on my recent incarceration.

There didn't appear to be anyone around. A couple of night-lights in the main entrance had been turned on, but the offices were dark, the blinds drawn.

The light in Celeste's office flickered on.

I ducked into an alcove and waited. Nothing. I took another step forward in the dim light, hoping to peek through a gap in the blinds without being noticed, when Mickey stepped out of the room, his hand on his gun belt, ready to draw and shoot. He looked very surprised to see me.

"For God's sake, Connor! What are you doing here?" Mickey held the journal in one hand; his key ring was bulging in his pocket.

"I . . . I was worried. You left so suddenly and looked upset. I . . . wanted to make sure you were all right."

Mickey's eyebrows pinched. He seemed agitated, rubbing his thumb over the edge of the journal and shifting his weight from leg to leg.

"Did something happen? Was that the sheriff on the phone at the café—"

He turned away suddenly, and I stopped talking. He was looking at Celeste's phone. And he didn't appear pleased.

"Mickey, what's wrong?"

He looked at me, then at the telephone again. The color seemed to drain from his face a second time.

"Is it the phone?"

He looked at me puzzled, then his face relaxed. "No! No, I'm just trying to think. Connor, it isn't safe for you to be here—"

Abruptly he turned his attention back to the phone. Again his face grew paler, and his forehead was sprinkled with diamonds of sweat.

The light on the answering machine began to blink.

Mickey was listening to a message.

The message machine light changed from a red blinking dot to the number "1."

Mickey looked back at me, his face masked in terror. He stared at me for several seconds, as if trying to read my expression.

He jumped, startled by something, and turned sharply toward the metal filing cabinet. His panic-stricken face looked as if it might break from the strain.

"Mickey, what's going on?" I demanded. The change in him was beginning to scare me.

"Nothing, Connor. Sit down. Don't move. There . . . may be a prowler in here. I'm going to check it out. Stay here, Connor. I mean it. This could be . . . dangerous."

He spoke slowly, using exaggerated lip movements, as if I were retarded, not deaf. I obeyed orders and sat down on Celeste's guest chair. Mickey left the room, one hand on his gun, the journal still clutched in the other hand.

There was something about the journal that bothered me. There wasn't anything truly useful in the thing. I had made up that stuff about revealing names and gaining information. And Mickey knew that when he helped me with the scene at the Nugget.

But that was it: He wasn't clutching the journal I had given him. Each journal Lacy owned had been a different shade in the pink and purple hues. That one had been, what, pale pink? This one was lavender. Mickey had found the missing journal!

When I had given him enough time to get several steps away, I moved to the metal closet Mickey had looked at with such terror, and tried the door. Had he found the journal inside Celeste's cabinet? Locked. I jiggled the handle a few more times, thinking it might open magically if I jerked it enough. Nothing.

I was about to take my hand off the knob when I felt something vibrate from inside. I placed my hand on the metal cabinet door. It hummed beneath my fingertips intermittently. Was it catching the vibrations of the air conditioning and heating? Trucks passing by? An airplane overhead?

Or something inside.

I needed a key.

I yanked open Celeste's desk drawer, checking the obvious hiding place. Nothing inside but some business cards, a few candies, and a half-used container of lipstick. Tropical Sunset. No key.

The key! That was it.

I had to find Mickey.

After a quick search of the main halls, I pushed open the door to the embalming room. Mickey stood next to a steel table, his back to me. He had set the journal down on the instrument table and was holding something else in his hand—

I must have made a sound because he whirled around with a terrified look on his doughy face.

"Mickey! I was getting scared and . . ."

He raised his hand. The thing he was holding, long and sharp and shiny, was glinting ominously off the room's dim lighting. He raised it higher.

A scalpel.

"Connor," Mickey said, shaking his head. "For God's sakes, I told you to stay put. You shouldn't have followed me here, not from the café, and not from the other room."

He took a step forward. I took a step backward.

"I didn't want you involved in this, Connor. That's why I told you to stop snooping around. Things are much more dangerous than you realize. I tried to warn you, Connor. Don't you understand?" It was difficult to read his face in the shadowy light. Was that a look of helplessness? Desperation? Or was that fear?

He took another step forward. I took another step back and hit the edge of the door. It swung shut.

"I wanted to help you with your newspaper stories, especially the murders, so you could make the *Eureka!* the newspaper you really want it to be. See, I understand you, Connor."

Mickey's face became a kaleidoscope of emotion. The look of alarm changed to compassion, to eagerness, to empathy, all within seconds. I tried to mask my own feelings of growing terror. I reached behind me, felt for the doorknob, slowly twisted it, and inched the door open.

"You could have helped me, too, Connor. Helped me get some credit for all the work I do to make this a safer place to live. I've done a lot for this town, but nobody knows that. I wanted you to know, so you'd understand me."

I almost felt sorry for him, he looked so vulnerable. But the scalpel in his raised hand reminded me constantly that this was no victim I was dealing with, and it scared the shit out of me. I hadn't made much progress with the door. Mickey stood only a few inches away. I noticed, with more than a little trepidation, that he was referring to me in the past tense. He definitely had something on his mind.

I knew there was no reasoning with him. He had already killed two people—maybe more. It was all part of his plan: Mickey Arnold wanted to be Super Cop.

Mickey moved in slowly, his face twisted into a look of barely controlled benevolence, as if I were a runaway rabbit he was cautiously trying to recapture, then have for dinner. With the door opened slightly, I turned to run, but he grabbed my wrist and yanked me back abruptly.

"Easy, Connor. You're with me now. We'll go to Celeste's office together. I want to show you something." His grip tightened with every word. Out of the corner of my eye I could see him caress the back edge of the scalpel with his thumb. There was a hint of mint.

I screamed, hoping someone might hear me.

Mickey just smiled. He must have known there was nobody at the mortuary but the two of us—among a couple of embalmed bodies. Holding the back of my hair, he pushed open the door and forced me down the hall to Celeste's office. There's something about a death grip on your hair that keeps you from doing much struggling.

Once inside the office, he closed the door and pressed me to the floor, next to Celeste's desk. The small lamp on the desk cast the room in a ghostly glow.

I sat up carefully as Mickey dropped into a chair opposite me. I looked at him while scanning the room with my peripheral vision. The lamp cord was only a few inches from my hand.

"You know that Smith guy, Connor?"

I inched my hand toward the cord, distracting him with my other hand by brushing my hair out of my face.

"He wasn't your type," he said with a chilling smile that set my skin tingling.

A few more inches. I desperately fluffed my hair.

"I found out some things about him and I had to—"

With a swift swing of my arm, I yanked the plug from the socket. The room went dark. I reached for the lamp, made contact, and threw it across the room to where I hoped Mickey would still be sitting.

I didn't know if I'd struck him or not. The room was pitch black and neither of us could see a thing. But he still had the advantage; he could hear.

I scooted under the desk, feeling my way, trying to figure out how to get out of the room without traveling by casket. I had to distract him if I wanted to get to the door, I thought, then bumped my head on the underside of the desk. Shit! I felt my hearing aid dangle out of my ear and fall.

My hearing aid! I searched the area around me, running my hand across the floor, and found it under my left thigh. I felt for the tiny volume control dial and turned it up full blast. Counting on the ear-piercing squeal that so irritated my hearing friends, I set it down on the floor and backed out quickly from beneath the desk. I hoped the screech would lead him to believe I was still there. If he didn't buy it, I was in more trouble than I counted on.

I scooted away in the darkness, not knowing where Mickey was or what condition he was in. Crawling around the edge of the room, I felt my way, terrified I'd bump into him.

If the lamp hadn't hit him, the hearing aid would probably only distract him for a few moments. Once he found I wasn't where he thought I was, he'd waste no time going for the door. And once opened, it would fill the room with light. If I didn't make it to the door by then, I wouldn't have a chance.

I kept inching along the wall, hoping I was quiet. It was an eternity before I reached the door frame. Moving in slow motion, I felt for the knob. A few more seconds and I'd be out of there. I turned the knob slowly—

Something stung my right ear. I touched it—it felt wet and sticky—and numb. Mickey had thrown something at me and narrowly missed. I didn't want to think what it might have been. I felt a drop of sweat run down my back. How did he know where I was?

My right foot was abruptly pulled from beneath me. I grabbed for the doorknob to keep from being swallowed up by Mickey's strength but I lost my balance and fell. Bracing my back against the door, I tried to kick him with my other foot, flailing blindly in the dark. Good old five-pound Doc Martens. The shoes carry quite a punch when they make contact. I managed to get off one good kick before I grabbed once again.

As Mickey tried to wrestle me to the floor, I reached out for the doorknob again and gave it a twist. The door opened slightly; light from the hallway filtered into the room.

Mickey had my foot in one hand and seemed to be scrambling on the floor with his other hand, likely searching for what he had thrown. I kicked and screamed, heaving the full impact of my Doc Martens into his contorted face. Suddenly he let go. In stunned pain, he covered his face, then wiped the increasing flow of blood from his nose.

He pulled his hands down and I could read his lips easily; they were outlined in red. "You ungrateful bitch!"

I scrambled for the door but he lunged, grabbed my arm and slammed me against the metal cabinet, knocking the wind out. I couldn't breathe for several seconds— enough time for Mickey to reach into his pocket for something: his keys. Quickly he fumbled for the one he wanted. As blood dripped down his face and onto his hand, he opened the metal closet.

Out tumbled Celeste, unconscious.

"And now for the big finale. Let's see, Connor. How

about this for a mystery puzzle? Celeste stabs you with the scalpel. And then she slits her wrists. I discover the bodies, realize who the murderer is . . . then I call the sheriff and wait for the TV cameras to arrive. Guess we'll have to forget about the local coverage. You won't be in any position to write a good story. But that's all right. I expect to make the *Sacramento Bee* this time."

Mickey raised Celeste's arm, about to drag the scalpel over her wrist, when I kicked the office door shut, dousing the lights once again. I felt for Celeste's guest chair where I'd seen it last, picked it up, and flung it in the general direction of where Mickey had stood. I had no idea if I'd made contact.

I scooted away from the door so Mickey wouldn't know my location, and groped for the phone on the desk. Fully aware I had very little time I removed the receiver. By feel, I punched what I hoped were the numbers 911, hoping the buttons made no sound, then left it off the hook. No need to say anything. If I had dialed correctly, they would hear the disturbance through the receiver and read the automatic location on the screen.

Except, I remembered, the dispatcher was at the café having dinner. Would the sheriff be there to take the call?

I couldn't wait around. Mickey would be finished with his plan long before the sheriff arrived. And ready to take the credit.

Scrambling on my hands and knees, I reached the door, which was now blocked. Celeste's body. I gave her a shove and rolled her over, then grabbed for the doorknob and opened the door as far as I could. It would only budge a couple of inches.

I looked behind me. Mickey's bloody, distorted face glowed in the eerie light. I gave Celeste another shove with my foot and squeezed through the door as Mickey leapt up in an adrenaline rage. I snatched the door handle and pulled the door shut behind me. It closed hard on Mickey's hand.

The scalpel he'd retrieved from the wall dropped to the floor at my feet. Quickly I scooped it up. As he reached out to grab me, I plunged the scalpel forward, ramming it through Mickey's already bloody hand.

I didn't wait to see his reaction. I took off down the hall, through the front door of the mortuary, down the driveway, to the dark street, and smack into what felt like a brick wall. Reeling back from the impact, I bent over to catch my breath, then straightened.

"Dan!"

I may be deaf but I ain't dumb.

I hate those women in movies who suspect there's something down in the dark basement and go investigate when they know there's a serial killer loose in the neighborhood.

I refuse to be that stupid.

I don't go places where I think murderers might be lurking—at least not without telling someone first. And I try to make sure backup is right behind me.

Only this time, there must have been a slip-up.

"Where the hell have you been?!" I flung the words out between gasps. "I was about to end up on display at the next funeral party!" Puff, puff. "I thought you were right behind me!" Wheeze.

"I lost you!" Dan said, throwing his arms in the air. "When you and Mickey—"

In the corner of my eye I caught Sheriff Mercer's car approaching up the road. I turned to flag him down, losing the rest of Dan's explanation. Breathlessly I explained to the sheriff what happened and told him to send for an ambulance for Celeste—and Mickey. I watched him pull out the car radio as he sped up the driveway. Dan and I followed him on foot.

"So, where in God's name were you?" I said, remembering my irritation as we approached the sheriff's car. "I was all alone up there! He was going to kill me and make it look like Celeste did it, then do her in a fake suicide. You were supposed to be right there!"

Dan looked helpless and a little frantic. "I don't know! You two must have left the café right after I placed that call to the deputy. I waited outside for a while but you never came out. When I finally looked inside, you were gone, and nobody could tell me where you went. So I went looking for you—not an easy task."

When I had stopped by earlier in the evening, just before going to the café with Mickey, I had told Dan about my plan; for several reasons, I was fairly certain the deputy was the one who killed Lacy, as well as the guy at the bed-and-breakfast inn. Dan had helped me make a copy of Lacy's voice taken from her telephone answering machine. Miah had spliced it together with his recording equipment—he's got all the latest stuff that young guys have to have these days just to get by: CD player, boom box, double cassette recorders, digital sound, speakers the size of small apartment buildings. We had him doctor the tape to say: "This is Lacy Penzance. I'd like to talk with you. It's important."

Apparently the quality wasn't bad. When Dan called the café and played the tape over the phone for Mickey, the result was just what I'd hoped for: panic. Of course, Mickey's no dummy, either. I don't imagine he thought for one moment that Lacy had risen from the grave. But he knew that someone was onto him. He just didn't know who.

"You didn't hear me screaming?"

"Not until you got to the street. I'd already been to the sheriff's office, your office, Mickey's place, and back to the café. I didn't know where to go next."

Outside the mortuary we found the sheriff's abandoned car, lights flashing, door open, exhaust spewing from the tailpipe. Dan stopped a few feet from the mortuary door and turned to face me.

"Are you all right?" Dan took my still shaking hands into his own. "Your hands are trembling," he said, caressing them lightly. If he didn't stop, my hands might never stop shaking.

Still wired from the excitement, I pulled my hands from his and searched the visible parts of my body for new bruises, peering through torn and disheveled clothing. I counted four major injuries: One on each shin where I'd bumped into Celeste's desk on my way out the door. One on my arm where Mickey had held me a little too tightly. And I felt one on my temple where he'd slammed me to the floor. I also had a skin burn, some fingernail scratches on my ankle, a bloody ear, and a lump on the top of my head where I'd hit the desk. I was actually kind of proud of all my injuries. They beat that wimpy old poison oak.

"I'm fine, really. Just a little shaky. A few nicks here and there. I guess things didn't go exactly as I planned."

"No kidding," Dan agreed, taking my hands again and massaging them gently.

"God, when you called Mickey at the café and played that tape of Lacy's voice, he completely freaked."

Dan grinned. "So the phone call worked?"

"I guess hearing her voice disoriented him enough to make him scramble for the journal he'd hidden at home. He had it with him when he arrived here at the mortuary."

"Did you see anything at his house?" Dan asked.

"Only what I could see from the window: a bunch of police fanatic stuff. But he had this massive brass ring, loaded with all kinds of keys." My forehead ached. The rest of my bruises began to throb in support.

An ambulance drove up and parked next to the sheriff's car. The two paramedics I'd seen hoisting Sluice out of the open grave ran past us with medical bags and a stretcher.

"There's a woman in there. I don't know if she's—"

"We better keep out of the way," Dan said, pulling me aside as I started to follow them in. He was right.

"God, Celeste—"

"You said you thought Mickey probably got Lacy's keys when her purse fell open, that day they crashed into each other at the Nugget. Do you think he planned that little encounter?" Dan asked, distracting me from my frustration at not being able to do anything more.

"It's possible. It's also possible he already had copies of her keys. Making copies of everyone's keys was part of his master plan to clean up the neighborhood."

"What about your keys? How did he get hold of them? He *was* the one creeping around your house, wasn't he?"

"He could have taken them from my purse any time he visited my office. Maybe when I was next door with you, even. He probably had them copied at the hardware store and returned them before I knew they were missing."

Mickey came stumbling out of the mortuary doors, shackled in handcuffs, his wounded bloody hand bandaged by the paramedics. The sheriff was right behind him, rubbing his head in disbelief as his deputy resolutely entered the patrol car, this time as a backseat passenger. I went over to the car window and bent down to talk to him.

"Why, Mickey?" I asked. "All this, just to be Super Cop?"

He gave a small laugh, as if I would never understand him. He was right.

The sheriff got into the driver's side and closed the door. He leaned over toward the front passenger window to make sure I could read his lips.

"Don't touch anything, Connor! Don't even go in there! I'm going to run him to lockup, then I'll be back to check the place out. The EMT's are taking care of Celeste, so stay out of their way, Connor. Goddammit, I mean it! You hear me?"

Nope, I thought, and waved him off as he drove out of sight. Then I turned toward the mortuary and practically ran inside. The emergency medical technicians in the hallway were wheeling Celeste out on a stretcher. She was hooked up to oxygen, an IV, and a monitor.

"Is she—"

The paramedic cut me off. "Please clear the way. She'll be at Pioneer Hospital over in Whiskey Slide."

"Nice place," Dan said, following me into Mickey's front room. "If you're a cop fanatic."

After a thorough but unobtrusive search of the mortuary, Dan and I had decided to check out Mickey's place, to see if we could find a link to Boone. We stopped by the hotel building and picked up the Bronco.

Ironic, I thought. In his hurry, Mickey hadn't bothered to lock up his own home. We had come by for a quick look around but I still had to promise Dan, ever the ex-cop, that I wouldn't touch anything. Ha.

We found the bedroom in chaos. Clothes were strewn about, a chair had been upturned, and most of the contents of Mickey's closet had been tossed out on the floor.

Peeking inside the closet, I found a key-making machine and a sheet of plywood covered with small hooks. Dozens of keys hung from the board, each labeled with a name. Celeste. French. Jilda. Beau's keys were there. Lacy's, of course. And mine.

I bent down to check out the cache in Mickey's closet. Lying on the floor was the pink journal I had given him at the office. The lavender one, the volume that had been missing from Lacy's collection in her bedroom, was now in Dan's car. I had picked it up at the mortuary after the EMT's rushed out. A page had been torn out from the blank ones at the end. I felt sure it was the sheet Mickey had used for the fake suicide note.

Why had Mickey tried to make Lacy's death look like a suicide? He must have known her body would be examined and the trocar wound discovered.

"Look at this." Dan came up beside me. He had been searching Mickey's drawers. In his palm he held a tiny gold earring. The one missing from Lacy Penzance at the crime scene?

"I thought you said not to touch anything."

He ignored me. "Check out this scrapbook," he said, holding up a leather-bound album. "Guess who's the star?"

I took it from him and lifted the cover. Taped to the front page was the first edition of the *Eureka!* My name had been highlighted in yellow felt-tip pen.

I turned the page and found a letter from my ex-boyfriend. I opened the envelope and read the contents, a bunch of ramblings about how sorry he was and would I please call. It had once been tucked away in my top drawer—right next to my underwear.

The next page held a Polaroid picture of me sitting at the Miwok Reservoir eating lunch. The next, one of me riding my bike down Main Street. And another taken from behind as I walked toward my office building. I frowned at that one.

"I should never wear stripes," I said.

"I think you look great," Dan replied.

The next page featured the cover of one of my comic books, a *Heckle and Jeckle* that had been missing for a couple of months. Then came a ticket stub from the night Mickey took me to the pasta festival in Rough & Ready, a photocopy of my driver's license, a computer printout of my driving record—two parking tickets and an unfair violation for driving fifty in a thirty-five zone.

Bits of my first six months in Flat Skunk were spread out before me via the scrapbook; every third or fourth page featured one of my mystery puzzles from the *Eureka!* The last filled page contained the missing napkin with the unfinished puzzle.

"I think he's hot for you," Dan said, holding a pair of lace panties I'd been missing for some time. I thought they'd been sacrificed to the Dryer God, the one who collects single socks. I could feel the heat fill my chest and neck as I ripped the panties from his fingers and stuffed them in my pocket.

"Uh-uh-uh," Dan said, wagging a finger. "Sheriff will need that for evidence."

He put out his hand. I slapped it.

"Not a chance in hell," I said.

Dan drove us to the sheriff's office by way of the late-night drugstore so I could patch myself together. There wasn't much I could do with the clawed ankle except put some disinfectant on it, but my left earlobe required a major bandage where the whizzing scalpel had kissed it.

Dan picked out some cartoon Band-Aids and stuck them all over me, everywhere he saw a mark, cut, or scratch. The box was empty in a matter of moments and I soon looked like a kid who'd sneaked into the medicine cabinet. The hurt from ripping them off later would probably exceed the good they were doing me now, but the attention was kind of nice.

I waved to the sheriff, as we walked into his office. He was filling out paper work at his desk.

"Can I see him?" I asked hesitantly.

The sheriff gave a single nod. "But I want to talk with you, Connor. He's confessed, but there are some holes I need filled. Deep holes."

Dan pulled up a chair from the sheriff's desk and sat down. "You go ahead, Connor. I want to talk to the sheriff a few minutes."

I nodded and headed down the hall.

Mickey sat in the cell at the back of the sheriff's office, his head in his hands. When he saw me, he wiped his nose with the back of his uniform sleeve, stained dark red from the nosebleed I'd given him earlier.

I sat down on the floor across from the bars so I could be at eye level. "Mickey, tell me why?"

He didn't look up.

"Mickey, did you take Lacy's keys when she dropped her purse that day in the café?"

No answer.

"Did you plan to kill everyone on that board of keys?"

He finally looked up angrily. "I didn't plan to kill anyone! I just wanted to see Lacy's place, find out if she . . . had any secrets. Everybody has secrets, you know. Especially the ones who look so perfect."

"So you got her keys and . . ."

"I figured I'd find something there if I looked hard enough. I borrowed her keys, made copies, then went back when I knew she wasn't at home and had a look around."

"What did you expect to find?"

He shrugged. "I'm a cop—it's my business to know if people are breaking the law or up to no good. The police can't do everything by the book, you know. Our hands are tied most of the time. I had to bend the rules now and then, for the good of the town."

"So you helped yourself to everyone's keys to unlock their secrets."

Mickey swiped away something from under his eye. "Yeah. And I'm glad I did. That's how I found out the Penryn brothers were growing smoke in their bathroom. And old man Cabral was skimming off the accounts at the post office."

"But Lacy? She was always doing something good for the town. All those charities and benefits and—"

"Ha! Those are the ones you never suspect, while they poison their renters for retirement checks and bury bodies in the backyard."

"What did you discover at Lacy's?" I asked gently.

He gave a sardonic smile. "Jewelry, lots of it. I figured she bought it from that flake, Wolf, but it got me thinking. I knew Wolf and Celeste were up to some kind of jewelry scam, because Celeste had a stash of gold necklaces and rings herself. I found them when I checked out her place. But I didn't know how they were pulling it off, until I got the key to the mortuary. I thought maybe Lacy was in on it."

"But she wasn't?"

His body language spoke volumes while his lips said nothing. He rocked back and forth, shook his head rhythmically, and tapped his feet.

"Why did you kill her?"

"Because! Because she walked in on me while I was looking through her stuff. I'm usually real careful. I thought she was going to be gone for a while. She went out every night about the same time and met some guy that nobody knew about—except me, of course. But she came back early that night and caught me snooping around."

"So you killed her?"

Mickey rocked a little harder.

"I didn't mean to kill her. I didn't mean for anyone to die. Not even Reuben. It doesn't make me a killer, does it, just because I was there and didn't do anything?"

So Mickey had been at the lake when Reuben had fallen over in the boat? Reuben had drowned and Mickey hadn't done anything to save him. That's why he knew so much about Reuben's death.

"What happened that night?" I asked.

He opened and closed his knees, unable to keep them still. "Reuben was cheating on Lacy. He used that boat to meet other women. I was there—"

"Spying on him?"

Mickey glared at me. "I was watching him. I knew he was up to something. I was just waiting for him to make a mistake. He was drinking, not paying attention. He rammed the boat on a big rock, it began to sink, and he went under—" He paused, looking off to some far horizon only visible to Mickey from that cell. "I couldn't do anything. I wasn't even supposed to be there. The sheriff thought I was watching the high school football game."

"I still don't understand what happened with Lacy."

He looked down at his restless feet, then at me.

"When she caught me going through her stuff, she said she was going to tell the sheriff, like I was some kind of criminal or something. I . . . I couldn't let her do that. Not after I'd worked so hard to be a good cop."

"So you stabbed her?"

"No! No . . . I pushed her, you know, when she started to call the sheriff. She reached for her purse; I didn't know what she was going to do next—maybe pull a gun . . ."

Mickey checked to see if I was understanding what he was trying to say. I tried to look supportive. It wasn't easy.

"So I pushed her to the floor and got a knife from the table when she pulled out something from her purse. I tried to grab it away, but the knife kind of caught on her . . ."

He stopped and hung his head.

"What did you do then?"

"I didn't know what to do. I sat there for a while, trying to figure it out. I knew I hadn't meant to do it, so it wasn't really my fault. I thought maybe I could put the blame on someone who really deserved it. That's when I got the idea about making it look like a phony suicide, to hide a murder that was supposedly perpetrated by Celeste. I thought it would make a good mystery, you know?"

"Why Celeste? You said you knew about the jewelry scam? Why not just arrest her for that?" I asked.

Mickey looked at me pleadingly. "I knew about the jewelry, but I couldn't prove it. I figured she deserved to go to jail anyway, and while I was at it, I could give you a shot at putting your paper into the big-time with a real murder mystery to solve."

"Why the trocar?"

He nodded repeatedly, like an autistic. "Like I said, I thought it would be a good puzzle. I liked working on those mysteries with you, Connor. It was something we had in common. I thought, if we worked together, we might become closer, you know. So I used the trocar to cover the knife wound."

He paused for a moment, then went quickly on, as if afraid to lose momentum.

"No one seems to be able to do anything about crime any more—drug dealers, thieves, smart-ass teenagers—not even the police. Don't you see? I had to do something!"

"What about Sluice? Did you try to kill him too?"

"No, he wasn't a threat, really. I pushed him into the grave so he'd shut up for awhile, put him in the hospital, keep him out of the way. I had a feeling he had some jewelry in his backpack. But I couldn't find it. Then I spotted Wolf and had to get out of there."

"Why did you kill James Russell?"

Mickey sat quietly for a few seconds before speaking.

"I . . . followed Celeste that night. I thought she was going to see Wolf about the jewelry."

I watched him intently.

"But Celeste went to the Mark Twain instead. She was acting real strange, kind of sneaking around, you know. And wearing these dark, manlike clothes. She went in through the window instead of the door. Tell me that's not weird."

"That is strange," I agreed.

"I hung around outside, listening through the open window, but what I overheard wasn't what I expected."

He looked at me for a reaction, but I knew what he was about to say. "It wasn't the jewelry scam," I said.

Mickey laughed. "Hell, no. Celeste and this guy were conning rich old widows out of all their money. It was incredible!"

"And they had to be stopped . . ." I suggested.

Mickey rubbed his hands together feverishly. "After Celeste left, I climbed in the window. Shoot, was that guy surprised to see me. I told him I knew what he was up to. But he laughed and said I couldn't prove anything. He was right. I didn't have anything. But I couldn't let him get away with it."

"So you took that old mining pick down from the wall and stabbed him with it."

Mickey's eyes filled with tears.

"Connor, don't you get it yet? He was no good. And I couldn't have done anything about it within the law. I'm a lawman, and it's my duty to do the right thing. It seemed the only way."

"I guess I know how Celeste's hairs and threads happened to be at the inn, but what about the fingerprints? Were they Dan's?" I asked.

Mickey tilted his head to one side.

"I didn't trust him, Connor. He was a stranger in town, always snooping around, taking up all of your time. Nobody knew much about him. I still don't know what his game is, but I figure he's into drugs or something like that."

"Did you kill his brother?"

I didn't think Mickey was going to respond, he paused so long. Finally he took a deep breath, scratched the rash on his arm, and began to answer.

"Boone knew too much about my connection to Lacy Penzance. All that investigating he was doing was becoming a problem. He called from Rio Vista needing some information from the sheriff, but I took the call."

"What did he want?"

"He said he knew something about Lacy's death. But he wouldn't say more."

"So you went to Rio Vista."

"I had to know what he'd found out. I drove down and met him at a bar. He'd been drinking again—he was pretty far gone. He had a few more shots in the car and was getting really drunk. Seemed really upset about something. I kept asking him about his investigation and he wouldn't say anything, even as drunk as he was."

"Then why did you kill him?"

He gave me another piercing look. It was alarming how quickly his moods changed. "Would you wait! I'm trying to tell you!" He took another deep breath, wiped his nose, and resumed his story, speaking calmly. "He wouldn't say anything for the longest time. Finally he said he'd seen me go into Jilda's house one night when she was at the café."

"So he figured out that you were entering illegally."

Mickey raised his eyebrows. "I tried to convince him he was wrong, but he just opened the car door to get out—and fell. He was so drunk. I rolled him into the water, you know, to sober him up. But he rolled in too far, you know? And, well, he drowned. Like Reuben; he just drowned."

"And you didn't try to save him."

"I didn't see the point," Mickey said, completely devoid of expression.

"How're you doing?" Dan asked over a light beer in my diner kitchen. I chugged a couple of swallows before I answered, then set the pale ale down on the swirled Formica top.

"God, he was here! In my home! Going through my things!" I visualized Mickey running his hands through my Miracle bras and bikini underwear. "He went into my drawers—he read my mail. He tried to find out all my secrets."

"Got any?" Dan asked.

"Tons. But none that he'd ever discover. I don't leave them lying around where just anyone can find them."

"Sheriff says he's being transported to Calaveras County Jail tomorrow. There's going to be a lot of publicity."

I nodded and rubbed my chest. It was itching. I pulled down the collar of my shirt and saw the red rash.

"Poison oak?"

"The patch on my arm is starting to dry up, but now it's on my chest, and I can't stop scratching it. Oh, well, poison oak isn't all bad. It helped me figure out Mickey was Lacy's killer."

"What? How?" Dan said, scratching his cheek. Uh-oh.

"You getting it too?" I remembered the time we kissed. I touched his cheek, probably right after I scratched my arm. I could have spread it to him then.

"Nah. My beard itches. I never get poison oak. I'm immune. So how did getting poison oak help you figure out Mickey was a killer? That's quite a long shot."

"There were bunches of it in the older cemetery, where Reuben and Lacy's gravestones are, remember? You almost sat in it. The stuff hadn't been cleared away like it had in the newer section. When Mickey dragged Lacy's body up there and spread it out on the gravestone, he got into the poison oak without knowing it. Mickey and I were both there the next day—that's when I must have touched it. But he broke out at least eight hours before I did. I remember him scratching it early the next day."

"I don't think it's enough to convict him on."

I laughed. "Exhibit A: calamine lotion. Speaking of which, that's what was missing from my medicine cabinet. It got me thinking about him. Anyway, there's plenty of other evidence. The keys he copied, the stash of jewelry he'd hidden in his closet and drawers, Lacy's earring, the journal. That scrapbook—with my half-finished mystery napkin taped inside. He must have picked it up that day he came to return Lacy's keys. And the minty breath—I knew I smelled something besides that horrible stuff he put over my face. But I suppose his confession is the clincher."

"If it holds up. He knew his rights and he waived them, but these days the law seems to do everything it can to protect the criminal."

"I guess that's why Mickey did all this," I said. "He felt frustrated at the system and wanted to put the bad guys away himself—only he didn't even know he was one of the bad guys, too. Just like this movie back-lot town. Mickey was a false front with a hidden interior that didn't much resemble what he presented."

"These people aren't all 'bad,' except in Mickey's

eyes," Dan said. "He wanted to be Super Cop, adored by the public. And by you, especially," Dan said.

"That reminds me. How did you know those were my underpants at Mickey's? They could have been anyone's."

Dan smiled. "Because underneath that tough-gal facade of yours a very sexy woman is hiding."

I blushed, pulled a jar of cashews from the cupboard, and opened them into a bowl to distract myself from Dan.

"How's Celeste? What did the sheriff say is going to happen to her?"

"She's under house arrest at the hospital. She committed fraud, theft, and bigamy once removed. She won't be dancing on anyone's grave for awhile."

"And Wolf?"

Dan shrugged one shoulder and ate a cashew. "I don't know what they can prove. Celeste could implicate him, but to what degree there's no telling. He's a modern-day grave-robber. Hopefully he won't get away with it. But proving it won't be easy, without exhuming a few graves. That won't be pleasant."

"Poor Sluice," I said, with a mouthful of cashews. "Do you think he'll take any blame for this?"

"What?" Dan said. I chewed up the nuts and repeated the question.

"I don't know. Everyone seems to know his shirt is missing a few buttons."

"What?"

"His pocket's half empty. His shoes have no traction. His cortex is missing a few synapses. You know."

I giggled. "The sheriff said he probably aided Celeste and Wolf without really knowing what he was doing. He was just the go-between with the jewelry. The sheriff took him to a shelter tonight, over in Whiskey Slide. He needs someone to look after him. Poor, lonely old guy."

Dan filled his mouth with cashews, then tried to speak. All I saw were cashews. When he finished, he repeated his question. We were clearly going to have to give up eating if we wanted to communicate.

"So your suspicions began when Mickey alluded to an inconsistency in Lacy's wound?"

"Not really. It was Lacy's body language while she lay on the grave. It just spoke to me when I saw that snapshot of her dead body."

"When did you first suspect Mickey? An itchy arm isn't much to go on."

"I was never really certain, not for a long time, just something in the back of my mind. He knew a lot more about Reuben's drowning than any of the reports I had read. He seemed to know a lot about me, more than I ever told him. He was almost intuitive about what I liked to read and eat, and what I was interested in. I guess he researched me, but it was superficial. He said he loved the *Little Lulu* comics, but he knew nothing about Witch Hazel."

"I don't know anything about Witch Hazel."

"But you don't pretend to know anything about Little Lulu either."

"So who's Witch Hazel?"

"She's a witch Lulu created to get Alvin to sleep at night."

"Who's Alvin?"

"I'll let you read one later."

The light on the TTY flashed at the doorway that leads to the back part of the house. I had it placed there so I could see it from most areas in the diner. I picked it up; it was the sheriff—I could tell by his typing.

"C.W. HOw you doing? GEtting a little R & R? GA."

"Hi, Sheriff. Doing OK. How's Mickey? GA."

"NOt good. HE's really a messed up guy. GOt a new deputy coming in tomorrow to filll in until I Find a replacement. NAme's HEather. HOw am I going to work with a deputy named HEather, for God's sake?"

I waited for the GA. It never came. "It'll be great for your image, Sheriff. Think about it. With a woman for a partner, maybe you won't have to go to all those self-help groups or counselors anymore. She'll help you get in touch with your feelings. How's Celeste? GA."

"IN a heap of trouble, but recovering. GA."

"Hey, Sheriff, was French involved in any of this? GA."

"DOesn't look like it. HE didn't know what was going on under his own roof. He's got a lot of P.R. work ahead of him, though, I'll tell you that."

"Thanks for calling, Sheriff. GA. SK."

"10-4. SK."

Dan had come into the living area while I was on the phone. He was lying on the couch playing with the remote control.

"That's another thing," I said, sitting next to him.

"What is?" Dan asked.

"The typing. People have different ways of communicating on the TTY. Most Deaf people type in all caps, use abbreviations, and not much punctuation. But hearing people are used to typing more formally. The sheriff always holds his shift key down too long so that more than one letter is capitalized."

"So?"

"Mickey never used capitals or punctuation. It was his style. When I got that threatening message on the TTY, I had a feeling it was from him. I always wondered how he knew I'd been up to Whiskey Slide to see Risa Longo. When I called the sheriff's office from the pay phone using the TTY, I thought I was talking with the sheriff. But it was the deputy I was spilling my guts to about someone being in my house."

"Typewriting analysis, eh? Something like handwriting analysis in the computer age? Pretty clever. Hey, what about the five-thousand dollars waiting for you at the attorney's office?"

"I don't know. It's not really mine."

"The sheriff thinks otherwise. He said you not only found the woman Lacy was looking for, but you found out who killed Lacy."

We were quiet for a few moments, each contemplating the remnants of the week's excitement. I placed a hand on his knee and said, "Sorry about Boone."

Dan nodded. "I wish I'd known him better. I was looking forward to getting reacquainted. He didn't have an easy life."

"You told the sheriff?"

"Yeah. He asked where I wanted to body sent."

"Not Memory Kingdom, I assume."

"Neptune Society. No funeral. I think I'll just scatter his ashes over the Mother Lode hills."

I gave Dan's knee a pat and removed my hand. I still wasn't much good with words of sympathy.

Dan punched the remote around a few stations and landed on a screen featuring a woman in a police uniform. "Looks like there's a good mystery on right now. Just started. One of those Jane Tennison stories. The female chief inspector?"

I took the remote from his hand and settled back on the couch. "I've had enough mystery for a while, thank you. How about something predictable?" I punched a couple of buttons and up popped a sit-com about a pair of newlyweds trying to figure out their relationship.

Dan leaned back, took the remote, and punched the button again. He found an ice hockey game on the next channel. "Sports?"

My turn. "MTV?"

"What do you get from MTV?" he asked, cautiously surprised.

"Fashion tips. Where to pierce my next body part. What tattoos look good with what outfits. Hairstyles, makeup, everything you need to know to be hip."

He punched the button. An old black-and-white western. We wrestled over the remote until the wrestling turned to more playful physical contact. Dan punched the "off" button—left-handed, under the leg. Impressive.

"Teach me the sign for 'mystery,' " he said, sitting up, but not removing his arms which had encircled me.

"There are several ways you can sign it. I like this one."

I moved my right fist, thumb up, under my left facedown palm. He pulled his arms away and imitated me, awkwardly at first, then more smoothly the second time.

"Good. Anything else?" I asked.

"Naw. I don't need any more signs. I can read your body language."

"Oh, really? What am I saying?"

As if we both didn't know.

About the Author

Penny Warner teaches child development and special education at Diablo Valley and Chabot College, and teaches creative writing at Cal-State University, Hayward and U.C. Berkeley Extension. She lives in Danville, California, with her husband Tom, where together they write and produce mystery events for libraries, corporations, and other organizations across the country.